The Flu is Coming

Science Traveler Series

Book 1

The Flu Is Coming

Science Traveler Series

Book 1

J. L. Greger

Bug Press

New Mexico

The Flu Is Coming

Text edited by Zelda Gatuskin.

Cover design by Barbara Hodges for Got You Covered Bookcover Design © 2018

ISBN (Bug Press paperback): 978-0-578-4325-8

LCCN: 2018914033

Bug Press

Bernalillo, New Mexico

www.jlgreger.com

DEDICATION

To Bug who stayed by me during the whole writing, editing, and publishing process.

ACKNOWLEDGEMENTS

Thanks to Zelda Gatuskin for editing the text and Barbara Hodges for designing the cover for *The Flu Is Coming*.

A special thanks to Marilyn Olsen and the late Billie Johnson who had faith in me when I started writing about Sara Almquist.

CHAPTER 1: May — Sara Almquist

Not one but two garbage trucks chugged into the upscale community of La Bendita once a week. Sometimes as Sara Almquist watched her neighbors roll out overflowing cans from their garages weekly, she was reminded of T.S. Eliot's line, "I have measured out my life with coffee spoons." She thought the residents of La Bendita could say that they measured their lives with garbage cans.

Life in the adult-only community was uneventful. Many of her retired neighbors did little but talk, play cards, drink, and talk more. Usually they spoke about their real and imagined ailments and fears and, of course, each other.

Jane Lane braked her bicycle to a stop as Sara placed her garbage can at the curb. "Are you going to the sunset wine and cheese event at the clubhouse on Saturday? Jean Peterson is in charge. Last week Hank Crockett told her to stop 'clucking like an old hen 'fore they chop its head off for Sunday dinner.' It was the highlight of the evening."

Sara wondered whether the redheaded, retired sales rep was as bored as her conversation suggested. "You'd be devastated if anything happened to Jean. You'd have no one to talk about."

"You're wrong. I could talk about you. You're the biggest enigma at La Bendita — the tall blonde who seldom talks about her past but seems to have been everywhere."

"I guess I should be flattered." Sara turned and rushed up her driveway. Once inside she slammed the door. "I gotta get out of here."

Bug, her black and white Japanese Chin, jumped up, wagged his plumed tail, and headed for the door. He snuffled noisily when she did not follow immediately.

"You're right. We need to go to the savanna."

Sara smiled as she thought about the savanna. It really was an old cow pasture with patchy weeds and no real paths. The occasional trees on the savanna were more creatively contorted than those in the bosque, the woods along the Rio Grande River. An uncontrolled fire about five years before had left several trees on the savanna permanently leafless. They looked like stark modernistic sculptures in white, gray, and black. In summer, the remaining massive cottonwoods provided islands of shade from the blazing sun. In fall, the wind rustled their yellow leaves to sound like applause. Now in May, the cottonwoods coated the ground with the cotton from their seedpods.

Sara hated to admit it, but one reason she preferred the savanna to the bosque was her neighbors seldom visited it. They walked along the groomed trails within La Bendita through a wrought iron gate, which locked out everyone who did not live in the community, and onto the gravel paths of the bosque. Sara liked the freedom of meandering without a structured path and thinking not talking.

Today, Sara and Bug walked along Willow Drive, lined with stucco houses set on small yards with desert landscaping. They came to the wide bricked driveway that connected the double front gates of the community to the circle drive in front of the large, stone clubhouse. Bug enthusiastically sniffed the lush grass, the ultimate luxury in a water-restricted area, surrounding the clubhouse. Then Sara led Bug down another street until they reached one of the few unsold lots in La Bendita. Bug took control and pulled Sara to a low spot in the perimeter wall. They clambered over it and walked along a sandy path in the shade of the wall as it wound around La Bendita, until they crossed the gravel road leading to the community's emergency back exit.

Together they climbed down the steep concrete abutment to the bottom of the flood control channel eight feet below. She'd never seen more than an inch of water in the channel, but old-timers claimed severe storms had created even deeper natural gulches, called arroyos. As she stood in the bottom of the trough, she knew why few of her neighbors were willing to cross it. Bug and Sara scaled the other side of the abutment and crossed to the savanna.

Bug gamely trotted the whole distance even though he took four or five steps for every one of hers. In the savanna, he started to lag. She stopped and cradled him in her arms as she studied La Bendita with its combination of flat and red tile roofs on stucco buildings.

English Construction Company, the community's developer, had wedged La Bendita between the bosque along the Rio Grande River and the flood control channel, with the community's front gates facing west in the middle of the widest side of the property. They had created a cobweb pattern of streets radiating from the clubhouse by the front gate with pools, terraces, putting greens, and bocce ball courts cascading toward the back of the property. The resulting confused traffic patterns had been further complicated when the developer panicked about lagging sales of homes five years previously. Agents had sold only twenty percent of the planned lots in the first two years of the development. Accordingly, English Construction had struck two deals. They had built a three-story assisted living and nursing home facility for Progressive Health Care Corporation and a three-story clinic for University Hospital's Medical Group, Inc. at the back of the community. The net result was that about six hundred lived within the adobe walls of La Bendita with only about half in the one hundred-seventy homes.

Although the physical setting of La Bendita was idyllic, the internal politics was not. Board meetings for the Homeowners' Association were stormy. Sara wasn't sure why, but she suspected the high crime rate in nearby Albuquerque and the headlines in the *Albuquerque Journal* stoked her neighbors' fear of drugs and crimes. Thus, her neighbors often discussed security issues at board meetings, particularly the community's perimeter wall and gates. Sara thought the wall was a joke because even house cats could scale it.

She also thought the animosity between the homeowners and the health complex within La Bendita reflected the composition of the HOA Board. Until all the lots were sold, the board consisted of two members elected by the homeowners, two representatives of the health complex, and a representative of the developer. When the last twelve lots were sold, hopefully within a year, the homeowners would elect three members on the Board and the construction company would lose its seat. The developer's representative was currently the board president, and Sara thought he fanned gossip within the community with his frequent innuendoes. She eagerly anticipated his departure.

Finally, Sara hated to admit the third reason for the unhappiness in La Bendita. A number of her neighbors referred to the Hispanic and Native Americans who worked at the clinic and health center as "riffraff." At best these neighbors were snobs, and at worst they were racists.

As Bug nestled in the crook of her arm, her anger ebbed and her shoulders relaxed. She wasn't angry with her neighbors but with herself. She didn't want to talk about her past. She didn't want to remember how hard she'd tried to fit into the all-male club known as the Statistics Department at Michigan State University or why her marriage failed.

Sara placed Bug on the ground, straightened to her full height of five foot-eight, and rolled her shoulders back. She'd gotten what she wanted at Michigan State eventually — a full professorship, tenure, and the creation of a Department of Epidemiology separate from the Statistics Department. Her research in the epidemiology of diseases had taken her to many exotic spots. Not bad for a Midwestern pig-farmer's daughter. She figured many of the problems at La Bendita would also be solved with patience and work.

On the way back from the savanna, Sara spotted two new neighbors wrangling over the placement of rosemary plants in their front yard. Sara would have quickly slipped by them but Bug pulled her toward a dumpster emanating a disgusting odor in their yard. They quickly introduced themselves as Marv and Marcia Morton.

When the short, plump woman noticed Bug's avid interest in the dumpster, she said, "Please don't report us to the Homeowners' Association. I know it stinks to high heaven."

Her husband interrupted, "Nothing to apologize about. We drove to El Paso to pick up this special fertilizer made from the manure of active roosters. Wait until you see what it does for my plants."

Sara coughed. "I'd never report anyone to the HOA. That's what we call the Homeowners' Association. But why did you drive all the way to El Paso for chicken manure? They have plenty in nearby Mercado."

"The stuff in Mercado is the debris from egg layers. I want the manure from active roosters."

"What's the deal with active roosters?"

Marcia rolled her eyes. "Don't ask."

CHAPTER 2: Five Months Later — The Crisis Begins

"Breathe deeply, Mr. Morton."

"C… Can't." He choked and gray foamy slime dripped from his mouth.

Tears splashed down Marcia's ashen cheeks. The young emergency room doctor could see she was past being worried. She was scared and on the verge of becoming hysterical. She'd described her husband as a lean, but vigorous, man. He saw grayish skin stretched over a skeleton.

"Two days ago, Marv started coughing violently. He kept saying that he didn't need a doctor to tell him his allergies were acting up." Marcia wiped her eyes with a tissue. "He got quieter when he started spitting up blood last night."

"How about today?" The young doctor avoided looking at Marcia because he couldn't fake a smile to reassure her.

"He could hardly move and didn't even comment when I got a neighbor to help hoist him into the car to bring him here."

When Marcia began to cough violently, the doctor motioned for a nurse to steady Marv while he checked Marcia's breathing. She deserved to hear the truth, but he couldn't force himself to say it. Again, he avoided looking at her face.

After his shift ended two hours later, the young doctor broke one of his personal rules. He checked on the Mortons, even though they were no longer his patients. Both were covered with *i.v.* lines and monitors and lay in hospital beds in an isolation room in the ICU. Marv was attached to a ventilator with a tube down his throat and Marcia had a cannula in her nose. The doctor stared through the window of the door to their room. He heard the clicking sounds of medical devices and occasional sobs from Marcia. He tried to smile at her but left quickly. He could do nothing for them, besides, a large red sign on the door declared: *CONTACT RESTRICTED. NO VISITORS.*

During his next shift on Wednesday, public health officials bustled into the emergency room and questioned him and everyone else about their vaccination histories and their exposure to the Mortons. They whisked away a clerk who had not been vaccinated and ordered the young doctor and the rest of the staff members to a meeting.

The officials were in a hurry and conducted a brisk session. They made quick announcements. Marv Morton had died the previous night. His wife Marcia was not expected to survive the day. The Mortons' daughter had been banned from entering her parents' room to say good-bye. Then they instructed the emergency room staff on the triage procedures to be followed with all patients showing any symptoms of this new type of flu — the Philippine flu.

The young doctor wished he had smiled more at Marcia. He didn't want to become like these officials. They were so concerned about the welfare of citizens throughout the Albuquerque area that they had no time to sympathize with individual patients. They had decreed new severe triage procedures. Worst of all — they'd forbade him to tell anyone outside the emergency room about the new rules.

CHAPTER 3: Wednesday, Day Two of the Crisis — Sara

Sara Almquist visited her sister Linda, a physician in the Department of Internal Medicine at the medical school in Albuquerque on Wednesday evening. Linda, a wren-like woman with graying dishwater blonde hair, listened intently as Sara summarized the Mortons' story.

"It's hard to believe they're both dead. So fast." Sara stopped sniffling. "Could it be the Philippine flu?" She continued without waiting for an answer. "The Centers for Disease Control reported last week in the *Journal of the American Medical Association* that this flu has killed over a hundred thousand in the Philippines in the last four months. Experts assume this flu is the result of a still-unidentified mutation in a flu virus common in poultry in the Philippines."

Linda stopped biting her already short nails. "I wish I had the time to keep up with the medical journals as well as you do."

"One of the joys of an early retirement." Sara was about to add one of the deficits of an early retirement was the inability to discuss scientific issues with informed colleagues, but that wasn't a problem for her because she had a built-in informed colleague in Linda. As Linda bit her lip nervously, Sara decided not to interrupt her sister more.

"Another is you miss the memos. I think we get more of them during the fall semester. We got one from the dean and the hospital administrator today. Strange, they seldom cooperate."

"So?"

"They noted that the CDC was investigating fifty deaths in Juarez from the Philippine flu. The CDC assumed the flu had already spread to El Paso. Anyway, they ordered all medical personnel to be vaccinated immediately."

"Weren't you vaccinated against the Philippine flu months ago?"

"Yeah, most of us at the hospital were, with an experimental nasal spray of the live attenuated vaccine."

"I read about that vaccine," said Sara. "The CDC was in such a hurry to get it out before the Philippine flu reached the U.S. that the virus wasn't attenuated, or weakened, much. They made it heat sensitive so it could survive in the nasal passages but not in the hotter lungs. Otherwise, the virus was unchanged."

Linda shook her head. "Gave me a sinus headache for the two days. It could be really dangerous for anyone with a weakened immune system."

"Did the memo mention the Mortons?"

"No, wouldn't be like our hospital admin to be that straight with the docs."

"Maybe they're following orders from the CDC."

"Doubt it. Our dean doesn't listen to anyone. Neither does our hospital administrator. That's why they're always at war."

"That's the story at most med schools. Back to the flu. There's been a lot in *Science* and other journals about how the Surgeon General and the CDC coerced the Department of Agriculture to ban shipment of poultry and poultry-products from the Philippines to the U.S. almost two months ago. Several experts noted the meat and birds weren't dangerous because of common flu viruses in birds but because of a mutated virus now also transmitted among humans. Accordingly, the State Department issued a level three travel advisory for travel to the Philippines three weeks ago."

"Looks like it wasn't enough to prevent the spread of the flu."

"Did anyone say what the source of the flu virus in Juarez was?"

"Funny thing, the memo did. Filipinos who smuggled fighting cocks from the Philippines. Evidently, they doped the birds and hid them in sleeves of their jackets during flights. They warned us to be particularly vigilant if we saw flu symptoms in Hispanic men or teenage boys with ties to Mexico or to cock fighting."

"That's not helpful. Cock fighting is illegal in New Mexico. No one would admit participating in that so-called sport."

"No kidding, but typical of the advice from the hospital admin."

"Anyway, Marvin Morton from New Jersey sure doesn't fit the profile." Sara wiped tears from her eyes. "He's been gardening and delivering potted mums to shut-ins for the last two weeks. Of course, he took breaks for poker games with the guys."

The sisters continued their discussion but quickly agreed on two points. Sara and Bug should move to Linda's house for the next week, just in case any of Sara's neighbors had caught the flu from the Mortons. They would hope Sara had not been exposed.

CHAPTER 4: Thursday, Day Three of the Crisis — Dr. Linda Almquist

Linda trudged into her dining room, dropped her heavy book bag, and gawked at the scene. Usually the crystal chandelier softly lit the surface of her mahogany dining table. Now the room was awash in light from two floor lamps. Sara had moved them from the den. A loom with a partially completed piece of nubby ivory fabric streaked with fluffy white areas and silver slashes sat by the front window. Four three-dimensional, beaded pieces of art were aligned against the walls. At least five piles of crystal beads, white ribbon, and silver cord on the dining room table were merging into one big heap. Sara was bent over a beading loom in the middle of the heap. Bug snored at her feet.

Linda thought the next week would be a rough one. The sisters were female versions of Oscar and Felix in the *Odd Couple*. Linda liked her traditionally decorated house to be neat and organized, a refuge from the pandemonium of her clinics.

Sara thrived on chaos. When she had worked as an epidemiology professor, she always kept one suitcase partially packed at her home in case the World Health Organization asked her to inspect the site of a developing epidemic, or a university invited her to speak on her latest scientific findings. Her overstuffed office had contained ten steel file cabinets, computers with screens usually filled with spreadsheets, and two bookcases filled with books on statistics, epidemiology, microbiology, and pathology. Graduate students and post docs had scurried in and out without knocking to consult with Sara, to borrow books, and to inspect files in the open drawers of the file cabinets.

Linda suspected Sara missed the excitement. When Sara retired she had traded in all the files and data for art and weaving supplies and had adopted Bug as a puppy. Bug was good for Sara. She no longer — well, very seldom — erupted into tirades at those who failed to grasp new ideas quickly. However, she still kept four or five ongoing projects strewn around her eclectically decorated house.

"I see you made yourself at home."

Sara did not look up from her loom. "You saw everything last night."

"But you didn't unpack your car last night. Feel any side effects from the vaccination yet?"

"Nope, that's why I made a good supper for tonight. Meatloaf and scalloped potatoes. Figured I might not feel like it tomorrow."

Linda went to her room and took a shower. Ten minutes later she looked at the full dinner laid out on the kitchen table. "I'm not hungry."

"I fixed your favorite foods." Sara scooped a serving of steaming potatoes onto Linda's plate. "I know on clinic days you don't get much of a lunch."

Linda studied the meat loaf that Sara had glazed with Dijon mustard and brown sugar, just the way Linda liked it. She selected the smallest piece.

Sara frowned and handed her a bowl of coleslaw. "How was your day?"

"The usual. The clerks overbooked my morning clinic assuming half wouldn't show. God, I hate when they do that. Today almost all my appointments showed. My nurse practitioners and I felt like we were on treadmills running between rooms. Finally, saw all of them by two, but the last ones were pretty cranky. When I went to the cafeteria for coffee before I started my paperwork for the day, I heard the rumor that they had run out of flu vaccine."

"Glad you called at nine and told me the hospital would vaccinate volunteers, especially those who worked with children like Bug and I do in pet therapy. I was in line by ten. Waited in line for over an hour." Sara chewed a mouthful of meat loaf. "Any announcements to the docs about the flu?"

"As usual, the hospital administration let the docs swing in the wind most of the day. About three, all section heads got a terse email announcement from the head of the hospital stating two patients in the hospital had died of the Philippine flu and five others were in critical condition."

"The Mortons. But who else?"

"Don't know. They noted the CDC and state health officials were on the premises and meeting with staff in the infectious disease sections of internal medicine and pediatrics. They ended their email by saying a major announcement would be made at a meeting for all section heads tomorrow at eight."

"You'll go?"

"Yeah."

"Any scuttlebutt?"

"Talked to Martin Bloom."

Sara looked blankly at Linda.

Linda scowled. "You've met him. The redhead. He's in the infectious disease section of internal medicine. He hinted all suspected flu cases would be sent to a satellite clinic that would be quarantined."

"How'll they do it?"

"Probably assign a couple of attendings, a bunch of medical residents, and three shifts of nurses to stay at the site so they don't expose their families."

"Most small hospitals and clinics couldn't house that many staff as well as patients, could they?"

"No, the logistics will be a nightmare."

"What if they need more docs?"

The creases between Linda's brows deepened. "It'll be a problem. We're short staffed now at the University Hospital. Clinics elsewhere in the state, or for that matter in the Southwest, won't want to send their physicians to help us because they'll figure it's only a matter of time before the flu reaches them."

"What will happen?"

"They'll probably pull nurse practitioners from our clinics to work with flu patients." Linda sighed. "I'd be lost without mine. And I can't work more hours. I already work sixty hours many weeks now."

"I know. Usually you're home by seven. Tonight it was eight."

"No kidding, Sherlock."

Sara tensed slightly. "Guess that's enough about your day. Did you see all my wall hangings in the dining room?"

"Be hard to miss them. I also saw several shipping crates in my garage. Can I hope you'll be sending them off tomorrow?"

"Not tomorrow but probably early next week. The galleries want them for holiday shopping. The big one that I'm working on now is for the charity art auction for the University Hospital."

"Bet there won't be an auction this year."

"They'll hold it. Maybe online. But they'll hold it because they'll want the money. A flu epidemic will make people want to support their local hospitals." Sara ate several mouthfuls of potatoes. "Maybe, I should rework my piece for the hospital auction a bit and weave the word hope into a narrow banner that I put across the top of the piece."

“Sounds cheap.”

“Subtly, so it’s not kitschy. Upbeat stuff sells in sad times. With luck, my piece could be picked for the advertising poster for the auction. Then I’d move from being a local craftsman to being a recognized artist.”

“Hmmf. I’m going to bed before you think you’ll become Picasso.”

“Nothing wrong with dreaming. That’s what got me through all those years at Michigan State.”

CHAPTER 5: Friday, Day Four of the Crisis — Sara

Sara made slow progress with her weaving the next day. Her head ached. She wiped drips from her nose more than she twisted fibers into place on the loom. Her phone rang around nine.

Linda's usually alto voice was in the soprano range. "They're going to isolate all the flu patients at the La Bendita Assisted Living and Nursing Home Center and the La Bendita Clinic."

"What?"

"That's what they announced at the briefing for the section heads. Four of the five patients in critical condition yesterday died. All were from the nursing home part of the medical center at La Bendita."

"Oh, my God."

"That's just the beginning. They claimed at least fifty of the residents of the center exhibited severe flu symptoms at six this morning."

"A fast onset," said Sara. "What about the residents of homes like mine in La Bendita?"

"Don't know. I bet they'll quarantine everyone."

"Who'll head up the medical team?"

"Martin Bloom. He's going to man it with the two physicians who staff the La Bendita Clinic and the nursing staff of the La Bendita's center and clinic. He's also taking several medical residents and fellows from the University Hospital."

"Will that be enough?"

"Who knows?" Linda's voice lowered. She spoke rapidly but not at the supersonic speed of the previous exchange. "Evidently the CDC, state health officials, and politicos from Mercado and Albuquerque met with reps from the clinic and the assisted living center at La Bendita. The governor sent reps, too. The center and clinic management agreed to turn the clubhouse over to the CDC."

"Damn. Damn. Damn." Sara voice became shriller with each word. "I always knew those stupid governance covenants for La Bendita gave those two health care facilities all the power and the residents none."

"What are you ranting about?"

"Under our covenants, the leadership of the center and clinic can make decisions for all of La Bendita without contacting the homeowners if Paul Owens, as President of the HOA Board, agrees. For this kind of decision, it's unfair, but of course Paul wouldn't care."

"Probably he didn't have much choice once the politicians got involved."

"Guess so." Sara's voice had returned to its usual clipped alto tones. "Did anyone say why La Bendita was chosen?"

"State health officials believed the quarantine would be easier to maintain in a walled community with no school-age children or teens."

"I wouldn't bet on that."

"They also noted the center and clinics had lots of rooms that could be used for patients. And the clubhouse with its gym, kitchen, and more importantly showers would be a good place to house staff. Even so, they plan to put up two large tents to house staff."

While Linda gave more details about the briefing at University Hospital, Sara checked her emails. "Wait a second," interrupted Sara. "There's an emergency meeting at the clubhouse at ten. All residents are expected to attend."

"Don't go." said Linda. "Bet they'll announce a quarantine for everyone in La Bendita. You're out; stay out."

Sara debated whether to call or email Jane Lane. Anything she told Jane would be conveyed, probably incorrectly, to everyone at La Bendita. She called Jane, but all she got was Jane's answering machine. She sent an email to Jane and called the Benders, one of her favorite neighbors. After the phone rang more than thirty times, a recording directed her to call another number. Finally, she called the Crocketts.

"Sara, where are you?" Marian Crockett continued without waiting for an answer. "You can't believe what's happening here. Elsie and Herman Bender disappeared yesterday."

"What do you mean they disappeared?" asked Sara.

"The Benders' house is still as a snake before it strikes. No one's there. They must have taken them away?"

"Who are they?"

"Yesterday about noon a bunch of white vans came in. I'm a thinking they said they were from DCD, no CDD."

"CDC?" said Sara.

"Could be." Sara could hear Marian conferring with Hank before she responded more. "Federal folks with badges and state people. All of them wore yellow paper robes over their clothes and masks. They went door to door. They took everyone's temperature with fancy thermometers and took notes on laptop computers as we answered their endless questions."

"Did they mention whether they would take anyone who was sick to the center?"

Marian was silent for several seconds. "No. But they said we were fine and put two yellow suns on our door. Ordered us to leave them there. Why did they do that?"

"Staff in several Albuquerque hospitals put paper yellow oak leaves on the doors of patients who are prone to falling. Maybe the officials are marking houses as to the number and health of the residents. Did you happen to notice whether they put anything on the front door of the Benders' house?"

The phone clunked on a hard surface. Marian yelled, "Hey Hank, you notice any signs on the Benders' door?" After a minute, Marian spoke into the phone. "Hank just looked. There are two black clouds on the Benders' door. What are you thinking that means?"

"I'd guess both Hank and Elsie have the flu, but I'm guessing."

Marian turned and loudly relayed the information to Hank. There were muffled whispers between Hank and Marian.

"Hank thinks you, as a scientist, might find this interesting."

"What?"

"The people in the vans. They kept asking when was the last time we spoke to or saw the Mortons. And did we know what the Mortons did the week before they got sick? How would we know?"

"They were probably trying to figure out how the flu was transmitted." Sara didn't want to break Marian's train of thought and didn't ask for details.

"They also gave us a brochure on the Philippine flu. They told us how the flu bug could be spread through the air when someone coughed or sneezed. They said the bug could also stick to objects that flu patients touched and then come off on someone else. Stuff we hear every flu season. Course, they said this bug could last longer on surfaces than most flu bugs."

"So, they tried to be helpful?"

"Guess so," said Marian. "They said we'd come down with symptoms within one to four days after we were exposed to the flu bug. Even told us what symptoms to look for."

Again Sara could hear indistinct whispers on the other end of the line.

"Sara, are you coming to the meeting at ten?"

"I'm at my sister's. I've been here since Wednesday and plan to stay here. If they ask, you might tell them I was vaccinated with the attenuated flu virus yesterday. I think it's best if I stay here."

"We'll pass your news on."

"Thanks. What about Jane Lane? I couldn't reach her."

"You know Jane. She's riding her bike all the time now in big circles around the place and spreading gossip. She calls it news. Well, better be going to the meeting. Bye."

Sara returned to her weaving but her head ached. She decided to take a short nap. The ringing of her phone woke her.

"What time is it?" squeaked Sara. "I laid down for a short nap at ten."

"It's two," said Linda. "You sound terrible."

"I developed a sore throat while I napped. My head feels like it'll split."

"You've probably reacting to your vaccination. I warned you."

"Yeah. Would any antiviral medication help?"

"You can't take an antiviral. It would prevent your body from reacting to the vaccination and keep you from developing immunity to the flu. Besides, the Philippine virus is resistant to Tamiflu and all standard antivirals. It may respond to a couple of experimental antivirals, but probably only before symptoms appear."

"Tell me about them."

"All I can tell you is what Martin Bloom said at a seminar that I attended a few weeks ago. The CDC invited Martin and a couple hundred other physicians from around the country to Atlanta for a workshop on the Philippine flu in August. The CDC insisted the attendees present the data to other physicians at their home institution."

"So?" When Linda didn't respond, Sara said, "So, what did you learn about the experimental antivirals?"

"Let me think. Scientists at Boston University tried to develop an antiviral medication against the Ebola virus. Seems they took pieces of small interfering RNA often called siRNA."

As an epidemiologist Sara was familiar with general medical terminology but not the latest biochemical techniques. She said, "How do these snippets of siRNAs work?"

"Martin didn't explain any mechanisms. He only said they prevented symptoms produced by the viruses."

"Okay," said Sara. "Why haven't scientists used these pieces of siRNA before?"

"The body degrades them rapidly. The researchers at Boston University packaged them in stable nucleic acid-lipid particles."

"How?"

"Don't know. Anyway they found if this packaged siRNA was injected frequently enough in mice infected with the Ebola virus, it interfered with the Ebola virus's ability to take control of cells in patients and replicate. They injected them repeatedly into a woman who accidentally injected herself with Ebola virus while doing studies on it in a lab. She survived."

"Did they do clinical studies on patients exposed to the Ebola virus in Africa?"

"Not really." Linda was silent for several seconds.

"So, how much work has been done with these pieces of siRNA in flu patients?"

"I'm trying to remember what Martin said. I think several groups of scientists have hypothesized packaged siRNA particles would be effective in preventing other viral diseases, like the Philippine flu. One group found some of these packaged siRNAs could stop the development of flu symptoms in mice and monkeys if given fast enough after infection and often enough."

"How much have they been tested in human flu patients?" asked Sara.

"Very little."

Sara paused and thought. She hadn't gotten into such an interesting discussion of science since she retired. "So, no info on toxicity or effectiveness in humans exposed to any type of flu."

"Don't think so," said Linda. "They may not even know the side effects. That's why they've only been used to treat humans exposed to the Ebola virus."

"Expect you're right. Those exposed to Ebola, which has a mortality rate greater than fifty percent, are more apt to try risky experimental treatments."

"True." Linda paused, "Why are you so interested in the antivirals?"

"A number of people I know in La Bendita have come down with the flu."

"So, it's spread into your community from the assisted living center and the nursing home."

"Appears so. And that means I could have it. My symptoms might be the start of the real thing, not a reaction to the vaccination. But as you said, I can't take antivirals right after I've been immunized."

"Yeah, antivirals prevent the vaccine from working."

"So, I could be up a creek. Getting vaccinated was a mistake if I was already infected with the flu virus."

"Oh dear." Linda suddenly assumed her "doctor" tone. "Get a thermometer and take your temperature."

A minute later Sara returned to the phone. Linda began to dispense medical advice.

Sara listened a couple of seconds. "Looks like I don't have a temperature."

"Leave it under your tongue longer while I tell you what I learned at the meeting this morning. Although fifty at La Bendita have severe flu symptoms, over a hundred more are sniffling and coughing occasionally. Our docs in infectious disease think all patients in the assisted living center and nursing home have been exposed to the flu and they consider the whole center to be an isolation unit."

"Do they know the source of exposure?"

"You're not supposed to talk while you have the thermometer in your mouth. No, but figure it must be through your friends, er, er…"

"The Mortons."

"Yes, and thirteen have died."

Sara was stunned. "So many? So fast?"

"You're not a cooperative patient. What's your temperature?"

"A little less than a hundred."

Sara listened half-heartedly to Linda's medical advice as she scanned her emails. "Wait a second, I got an email from someone named Ellen Behren of the CDC. She's ordering me to return to La Bendita. She's also accusing me of lying when I told the Crocketts I was vaccinated yesterday. She says she can file criminal charges against me for reckless endangerment of others. She's threatening to send police to arrest me and bring me back to La Bendita."

"Oh dear."

"Don't worry. I'll reply with a one-line email:

Check the vaccination records at the University Hospital.

"I'm too experienced to respond to an emotional email with another emotional email. I'll let this officious lady cool her jets while I take a nap for an hour or two."

"If you feel worse, call me. I really don't want to see you sent to the La Bendita medical center. It's too…"

"Risky. Yeah, I know. Medical care is not good in an epidemic situation when docs run out of time and supplies." Sara paused. "I'm not old and infirm like the nursing home patients, and don't have chronic conditions like a lot of the assisted living residents."

"You're always the cheerleader."

"Optimism is good."

"Call me."

The phone rang about an hour later. Sara expected to hear her sister's voice. Instead she heard an unrecognizable, high-pitched moan. "Help me, Sara. We're all going to die here." There were sounds of a bit of a struggle and the phone went dead.

Sara replayed the message but couldn't identify the voice. She didn't recognize the number shown on Caller ID. She went to her computer. None of the residents of La Bendita had emailed her, but Ellen Behren had. The email said:

Dear Dr. Sara Almquist,

The University Hospital confirmed you were given the attenuated vaccine yesterday. You will not be included in the quarantine of residents of La Bendita as long as you do not return to your home in La Bendita or develop the flu.

Sara was glad she hadn't wasted a lot of energy stewing over her last email and continued to read the memo.

I recognize your name and have read several of your papers tracing the spread of epidemics. Would you be willing to help the CDC chart the course of this flu epidemic in the Albuquerque area?

Ellen Behren, M.D., Ph.D.

Sara emailed a quick response to Ellen Behren and debated what do about the odd phone call — the cry for help. It was probably Elsie Bender. She punched the number that the recording had given her when she called the Benders and worked her way through an automatic telephone tree. After five minutes, she reached a real person who nicely but firmly stated that no information could be released on Elsie and Herman Bender except to their family.

Sara shivered. Could the Benders have died?

CHAPTER 6: Day Four Continued — Sara

"Sara, thank God you emailed me." Jane's voice was so shrill that Sara pulled the phone away from her ear. "You can't believe what they did here yesterday."

Sara resisted the urge to remind Jane that she had earned her living by investigating epidemics. Instead, she said, "Did staff from the CDC interview you? Or was it someone from the New Mexico Department of Health?"

"Yes."

"To which question?"

"To both of them. Doesn't matter who did the interviews. They're all Nazis. Two of them came to my house yesterday afternoon and demanded that I answer their questions. They treated me like I was a potential murderer."

Sara didn't want to inflame Jane with a professional comment. To public health officials studying an epidemic, anyone transmitting a deadly infection, in this case the flu, was a potential, although unintentional, murderer. It was like an AIDS patient having unprotected sex. Sara waited for Jane to continue.

"I had to tell them every place I went and everyone with whom I spoke since last Saturday. It's none of their business."

Sara spoke softly hoping to calm Jane. "Didn't they explain why they needed the info?"

"Yeah, they tried to scare me about how easy it was to spread the flu virus. They told me epidemiologists would use my answers, really everyone's answers, to figure out who had been exposed to the flu."

"So?"

"I don't want them to know if I might have been exposed. They'd watch me more."

Sara realized Jane was cleverer than she often appeared. "You'd be a hard person to interview."

"Hmmf. One of them pecked at her computer during the whole conversation. It took more than an hour. It was odd. Both of them wore plastic gloves, a yellow paper robe over their clothes, and a mask. When they left, I rode my bicycle around the neighborhood. I tried to enter the clubhouse. They barred the doors and told me to go home."

"Did you?"

"Yes, for a while. The more I thought about it, the more steamed I got. I looked out my door and watched men and women in yellow streaming in and out of every house on the block. Then suddenly around six, all the vans pulled out."

"What do you mean pulled out?"

"They all left through the front gate," said Jane. "I got thinking. This would be a good time to take a look-see in Riverview, the development next to us on the west. See whether those public health officials were harassing people there too. I jumped in my car and drove out the front gate. The next thing I knew, a police car with sirens blaring and lights blinking was following me. The officers waved at me and yelled for me to stop."

"What did you do?"

"I ignored them and kept on driving. Suddenly the police car roared past me and swerved in front of me. If I hadn't braked fast, I would have hit the police car."

Sara resisted the urge to snicker. Public health officials had underestimated the feistiness of older adults in La Bendita. "What happened next?"

"Two officers jumped out of the police car and strutted over to my car. They yanked open the front doors of my car on both sides. They ordered me out. I was little slow. Then one ordered me to stand with my hands on the hood of my car. I refused. I'm too old for such nonsense. The other one took the keys out of my car's ignition. I couldn't escape."

"What did they say?"

"Ma'am, weren't you told earlier to stay in your home?"

"So?"

"I just smiled," said Jane. "They lectured me about not stopping when they asked. I told them something like — this is America. They lectured me more and told me the quarantine would be explained the next day — that is today."

Sara thought Jane was lucky they didn't arrest her. On reflection, she decided they couldn't arrest Jane because probably no jail was prepared to take a potential flu patient. Besides, Jane and everyone else at La Bendita were already sort of in a jail with the quarantine. Sara had often thought quarantines were an infringement on the rights of those exposed to an uncontrollable infection, but she'd never known personally those quarantined before. Jane had a good reason to be upset but giving her sympathy now would be counterproductive. "Then what?"

"They shoved me into the back seat of the police car where I was locked in. One drove me to the front gate. The other drove my car. Then they pulled me from the police car and told me to drive my car home."

"Did they follow you?"

"No. They never stepped past the front gates of La Bendita. They closed them after I pulled away."

Sara was surprised officials had implemented the quarantine so quickly, but she guessed their decision was wise. "So, they were nice but insisted you stay in La Bendita."

"Hmmf. I wouldn't call being handled like a criminal nice," screamed Jane. "Then do you know what they did? The Nazis sent out an email saying they would meet with all of us today at ten."

"I got the message."

"Made me mad. They were ordering us to a meeting. I thought about it and then I cycled down to Howie's house and demanded he do something."

Sara was surprised Jane trusted Howard Steele, better known as Howie. He was one of two elected members of the Board of Directors of the HOA. "What did he say?"

"You know Howie. He's always kind of secretive. It's hard to know what really happened."

"Did he say anything useful?"

"First, he mentioned that Dr. Gaspar Gonzales, you know the head of the La Bendita Clinic and a HOA Board member, called him before the vans arrived. Then the truth came out. Dr. Gonzales got the mayor of Mercado to call Howie. A woman official from the CDC met with Howie and George Kent. Howie bragged she called them La Bendita's leaders or some bullshit like that."

Sara had never thought of George and Howie as the leaders of the community but they were the elected members on the HOA Board. Sara decided it was best not to agree with the official because it would rile Jane. "So, what happened this morning?"

"It was bad. They stopped us in front of the clubhouse."

"Who are they?" said Sara.

"Dr. Gonzales and nurses from the clinic. They gave us packets of hand wipes, plastic gloves, and masks. I felt like a baby chick being watched by chicken hawks. We couldn't enter the clubhouse until we used the junk."

"Scary but a good idea."

"The next part was unbelievable. A woman announced the CDC and the New Mexico Department of Public Health with the Mercado Police and the New Mexico State Police had implemented, get this, community containment measures at La Bendita as of last night. No one was allowed to leave. Police cars would be stationed night and day at our front gate as long as the quarantine continued."

"Did anyone complain?"

"It's not easy with a mask on. Jim Peterson tried. Then they turned on the TV and had some sort of video hook up with the head honcho of the New Mexico State Police. He talked about the Model State Emergency Health Powers Act. Unbelievable bullshit."

"Did they give you a copy of the act?" asked Sara.

"George and Howie claimed they got copies."

"So?"

"George played lawyer and gave us complicated bullshit."

"Well, he is a lawyer," said Sara.

"Yeah, he claimed the federal and state governments expanded their right to act in times of emergency after 9/11 and then again after the H1N1 flu scare in 2009. He added some malarkey that they always had the right to do whatever was necessary to prevent the spread of contagious diseases, but it hadn't been a big deal since the 1918 flu epidemic."

"It's true," said Sara.

"Bullshit. They can't do this. They can't turn La Bendita into a prison."

Sara knew George had been right, but knew she needed to listen to Jane and not correct her. "Did they say how you were supposed to get food and medicine?"

"Yeah, the turncoat Dr. Gonzales. I always thought he was a good doc, but he isn't." Jane took a deep breath. "He ordered us to give him a list of all medications that we take and how much we have on hand. The clinic will get our medications. They will distribute them in front of the clubhouse between ten and noon every day."

"How about food?"

"They'll email us when they figure it out. God knows when that'll be," screamed Jane. "They claimed they had to talk to FEMA and USDA. But it doesn't make sense. FEMA are the jerks that goofed in New Orleans after Katrina. USDA is for farmers."

"I admit FEMA has a checkered track record." Sara cleared her throat. "But it probably has more experience in distributing food during emergencies than other government agencies. USDA provides food commodities to schools and several of the Indian pueblos. Those commodities can be released to others in times of emergencies, such as epidemics."

"Who cares?" screeched Jane. "They're all fucking disasters. I want to bust out of here before it's too late. They won't even let the mail woman in here. We have to pick up our mail at the front gate. The mail we send out has to be irradiated or something before anyone on the outside can touch it."

"Didn't they explain they were trying to prevent the spread of the flu?"

"Yes, but I don't care about others. What about us? We're stuck here with flu all around."

Sara wondered how many others in La Bendita were as rabid as Jane. She wanted to calm her. "You can use your computer and phone as much as you want to safely communicate with others."

"I like to see people's faces when I talk to them."

Sara heard a crashing sound. Either Jane threw an object or tripped over something. Sara decided to ignore the noise. "They're enforcing the restrictions because the Philippine flu is highly contagious."

"I've heard that line. And here's another of their lines: There's not enough experimental drugs to go around."

Sara gasped. That added a new wrinkle to this mess. She wondered how officials would ration the experimental antivirals. Those infected who didn't get them were apt to die. Anything she said would make Jane more hysterical. Sara waited for Jane's next comments.

"My best protection is staying fit. Those Nazis won't let me use the gym in the clubhouse. All I have is my bicycle."

"Okay, but wear a mask when you talk to others. And maybe gloves so you don't touch contaminated surfaces."

"Don't worry, I'll wear a mask when we storm the gates in Jim Peterson's Hummer and make our prison break."

Sara called George Kent after Jane tired of ranting. George listened to Sara's story about her mysterious call and agreed Elsie Bender was the caller. When Sara asked how to contact Elsie, George surprised her.

"I don't think it's possible even if she's alive. Gaspar hinted they're too short staffed to do any more than the basics. Please don't spread that detail around. No need to add tension here."

Next Sara asked a question that had bugged her all day. "Where are they putting the dead bodies?"

Sara knew that transporting infected bodies to a morgue outside La Bendita would introduce all sorts of public health problems and accordingly was probably prohibited by the quarantine. On the other hand, pathologists probably would want to examine at least a few of the bodies eventually. To store them without an overwhelming stench required refrigeration.

This time George's answer did not surprise Sara. "They brought in a refrigerator truck, like ones used to transport meat, and parked it behind the center. Ellen Behren, the head CDC official here, thought no one would notice but it's the major topic in emails now."

"Is there anything I can do to help?"

"Don't think so. All the officials I've talked to seem to have thought through our problems pretty well. And Gaspar, well Gaspar is being himself. He's going all out to please. But communications is a problem. First off, it's scary being trapped here with the flu. Second, we're getting a lot of technical jargon when we ask questions. Finally, a lot of people are turned off by Dr. Behren's emails."

"Mmm. They are sharp edged."

"You mean rude and accusatory. Then people hear from Jane and the Petersons that they should demand open meetings."

"Group meetings are a mistake," said Sara. "They will spread the flu faster."

"I know. Gaspar explained. But Jim keeps riling Jane. And Jane keeps spouting off and making everyone nervous."

"Jane feels her rights are being trampled. It's a situation reminiscent of the case of Mary Mallon."

"Who?" said George.

"Typhoid Mary. She was imprisoned for more than twenty-five years on an island in New York harbor because she was a carrier for typhoid fever and refused to cooperate with authorities and stop being a cook. Her rights were trampled for the public good."

"I'd forgotten that case. It did set the legal precedent for this and any other quarantines in the United States."

"I tried to explain it to Jane."

"That was a waste of time," said George. "I've got a question for you. Why aren't you quarantined?"

"I am sort of, at my sister's house. I hadn't seen the Mortons in the last week. I didn't enter the clubhouse since last Saturday. So, it's likely I wasn't exposed. I went to my sister's on Wednesday evening and had a flu vaccination on Thursday before the quarantine at La Bendita was imposed."

"You played it smart."

Sara didn't feel as if she'd played it smart. Her head was screaming for relief. Her eyes and throat felt rough and she was tired. "That won't be clear until the weekend's over. If I'm okay then, I'll know I wasn't exposed to the flu."

"Uh-huh," said George. "Is the same true for us?"

"Only if you aren't getting infected at group meetings or by touching surfaces contaminated by sick individuals before they are hospitalized."

Sara went to bed as soon as the conversation ended. She woke when Bug licked her face and snorted. She looked at her watch. It was nearly five.

Her head was no longer pounding, just thumping softly. She sat up slowly and looked around the room. She sighed with relief. Her symptoms must have been a reaction to the vaccination, not the onset of the flu.

Two hours later Linda found Sara at her computer. The table was set for dinner. "What's up?"

"I'm working on a project for Ellen Behren." Sara looked away from her computer screen. "Thanks for getting your friend Martin to intercede with Ellen Behren today."

"Actually, Martin called me. Ellen had asked him about experts on medical statistics and epidemiology at the university. The CDC couldn't get any here because they sent their experts to El Paso. He remembered my comments about you."

"So, how is she using you?"

"Basic epidemiology. I sent her a list of data that I needed. She's already provided most of it."

"Like?" Linda looked over her sister's shoulder.

"The notes from the interviews with all La Bendita residents. Hopefully those notes will provide info on everyone's contacts during the last week. Thank God, the interviewers took notes on computers and transcription wasn't necessary."

"They must go on for pages and pages."

"They're not really notes. They're spread sheets, but they do go on for pages. She also sent me a list of all visitors to the assisted living center and clinic during the last ten days. And most importantly a list of the residents in the medical center and in the La Bendita community with flu symptoms, when they developed symptoms, and if and when they went into critical condition and/or died."

"I'm surprised," said Linda. "Sounds like you got everything she had."

"Yeah, with all of the data and my knowledge of the residents, I may be able to piece together a plausible history of transmission and progression of the flu among residents. Then I may be able to develop models that will help public health workers locate individuals before they have full-blown symptoms. Survival is more likely among patients with infectious diseases if treatment is begun early."

"Sound pretty tedious. Are you up to it? You look tired."

"That's the pot calling the kettle black. Besides, they need help."

Linda shrugged her shoulders.

"Did any cases of flu show up today at the hospital?"

"There was rumor that one case showed up from somewhere in or near Mercado and was transferred to the La Bendita Clinic."

"Any more details?" said Sara.

"No."

"What about your patients? Were they aware of the flu?"

"Most didn't seem to be until I gave them the card that the CDC prepared on what to do if they noticed flu symptoms among members of their family." She paused. "Not a bad idea."

"Generally, the CDC handles emergencies pretty well. Though, they don't seem to be communicating well with all of the residents of La Bendita."

"No one scores well with them," said Linda. "You know I hate to be around Jane Lane. Everything is a crisis with her."

"But they're my neighbors and Jane means well. Guess I'd bet serve dinner." Sara began to bustle about the kitchen.

After a supper of reheated scalloped potatoes and meatloaf, Sara checked her emails while Linda tidied up the kitchen.

"Damn." screamed Sara. "I know where the flu case in Mercado came from."

After a twenty-minute phone conversation, Sara walked into Linda's living room. Linda was seated in her favorite high back chair upholstered with a navy and maroon paisley print.

Linda did not look up from the latest edition of the *New England Journal of Medicine*. "What did the grande dame of art in New Mexico have to say? Did Aletha Bradley sell another one of your wall hangings, or as she calls them soft sculptures, at one of her galleries on Canyon Road in Santa Fe?" She looked up at Sara. "Judging from your face, no."

Sara plunked onto Linda navy sofa. "Do you remember me talking about Aletha's daughter Julia Chavez and her grandchildren Gabi and Lalo? They live in Riverview, the subdivision to the northwest of La Bendita."

"Of course, next to Bug, Lalo is your favorite hiking companion. What is Lalo, eight now? Pretty soon Gabi will be old enough to be a decent hiker too. And Julia is the buyer for the Gallery Store at the Albuquerque Museum. She's sold on consignment what I thought were your two best pieces last year."

Sara dabbed tears from her face.

"You weren't talking about art business with Aletha." Linda thought for a minute. "Oh dear, somehow they're involved in the flu case that showed up in Mercado."

Sara rubbed her eyes. "Appears Julia's neighbor Elena Pena had a bad cough and went to her doc this afternoon. She left her three-year-old daughter Maria with Julia to babysit a little before one. Then around four Elena's husband Cesar called Julia. Seems the Albuquerque Police grabbed him as he got off a plane at the airport in Albuquerque and rushed him to the University Hospital. They gave him two shots and asked him lots of questions. Finally, they told him Elena was in critical condition in the center at La Bendita."

"Oh dear."

"He had to decide whether he wanted to be with his wife Elena or with his daughter Maria. If he entered La Bendita to see his wife, he couldn't leave for at least five days and would be housed in a tent by the clubhouse. That is unless he developed flu symptoms; then he would be transferred to the clinic. He opted to stay with the daughter and showed up at Julia's house around five to pick up the daughter."

"So, Julia and her two kids have probably been exposed to the Philippine flu," said Linda.

"Looks like it. Evidently two state health officials showed up at Julia's home around six. Aletha said they really scared Julia. She and the kids cannot leave the house for the next five or six days. Local police will deliver needed groceries. They cannot have visitors, including Aletha."

"Bet that riled Aletha. She's used to giving orders not taking them."

Sara nodded. "The health officials gave Julia and the kids shots, but Aletha didn't know what type. Note the plural. The officials said that they will stop by twice a day to check on Julia and the kids. If they become ill, they'll be sent to La Bendita. Otherwise the health officials will continue to give them injections twice daily for five days."

Linda straightened in her chair. "In essence, they're under house arrest."

"That's tough with a hyperactive kid like Lalo. I'd like to help them. Over the last four years Aletha has been my main mentor when it comes to my artwork, even if she did call my original wall hangings "decorator fluff." And I meet the school bus most Mondays to pick up Lalo when Julia works late." Sara bit her lip. "You know if those injections, which I assume are antivirals, don't work, it's doubtful all three of them will survive. And Aletha knows it, too. She scared."

"Of course, she's a smart woman. What are you going to do?"

Sara was silent for about a minute. "Do what I always do in time of crisis — work. The best way I can help them is set any emotions aside and look for leads on the epidemiology of this Philippine flu."

"Are you up to it?"

"I feel pretty good now. Probably because of the almost six extra hours of sleep I got today."

Linda rose and felt Sara's forehead. "You don't feel warm."

"I really don't think I have the flu. Just a rough reaction to the vaccination."

"Probably right." Linda picked up the journals scattered about her chair. "It will be easier reading in my bedroom." She trudged off to her room.

Sara returned to the dining room. She'd already cleared the table of her artwork. Now her laptop computer sat on the table with piles of paper.

She knew this would be a long night and debated where to start. She scanned a document called "outpatients" that Ellen Behren had sent. It needed to be updated because the protocol listed was not consistent with what Aletha had said. She decided she also needed information on the antivirals, more than what Linda remembered. She sent an email to Ellen Behren and called Julia.

Bug watched Sara at first and then curled up on the chair next to her.

CHAPTER 7: Saturday, Day Five of the Crisis — Sara

Bug, lying at Sara's feet, looked up from under half-closed eyelids when Linda peeked in on Sara before she left to do rounds on Saturday morning. Sara groaned as Linda stuck a thermometer into her mouth.

Linda announced after a minute, "Your temperature is normal. How do you feel?"

"Sleepy. Bug and I are going to stay in bed for a while."

"When did you finally go to bed last night?"

"Around three."

The phone awakened Sara at nine. "Dr. Almquist, Dr. Sara Almquist?"

"Yes?"

"This is Dr. Dave Sedley. I'm one of medical residents Dr. Bloom brought to La Bendita. He wanted me to thank you for the work-up on Elena Pena that you sent him around one last night."

"Did Martin have a chance to look at what I sent?"

"Yes, and I have a few questions. Do you really think Elena had contact with only seven unimmunized people after she visited her grandmother in the center on Monday afternoon?"

Sara, still half asleep, stumbled to her computer in the dining room. "Well, as I outlined in my note to Ellen and Martin, Elena's husband was away on a business trip. She does telemarketing from her home and doesn't send her daughter to nursery school. She picked up groceries for the week before visiting her grandmother in the nursing home part of the medical center on Monday. I questioned her neighbor."

"Maria Chavez," Dave interrupted.

"Mmm. And I interviewed Elena's husband last night."

"Wasn't he pretty distraught?"

"Yeah, but he wanted to help." Sara reverted to a monotone voice as she recited details of the case. "Elena complained of flu symptoms on Wednesday and Thursday evenings when she talked to her husband by phone.”

Sara located her note to Drs. Behren and Bloom in her computer files while she talked to Dave. “Seems Elena was facing a deadline at her telemarketing job and logged into her computer for more than thirty hours Tuesday through Thursday.”

Sara now read straight from her notes. “Around noon on Friday, Elena delivered her daughter Maria to the Chavez home. Julia was alarmed about Elena’s coughing and isolated Maria in the front bedroom away from her two sons.” Sara stopped reading. “Of course, isolation of the child cannot be assumed just because it’s what Julia said she did.”

“So that’s the first four potential exposures to the flu: Maria, Julia Chavez, and her two children?”

“Right,” said Sara.

“How did you know who was in the doctor’s office?”

“I talked to Elena’s doctor last night. The only unimmunized individuals in the doctor’s office when Elena arrived were one other patient and the receptionist. The doctor and her nurses had been immunized against the Philippine flu about a month ago. As soon as she saw Elena, the doctor called an ambulance and had Elena taken to University Hospital’s emergency room. I assumed the ambulance crew and the staff in the emergency room were immunized against the flu.”

“Did you talk to the receptionist or patient?” asked Dave.

“No, figured it was Ellen’s or more likely your job.”

“Who’s Ricardo Vargas on your list?”

Sara suspected this resident either didn’t read her memo, had a short memory, or was a pompous fool. Most likely the latter. “If you had read my memo, you’d know he’s the janitor in the doctor’s office. I figured he could have come in contact with viruses on the work surfaces there.”

“Doubt it,” said Dave.

“Don’t be too sure. He’s the one who handles the garbage. It could include Julia’s used tissues. He really should be monitored.”

“Mmm.”

“Last night Ellen agreed someone would monitor all seven of the people who had contact with Elena.”

“We’ll see what we can do.”

Sara thought besides being pompous, Dave Sedley was lazy. She paused and assumed a professorial tone. “Furthermore, I noted twelve other individuals visited the assisted living center on Monday and Tuesday."

"That's all?"

"That's all who signed in. The center is strict about signing in. Sign-in desks block the two entrances that aren't keycard coded. So, the records are apt to be accurate. Well at least ninety percent accurate. Thank God, they closed the center to all visitors at nine on Wednesday morning. Those twelve need to be monitored, too. The good news is nine of the visitors are residents of La Bendita."

"I don't think we have the manpower."

"Do you realize if these visitors aren't quarantined and monitored, your patient load may explode?"

"No." he wailed. "You don't understand. This place is unbelievable. We have over a hundred seriously or critically ill patients here with at least fifty dead already."

Sara hadn't realized so many had died already. No wonder Dr. Sedley was distracted. However, she decided he'd fall apart completely and be more useless than he already was if she gave him sympathy. "I understand fine. Your treatments for the flu are pretty ineffective among the infirm elderly and those with chronic diseases in the center. That means the best treatment is prevention."

Dave didn't respond.

Maybe she'd been too rough on the resident. This was probably the first time he has come to grips with the limits of medicine. Sara took a deep breath. "Are you a first-year resident?"

"No, third."

She thought he was a slow learner but figured she'd better try to boost his confidence. "Tracking all contacts is important. That's why Dr. Bloom assigned you to talk to me."

"No." Dave hesitated. "It's… it's because I broke down in the wards last night. Dr. Bloom threw me out of the ward and said I might as well try to be useful in outreach."

Suddenly Sara heard shouting in the background. "What's going on?"

"What do you mean?"

"The noise in the background."

"Oh, it's probably another person trying to visit a friend or spouse."

"How can that be? It's posted at the door, isn't it?"

"Yes, but people try anyway. And now we have another reason. Late last night a woman brought a box of cookies for her husband. The clerk at the desk thought the box seemed heavy. The clerk opened the box after she forced the woman to leave. The woman had placed a loaded gun in the box with cookies."

"What did the clerk do?"

"Called the boss. That's another reason Dr. Bloom said I should work in the office by the front door. He thought the clerks needed help."

"What happened to the cookie baker?"

"Dr. Behren sent the ambulance crew to her house. She was coughing and sneezing. They brought her to the center as a patient after they patted her down to be sure she didn't have another gun."

The background noise increased.

"I got to check."

She heard the phone as it thumped down on a hard surface. The background noise increased, subsided, and increased again. Then heavy breathing on the phone.

"Oh my God." said Dave. "A man collapsed in front of the clerk's desk."

"So, the ambulance crew will take him to a bed in the center?"

"No."

"Why not?"

"He's... he's dead!" the young physician screamed. "Blood and foamy gunk all over the counter. He literally sprayed it as he coughed. What a mess. I can't take any more."

Sara wondered how the interviewers had missed the man's symptoms when they checked all the residents in their houses on Thursday. Then she realized that was about forty hours ago. Maybe he didn't have symptoms then. Obviously, Dave couldn't answer her questions. She rethought her earlier decision and decided Dave needed sympathy. "It's okay to be bothered by this situation. We all are. In situations like this, you've got to put your emotions aside."

"I can't." Dave sobbed loudly.

She decided it was time to trot out her old rah-rah story. It had helped many students when they were at a breaking point. "My grandmother didn't cry at my great-grandmother's funeral. I was only five, but I remember asking her why she didn't cry. She told me she had the rest of her life to cry. Now she had things to do. I think of that comment whenever I'm faced with a crisis. I think you need to do the same."

Dave continued to sniffle. "That's hard."

"No, letting your emotions cloud your judgment so much that you cause someone to die is hard. I'd better talk to Ellen or Martin."

"Don't tell them I cried. Besides, I didn't tell you Dr. Behren's main message yet."

"What's that?"

"The CDC sent a new experimental test for the Philippine flu virus to Dr. Behren yesterday morning. The test is from the WHO. I guess that stands for World Health Organization."

"Okay," said Sara. "How does it work?"

"Not sure. Somehow identifies slight changes in the virus's structure."

Sara decided that he was no science whiz and focused her next questions on practical problems. "Can this test be done on samples collected with nasal swabs, or will you have to do those horrible bronchoalveolar lavages to get aspirates from the lungs?"

"Dr. Bloom muttered something about this test worked with nasal swab samples. But I think he said you have to use the right swabs." Dave sighed. "Guess I'm through. I've given you their message."

"Wait a minute," said Sara. "Do we have a protocol for using the test here?"

"Oh, I forgot. That's why Dr. Bloom wanted me to call you. Dr. Bloom said he was 'up to his neck in alligators.' He wondered whether you could develop a protocol for using the screening test here."

"Do you have any more details on the test? How long does the lab work take? How much sample is needed? Who will perform the tests locally?"

"Don't know, but I'll forward the blurb on the test that the CDC sent to Dr. Behren and also a list of lab contacts at the CDC and at the state lab."

"Does Martin want to run any other tests on serum samples?" Sara paused and thought. "Researchers often report hemagglutination-inhibition assays to determine whether flu patients have antibodies that cross-react with known flu viruses."

"How would I know?"

"Find out. You are taking notes, aren't you?"

"Should I be?"

"Yes." Sara kept her voice steady and didn't show her annoyance as she reviewed the previous points with Dave. "Do we have to get approval of the human subjects committees at the CDC and at the university, specifically the one in the med school?"

"The what?"

"Human subjects committees, often called the IRBs. They review all research protocols with human patients to be sure the subjects understand the risk of participating in a study."

Dave laughed. "The first thing Dr. Bloom said when Dr. Behren told him yesterday about the test was the population of Albuquerque would be reduced to one-half before we'd get anything approved by the IRB in the med school."

"Yeah, it will probably take weeks."

"Dr. Behren may be a bitch." He added quickly, "Don't tell her I said. But she's effective on the phone. She made several calls. An emergency human subjects committee at the CDC will review any protocols and consent forms dealing with the Philippine flu within hours of receipt. She said this was possible because the line between research and best medical practice were blurred when it came to the Philippine flu and everyone was frantic for answers."

"What about the human subjects committee at the med school?"

"Dr. Behren performed a miracle. She forced the dean of the med school to call an emergency meeting on a Friday, no less. They ceded all review of protocols on the Philippine flu to the human subjects committee at the CDC. I don't know how she did it. Dr. Bloom only said that both the dean and the committee were afraid to say no."

"Okay, email me what you've got," said Sara. "Make sure you send me details on the CDC's emergency human subjects committee. You know, their rules and forms. Give Martin my questions and ask him to give me a call or email between patients. Thanks."

CHAPTER 8: Day Five Continued — Cesar Pena, Julia Chavez

Cesar Pena tucked his daughter Maria into bed early on Friday night. He watched two men dressed in protective clothing that looked like astronaut's gear decontaminate the surfaces in his kitchen and bathroom.

He thought the cleaning activity was useless. Elena had coughed on most of the surfaces in the house. No doubt, Maria was infected. He was exposed, too.

As the men continued the process in other rooms, Cesar pulled a beer from the refrigerator, contacted a lawyer, and drafted his will. He sent emails to family and friends. He couldn't talk to them and do what was important at the same time. He needed to listen to Maria breathe.

After he talked to Sara, a nice lady trying to chart the course of the flu, he went to bed but did not sleep. Around two in the morning he thought he heard a cough. He went to Maria's room. She was breathing heavily with her mouth open, but she was not coughing.

At three he woke in horror. There was no doubt Maria was coughing. He took her temperature. He cuddled her.

The state health officials had been clear on Friday night. If Maria developed flu symptoms — a fever and coughing, she had to be moved to the clinic at La Bendita. Cesar had asked whether she could be housed with her mother in the center. He'd been told it "would not be a good idea."

Cesar sat by Maria's bed and prayed. Neither he nor Maria was scheduled to get another injection of antivirals until six-thirty in the morning. That gave him three more hours to enjoy his princess. He decided he might as well go with her when she was taken into La Bendita. He hoped they would let him stay with her in the clinic. Tears coursed silently down his unshaven face as he sat and watched his daughter breathe. Finally, he packed her pink Cinderella case with a pair of pajamas, several pairs of panties, two favorite tee shirts, her Hannah Montana doll, and a picture of Elena. He also threw a few of his clothes in a plastic bag.

At six Cesar prepared Maria's favorite food, macaroni and cheese with hot dog pennies. He woke Maria just before the nurse arrived to dose them with antivirals. All the time the nurse was in his home, he prayed Maria wouldn't cough. His prayers were answered, almost. Maria didn't cough until the nurse was preparing to leave.

The nurse sighed and an ambulance arrived much too quickly. The ambulance crew handed him paper overalls, gloves, a cap, and a mask. The next few minutes were hazy to Cesar, except the moment when the ambulance stopped and waited for the gates of La Bendita to open. Then he and Maria were transferred to another ambulance inside the gates. He'd never forget the squeaks from those damn metal gates.

His cell phone rang while he settled his daughter in a room in the clinic. A tired voice said, "Is this Cesar Pena?"

"Yes."

"If you want to see your wife one last time, get to room 103 of the center within ten minutes. We'll keep her on life support until you get here."

The caller hung up. Cesar hugged his daughter as well as he could in the protective gear and ran to the center.

The only noises in room 103 were the sound of equipment — pumping sounds and hisses. The four patients in the room were surrounded by tubes, pulsating equipment, and green iridescent screen monitors. A nurse quickly put a screen around Elena's bed to give Cesar some privacy as he communed with his wife for the last time. The nurse mumbled that Elena was brain dead, shut off the ventilator, and removed the tube from Elena's mouth.

Cesar was stunned. Elena's face was pale — actually bluish white and drawn. After he got over his initial shock, he stroked her hand. He thought Elena fluttered her eyelids. He gently pulled a wisp of her wet hair from her fevered brow. He thought her lips moved a bit. He wondered whether she was trying to smile or to speak. He figured his imagination was working overtime but he talked to her about Maria and then about their lives together.

He thought she was making less noise as she breathed. Then he realized. She wasn't breathing at all. He prayed frantically but Elena remained silent.

After a couple more minutes the nurse tapped him on the shoulder and led him to an empty room that was more like an empty closet. She gave him papers to sign and told him to change his gown, cap, gloves, and mask before he returned to his daughter's room. Then she was gone, too.

Cesar sat in the room and thought. This was Saturday morning. Six days before on Sunday he'd left his healthy family to go on a short business trip. Now he was a widower. His daughter was apt to die like her mother in another two days unless the antivirals performed a miracle. And he was apt to die the same way in three to five days. A family wiped out in less than a week.

He could think of no one to call but Julia.

-/-/-

After Cesar's call, Julia dropped onto a chair in her living room. Elena was dead. She moaned and crossed herself.

She had listened carefully when Sara had warned her on Thursday to avoid all contact with La Bendita because the flu was deadly. This morning she had been alarmed when the health officials matter-of-factly stated almost fifty people in La Bendita had died already but she had reasoned those who had died were old. Elena's death changed everything. Elena is, no was, her age. She pondered her future. There was no doubt she'd been exposed to the flu. Elena coughed and hacked the whole time she was in her house. And she knew she could die like Elena tomorrow or in a couple of days. Of course, she was taking antivirals but she doubted that she got them soon enough. Her throat felt scratchy.

She was worried about her boys. Her mother would take good care of them after the "flu police" took her away. Funny, kids had a way with words. Flu police is what Lalo called the CDC and state health officials. It really described them well. They tried to be nice, but they were scary and bossy, even bossier than her mother and that wasn't easy.

Her biggest fear was she'd not protected her boys well. She'd kept the boys away from Maria, but they must have touched surfaces that Maria had touched. And besides, she'd hugged Maria as well as the boys. She'd been stupid and hadn't even changed her clothes until after supper last night. The realization she might have caused her boys' deaths horrified her.

The "flu police" had emphasized Julia and the boys needed to take the antiviral medication religiously. Sara had emailed her the same message. Sara must have told Aletha because Aletha had called three times to remind Julia. She knew her mother meant well, but she didn't need lectures now. If this was her last day with her boys, she'd make it happy. If Lalo and Gabi survived, at least they'd have good memories of her.

Julia called the boys to the kitchen. "I want you to make a list of your favorite activities."

Gabi, who was now five, gave a shy smile "Go to McDonald's."

"Let's think about what we can do at home. Like cook or play computer games. What would you like for dinner?"

"Chocolate chip cookies," said Gabi.

"No, enchiladas," said eight-year-old Lalo.

Her nerves couldn't take a long discussion. She gave Lalo a sheet of yellow paper and a pencil. "Write down what you'd like to do today."

The first item on the boys' list was to make cookies. After Julia and the boys had made chocolate chip cookies, they began the second activity on the list, play computer games.

They had played *Reader Rabbit* for five minutes before Lalo complained. "This is for babies."

Gabi screamed, "Is not."

"Gabi, you're a baby," said Lalo as he walked toward his room.

"Am not, am not, am not."

She felt the temples pulsing and fought the urge to scream. She wasn't up to arguments today. "How about *Nemo's Underwater Adventure?*" asked Julia.

Lalo slammed a disc on the desk. "I'd rather play *Electroplankton.*"

"It's too hard for Gabi."

Gabi began to chant again. "Nemo. Nemo. Nemo."

After an hour of playing computer games, Julia said, "Why don't we make dinner?"

Lalo looked away from the computer screen. "Dinner's in the evening."

"Let's pretend this is Sunday and have dinner around two. Besides, I don't want you to fill up on any more chocolate chip cookies. What will it be?"

"Enchiladas, like Granny makes."

Gabi sat quietly. "What would you like?" asked Julia.

"McDonald's."

She forced herself not to cry when she realized her little boy might never eat another McDonald's hamburger. "We can't go out. I'll make the enchiladas all cheesy and gooey — as you like them."

Lalo pushed Gabi aside as he threw open the cabinet doors and began to pull pans from the cabinet. After a lot of clattering, he handed Julia the pan she used for enchiladas. "Finally, something I want."

While the enchiladas baked in the oven, Julia called her mother. "Mama, this will be brief. I want to spend every minute I can with the boys. We're all fine. But when you…" She paused and bit her lip. "Get the call to come and to care for the boys, be sure to bring McDonald's hamburgers and fries. Gabi keeps asking for them."

After dinner she read to the boys. When a state health official stopped by to give them injections of the antivirals, Julia gave him a bag of chocolate chip cookies to give to Cesar and Maria.

Julia awoke with a start around five on Sunday morning. She couldn't breathe. She figured her allergies were acting up. Or she had the flu.

CHAPTER 9: Day Five Continued — Dr. Gaspar Gonzales

Dr. Gaspar Gonzales rushed into the main room of the clubhouse at two and groaned. It was really a waste of space, but Ellen Behren had insisted on commandeering the great room of the clubhouse with its mammoth fireplace as her headquarters.

Two clerks sat behind long tables banked with computers. Ellen Behren sat a table in front of them with her limp brown hair pulled back from her face by a telephone headpiece. As she frantically sorted through files, she periodically spoke into the phone, "We'll try," and "You don't seem to understand the situation here."

Only two others were in the large room. A tall, pale-skinned man in his early forties with matted red hair slumped in a chair with his head on the table. A forty-year-old woman fiddled with her long, black hair that was pulled back in a ponytail. Both were dressed in hospital-green scrubs.

"I see Ellen is on the phone. Who is it this time?" Gaspar didn't wait for an answer. "Her CDC bosses, the governor's office, or the Secretary of the New Mexico Department of Health?"

The red-headed man lifted his head slowly. "Not sure. I just got off duty, showered, and came in here for the tally."

Gaspar stared at Martin Bloom. He had changed in the last two days. On Thursday afternoon, Dr. Bloom, an internist in the infectious disease section of the Department of Internal Medicine at University Hospital, had smiled broadly when it was announced he would head the medical team at the La Bendita Clinic that included its two regular physicians. One of whom was Gaspar. Martin had arrived at La Bendita on Thursday evening full of confidence with three medical residents and a medical fellow in tow. On Friday, he seemed paler and more somber as he requested and got three physician assistants assigned to work with him. Today he looked ashen and frightened.

Sylvia Otega, on the other hand, had changed little in the last two days. She had efficiently and calmly administered more than sixty full- and part-time employees in Progressive Health Care's Assisted

Living and Nursing Home Center at La Bendita since it opened. Gaspar considered her features carefully. Perhaps, she had lost the usual glow in her eyes during the last two days.

Gaspar doubted he had weathered the last two days as well as Sylvia. He was older, in his fifties, and less fit. Although he was the Director of University Hospital's clinic at La Bendita and medical advisor for the center, his specialty was family medicine, not internal medicine. He'd gladly let Dr. Bloom head the medical team for the epidemic and had volunteered for two other activities. All patients who had been immunized or who had received the experimental antiviral medications before they developed flu symptoms would be under his care in the clinic. It was expected these patients would require less intense medical care than those in the center. So far, he had ten patients, mainly children of unimmunized staff. He had also agreed to spearhead the public health activities at La Bendita because he knew most of the residents in the private homes.

Gaspar muttered to himself. "Of course, knowing the peculiarities of the residents of the homes in La Bendita is not the same as knowing how to control them." No one paid any attention. He announced loudly, "You can't believe the problems I had today. They're ready to riot."

Ellen finished her phone conversation and announced, "Let's hear the report on the center first."

Sylvia grimaced as she pulled a sheet from a file in front of her. "I got these numbers from my nursing supervisors. As of one today, sixty-seven have died. Fifty-six were residents in the center. Nine were residents in the community; one was a clerk in the center; and one was a visitor to the center — Elena Pena."

Gaspar gasped. "The last I heard only fifty were dead."

"We had a busy morning. University Hospital, actually the State of New Mexico, ran out of ventilators." Martin turned to Ellen. "Are you sure Arizona and Texas couldn't send us more? Several of the ventilators we received must have come out of storage somewhere. The older nurses and I had to explain how to use them to the residents and young nurses."

Ellen flushed slightly. "I've tried, believe me, I've tried. I can't get any more."

Martin shook his head.

"What's the prognosis for those hospitalized in the center?" said Gaspar.

"At least half will die in the next three days," said Martin. "We don't have anything to save them. We're short of ventilators. Antibiotics are useless. The traditional antivirals, like Tamiflu, are useless." He glared at Ellen. "And she won't allow me to use the new experimental antivirals with any but sick staff members and their families."

Ellen looked up from a file and glared back at him. "The experimental antivirals are in short supply. I got the first shipment of them late on Thursday. The CDC doesn't think they will help patients who have developed full blown flu symptoms."

"Probably true," said Martin.

"I believe that describes most of the patients in the center now." Ellen sniffed. "Second, we shouldn't waste them on patients with potentially impaired immune function as often occurs in the aged. The FDA approved them for use in patients younger than fifty. Like most of our staff. I believe the average age of the residents in the center is seventy-nine."

Martin straightened in his chair. "FDA was covering the drug company's ass. We give other antivirals and vaccines to those over seventy routinely, even if their immune systems are less than optimal. I want to give the antivirals to all our patients when they first present with symptoms, at least for a day or two."

Ellen shook her head. "That's fine in a non-emergency situation. Officials in Santa Fe decided the state didn't have the manpower to inject everyone in the Albuquerque area with antivirals twice a day. Thus, they developed guidelines for the use of the experimental antivirals. Their criteria are the individual: was exposed to the flu, was not immunized against the flu, is quarantined here or in homes being monitored by public health workers, is younger than fifty, and does not have advanced stages of the flu."

Gaspar blinked his eyes. "So, I should give the antivirals to all the residents of La Bendita who are younger than fifty. Ellen, why didn't you tell me they were eligible on Thursday or at least yesterday?"

Ellen seemed to ignore him as she turned and studied her computer screen.

Martin cleared his throat. "Gaspar, I think you should be prepared to give the antivirals to everyone younger than sixty-five. Sara and I extracted a compromise from Ellen. She agreed to release the antivirals for use with those between fifty and sixty-five if we developed a protocol to test the effectiveness of the antivirals with that age group.

The CDC is reviewing the protocol now. We should have their answer in the next hour."

"Wait." Ellen sat up straight and tried to assume control of the room. "These new antivirals aren't perfect. Both Elena and the unimmunized ward clerk received antivirals. They died as fast as the elderly patients in the center who didn't receive the antivirals." Ellen returned to scanning her computer screen.

"Are you trying to obfuscate the facts?" Martin's face was flushed and his voice trembled. "Both Elena and the ward clerk had symptoms for more than three days before they received the new antivirals. They got the antivirals too late. Those unvaccinated staff and their families, who got antivirals after one day of coughing, are hanging in there so far." More quietly he added, "But I don't know for how long."

Gaspar wanted to curse at Ellen, but now was not the time for a power struggle. He shook his head. "Enough debate. I will give the new antivirals to all the residents of La Bendita who are younger than sixty-five today."

Ellen continued to stare sullenly at her computer screen.

Gaspar wanted to tell her to stop acting like a spoiled child but he'd learned when his children were teens that such confrontations were seldom useful. "Remember, the residents of La Bendita are foolish at times but they are quite capable of calling the governor, reporters, or even your bosses at the CDC if they think they're being cheated."

Ellen's upper lip quivered. "But first you have to get the baseline data."

"What baseline data?" groaned Gaspar.

"Martin and his staff collected blood samples and nasal swabs from all the staff, immunized and not immunized, in the center and the clinic, but no one has collected samples from the residents of the community yet."

"Let's get started." Gaspar jumped to his feet.

"It's not so simple. As you know, Sara emailed all the residents in the La Bendita community and asked for their dates of birth. Then three of the clinic's clerks, who were allowed to work from their homes because they have young children, phoned all residents who did not respond to the email — at least half of them."

"Yes, I knew that." Gaspar began to pace. "Some of the residents complained their privacy was violated. What did they find?"

"One hundred and fifty-nine are younger than sixty-five and are not already hospitalized. Here's the list of names with phone numbers and street addresses. When you're done collecting samples from all of them, the samples will be sent to the state lab for analyses. The lab should have the samples analyzed in two days."

Gaspar winced.

Ellen continued, "Sara will have to analyze the results statistically. You should be able to give the residents the experimental antivirals by late Monday."

Gaspar's jaw dropped. "Have you forgotten you're a physician as well as a bureaucrat? These delays can't be necessary."

"Let's try something different," said Martin, "and save lives. Let's start those under sixty-five on antivirals when we collect baseline samples from them."

"Can't." Ellen smiled. "The protocol states…"

"Baseline samples will be collected from patients before experimental antiviral treatment is begun," interrupted Martin. "Sara and I were careful. It doesn't state the analyses will be completed before treatment is begun."

Ellen looked dumb struck. "Are you sure?"

"We knew the new test for the Philippine flu virus would take at least two days, probably three, to complete. Patients could die waiting for those analyses." Martin smirked. "You would have known that if you read the protocol. The protocol must have sold itself to the CDC. You didn't even read it."

Gaspar looked around the room. "Who will help me draw the blood samples and inject the antivirals?"

"Sit down Gaspar," said Ellen. "First, I want to hear about your efforts at crowd control."

Martin buried his head in his hands. Sylvia, as she had for the last ten minutes, kept her hand in front of her mouth while she stared angrily at Ellen.

Gaspar sat down and scanned his notes. "Three picked up their medications this morning. Two didn't bother. I sent my outreach nurse to their homes. One was afraid to leave her house because she thought she might catch the flu."

"Not an illogical decision," said Martin.

"Not when you have congestive heart failure and have run out of your statins." Gaspar paused. "The other one had started to cough and didn't want us to know. His wife tried to keep my outreach nurse from hearing him." He paused, scanned his notes, and closed the file. "And now we get to the real circus — food distribution. We explained in phone and email messages on Friday we would have only basics for sale. And the residents should place their orders from our checklist of twenty items by ten last night."

"Who's we?" asked Ellen.

"Me, my outreach nurse, and George Kent and his wife. The other damn HOA Board member Howie Steele is useless. He acts like talking on the phone to potential flu victims might infect him. He'll starve before he leaves his home, and he's not the only one."

Sylvia smiled at Gaspar. "You've done an amazing job of handling the crowd. I really doubt any will starve."

"Problem is when they sit home and stew, they're more apt to plot escapes."

Ellen glared at him. "Back to reality."

"About fifty households purchased food. We assigned them staggered pick-up times. George Kent and I told them it was to reduce chances for transmission of the flu, but we also thought it would reduce the risk of an uprising. Several were belligerent. Almost everyone complained about the lack of variety in the foods we offered but we can't handle more choices."

"How did you get the food?" asked Martin.

"Same way we get food for the center," said Sylvia. "My dietary department orders the food. The vendors leave it outside our front gate. The ambulance crew brings it inside the gate for distribution or delivers it to the kitchen of the center. USDA is supposed to make a large delivery of staples on Monday."

"Did the residents pay in cash?" asked Ellen.

"Nah, we took checks and IOUs. It was a zoo. You've got to get us a way to accept credit cards." Ellen typed an email while Gaspar spoke.

"Done." she announced. "Besides, the cash and checks have to be held for five days or be irradiated before they can enter the general circulation. Credit cards can be wiped with alcohol."

"Now back to the urgent matter," said Gaspar. "I need help to draw blood samples today and then administer the antivirals twice a day to the…. what is it?" He looked at the sheet Ellen had given him. "One hundred and fifty-nine residents. We'll have to go house-to-house initially and may have to remove the sick forcibly from their homes."

Martin shook his head. "My docs and physician assistants are dead on their feet in the center. I can't ask them to do anything more. And I haven't slept for more than three hours at a time in the last two days." He rubbed his eyes. "Of course, there are the three that I threw out of center because all they could do was cry. That's Dave Sedley and two young nurses. You can have them."

"I can't spare any of the other nurses," said Sylvia.

"I'll assign the ambulance crew to help." Ellen emailed the two men. "They'll be at the front door of the clubhouse in ten minutes."

Gaspar noted Ellen's efficiency, but he did not compliment her. Instead he asked, "Oh, one other point. The residents want to know whether the families of the sick and deceased have been notified."

"Yes, the three ward clerks from the center who are quarantined in their homes call relatives when patients are hospitalized here, take calls from family twenty-four/seven, and notify them of deaths."

Sylvia said, "How are you handling the problem that the relatives can't say good-bye to their loved ones? It's pretty tough to find out Mom is going to be put in a refrigerator truck and the body can't be viewed, let alone buried, until this wave of the epidemic is over here."

"So far, the biggest problem is the families are upset they can't claim any of their parents' possessions until the epidemic is over," replied Ellen. "I've talked to the New Mexico Attorney General about extending the probate period for all flu deaths."

Sylvia shook her head. "What about pets?"

"An officer of the Sandoval County Animal Control Unit has agreed to pick up any unclaimed pets."

"They'll be euthanized in a week if no one claims them," said Gaspar.

"Sad." Sylvia sat quietly for a moment. "My nurses can't keep up this pace. Of course, our patient load is dwindling. Perhaps one or two cats or small dogs could be kept in the women's dorm tent. We need relief from the tension and grief. Pets would provide comfort to us."

"We're providing sleeping quarters for over seventy people. Besides docs, nurses, and aides, we have the ambulance, cleaning, and dietary crews." Ellen swept her arm toward one side of the clubhouse. "Most of the side rooms of the clubhouse are filled with cots. And the two tents pitched on the north and south sides of the parking lot by the clubhouse are full too. We can't handle the additional mess of pets."

"Perhaps not." Sylvia sighed. "But can we continue without hope?"

"The men's tent would probably like a pet too," added Gaspar. Martin lifted his head from his hands and nodded.

"Oh, you agree." Ellen sighed. "I'll have the ambulance crews deliver two or three pets to you, Sylvia."

"At least I saved a few of the residents of La Bendita today, even if it's the furry ones." Sylvia lips curved slightly.

CHAPTER 10: Day Five Continued — Sara

Sara thought she saw a trend. Residents on the third floor of the center, on average, came down with the flu almost a day later than those from the first and second floors. Many of the unimmunized ward clerks who worked on the first and second floors were ill. Only one ward clerk from the third floor was ill. The three visitors who saw relatives on the third floor hadn't developed flu symptoms. The visitors to the first and second floors were all ill or dead.

How could she explain those data? Part of the explanation was easy. All nurses and aides in the center and the clinic had been immunized against the Philippine flu two months ago because they were expected to have direct contact with patients. However, the center and the clinic, like most hospitals in the area, had not immunized kitchen staff, janitors, and clerks. Martin Bloom had recognized the problem on Thursday and had started treating all the unimmunized staff members under fifty years of age with antivirals. Unfortunately, the clerks working on the first and second floor of the center had already developed flu symptoms and the antivirals were less effective for them.

She figured someone or something originally exposed a number of residents on the first and second floor of the center to the flu virus on either last Sunday or Monday. Of course, that was based on two assumptions. One, patients developed symptoms one to four days after they were exposed to the virus. Two, the source of the Philippine flu in La Bendita was the Mortons. They were hospitalized on Wednesday and probably homebound on Tuesday. She needed to discover what the Mortons did on Sunday and Monday.

Sara called Ellen Behren to update her. At the end of their conversation, she asked, "Did Gaspar get the blood samples from our residents? Did he start them on antivirals?"

Ellen didn't wait for Sara to ask any more questions. "Gaspar and Dulce are walking in the door now. I'll put them on speakerphone so they can answer your questions while I talk to the governor's office."

Sara waited a moment. "Well guys, how'd it go?"

Gaspar groaned. "Awful."

Dulce Akee, his long-time clinic nurse, said, "Some are grateful."

"Most were angry they didn't get antivirals sooner."

"About what I expected," said Sara. "You can't blame them."

"Some sad cases," said Dulce. "Only one spouse eligible for the antivirals."

Gaspar blew his nose loudly. "The worst was Marian Crockett. She started screaming, 'I ain't got a life without Hank.' She wouldn't stop."

"I tell her she helps Hank by staying well."

Gaspar groaned. "No wonder your name is Dulce. You're all sweetness and light even with the most cantankerous residents of La Bendita."

Sara thought it was too bad Gaspar, really everyone including herself, didn't have more of Dulce's attitudes. Dulce always saw the best in everyone. Maybe it reflected her upbringing on the Jemez Pueblo. Her speech certainly did; she seldom used the past tense. Sara wondered whether Dulce's tendency not to hold grudges reflected her speech pattern — no need to dwell on the past. Sara's thoughts became practical. She decided humor might be the best way to snap Gaspar out of his funk. "Gaspar, you sound like our illustrious developer Paul Owens."

"Hmmf. I'm not that bad. Will talk more to you later. Have to settle a few issues."

CHAPTER 11: Dr. Gaspar Gonzales Remembers

"Ellen, is there any chance we could give the experimental antivirals to a few others? It's cruel to give the antiviral to one spouse who is younger than sixty-five and deny it to the other spouse older than sixty-five."

Ellen continued her conversation with the governor's office for at least a minutes before she put her thumb over the speaker on her head phone. "You know we can't."

Gaspar bit his tongue, partially because Dulce pulled at his sleeve.

"Maybe Sara can figure a way around the rules," said Dulce. "She fixes lots of things here. She got us bus service and started the pet therapy and volunteer programs in the center."

"Mmm. She is a fixer in more ways than you know." He recalled the day he first met her.

-/-/-

It was a blistering hot August day over a year ago. Progressive Health Care Corporation and University Hospital Medical Group, Inc. had hosted an open house of their new facilities for the residents of La Bendita.

Paul Owens had pulled Gaspar aside at the start of the open house. "Remember when University Hospital's Medical Group was looking for a site for your clinic. Your lawyers were sure we couldn't get part of the land in La Bendita re-zoned from residential to mixed-use."

Gaspar had wanted Sylvia, the director of the center, to hear Paul's comments. He'd motioned her to join them. "Yes, the lawyers figured, so did I, the residents of La Bendita community would agree to remove age restrictions on property ownership. Then you couldn't claim an operating emergency to negate their covenants."

Paul had grinned. "It didn't just happen. I made it happen."

"How?"

"I primed Howie Steele and Jim Peterson before the vote by telling them that four beaner families with teenagers wanted to move into La Bendita. But then the old bag Sara Almquist almost ruined the deal."

Gaspar hadn't known how to reply to the slurs. Sylvia had shown more character. "What do you mean?"

"Sara suggested compromise points. Ideas that might have made opening up La Bendita to all age groups acceptable to the other residents."

Sylvia had not hidden her contempt. "Normally what you'd want."

"Not when your bosses are demanding faster sales. They never anticipated we wouldn't sell all the lots in La Bendita in six years. With the creation of the medical clinic and assisted living facility, we should be able to sell the remaining lots in two more years and save my job." Paul had stalked away.

About an hour later Sylvia had approached Gaspar leading a tall, blonde woman. Sylvia winked at Gaspar. "Here's Paul's favorite resident — Sara Almquist."

Gaspar remembered he'd been flustered. Sara definitely wasn't an old bag. He had stammered, "You must be a real mover and shaker."

"Not really. But I have a couple of ideas that might ease tensions between the residents and you newcomers. Have you considered recruiting homeowners in La Bendita to be volunteers at your facilities? For example, my dog Bug and I could be a pet therapy team. We already visit weekly the pediatric units at University Hospital."

-/-/-

Gaspar felt Dulce poking him. "Dr. Gonzales, we should check on patients now."

CHAPTER 12: Day Five Continued — Jane Lane

Jane Lane rode her bicycle down Willow Drive, past the clubhouse, and onto Marigold Lane. She saw no one. Next she partially circled the clubhouse and rode down Cedar Avenue. As she approached the clinic, she saw Gaspar clamber into the front seat of the ambulance while his nurse Dulce and the ambulance crew loaded boxes into the rear of the vehicle.

She wondered what they were doing but figured they wouldn't admit the truth if she asked. She stopped her bike, pulled it behind a desert willow tree, and watched.

The ambulance driver drove toward her and stopped. Gaspar lowered the window. "Go home. If you want to talk to someone, phone or email them." He raised the window.

Jane tried to read his lips as the ambulance pulled from the curb. She thought he said, "Loco woman." She mumbled, "That's all right. I think you're Nazis." The ambulance turned onto Marigold Lane.

She didn't want them to know she was following them. She went down Willow Drive and then circled back to Marigold Lane. When she entered Marigold Lane, she saw the ambulance was parked in front of the Kents' house. The ambulance crew sat in the vehicle, but Dr. Gonzales and Dulce were not in sight. She parked her bicycle by the side of the Steeles' house and peeked around the corner of the house towards the Kents' house.

She suspected Doc Gonzales and George Kent were plotting against the rest of those in La Bendita. Before the flu, she thought they were good guys but not now. They were forcing everyone to stay trapped here while the flu picked off one after another. It didn't make sense.

Gaspar and Dulce appeared. The ambulance crew drove to Willow Drive. Jane followed on her bicycle after a few minutes. By the time she arrived, the ambulance was parked in front of the Crocketts' home, almost cater-cornered from her own home. She parked her bicycle in her driveway and watched.

Again, the ambulance crew remained in the ambulance and Doc Gonzalez and Dulce weren't in sight. After two minutes, she heard Marian screaming. Moaning was a better description of the sound. Jane stretched her neck. She could see nothing, but she heard, "I ain't got a life without Hank."

"Poor bastard must have the flu. They're going to cart him away to the center." But after another five minutes, Gaspar and Dulce appeared without Marian or Hank. They drove down the street past four houses and repeated the whole process.

Jane was tired of tailing the ambulance and rolled her bike into her garage. She called Jim Peterson. "Something strange is going on." Jane proceeded to explain what she'd seen.

He replied, "Keep with our plan. We'll meet at the designated spot at ten tomorrow night unless you hear otherwise from me or Jean."

Jane turned on the TV and channel surfed. "Nothing interesting again."

She turned the TV off and pushed buttons on her phone. "Hey Marian, I saw the flu Nazis attack you. Are you okay? What's up?"

Jane listened to the response.

"Let me get this straight. They have a medicine that can protect us against the flu. Why didn't they use it earlier? You know, the Benders and lots of others have disappeared into the center. No one who enters, except the staff, ever comes out. And at night they keep putting things, God knows what, into the meat truck behind the center."

Jane paced while she listened.

"A cock 'n bull story," she screamed. "So, Sara's working with the Nazis too?"

She listened again.

"Okay, maybe Sara is trying to help. But age discrimination is illegal. You should call a lawyer."

Jane's face became red as she listened.

"Okay. Okay. You and Hank trust Dr. Gonzales, Sara, and George Kent. Jim and I think differently. We're going to protect ourselves because no one else will." She slammed the phone down.

Jane suddenly felt tired. She lay down on her unmade bed. The next thing she knew, someone or something was knocking on her bedroom window. It was dark. She thought she saw a shadow cross her shade.

She feared the Nazis were spying on her because they didn't want to confront her directly at her front door. They must have figured that she wouldn't let them in the house again after the survey last Thursday. But why were they checking out her house? Could they have heard about her plans with Jim?

She decided to check her back yard and found her flashlight in the nightstand by her bed. She tiptoed to the front door, opened it as softly as she could, and ran. As she turned the corner of her house, she turned the flashlight on. Something rushed toward her. Jane braced for impact.

It was the Steeles' golden retriever Goldie. Goldie jumped up and put his big front paws on Jane's chest while his long tongue reached out to give her a sloppy kiss on the face.

She thought she heard the sound of stones striking stones as someone walked on the gravel. However, all she could see and smell was dog.

After a minute of confusion, Jane called, "Goldie. Goldie. Down. Down."

Goldie ignored Jane's commands and settled down at his own pace. Jane grabbed Goldie's leash and led him past the clubhouse to the Steeles' home on Marigold Lane.

She rang the doorbell. The television was blaring. She rang the doorbell again. Howie bellowed at Susan. She thumped on the door. Susan Steele opened the door enough to peek out. The cheeks of usually anemic-looking Susan were red.

Susan looked past Jane and stared at Goldie. "Goldie, have you been a bad boy? Did Jane have to rescue you?" She bit her lip, dragged Goldie into the house, and closed the door without ever speaking directly to Jane.

Jane stood there for a minute waiting for Susan to reopen the door and thank her. After a minute, Jane decided Susan wouldn't reappear and trotted back to her own house.

She thought Susan was always nervous, but tonight she was strange. Not surprising. Anyone married to Howie would be. Maybe the Nazis prowled near Jane's house too and spooked her.

Jane felt a shiver pass through her when she looked toward her house. The ambulance was parked in front.

"You're our last delivery," said Gaspar as he climbed from the vehicle. He gave her a long song-and-dance routine about the antivirals and ended by saying, "We need to give you an injection. Can we come in?"

"Do it here," said Jane. She slid out of her jacket and exposed her arm for the injection.

After the ambulance pulled away, Jane opened her front door cautiously. She looked to the left and right before she stepped into her house. As she paced from room to room, she checked to see whether the windows were locked and the shades were down. Then she pulled her backpack from a closet and crammed a pair of shoes and a change of clothes into it. She started to leave her house but returned inside and put the backpack under her bed.

As Jane rolled her bike out to the street, she looked all around. No one was out. Most houses were totally dark. She began to pedal around La Bendita. First, past the front gate. Two police cars were parked at the front gate. Two policemen sat in each car. Usually, well at least since Thursday and the Nazis' takeover of La Bendita, two policemen sat, or more correctly slept, in one car by the front gate.

She rode past the clubhouse and meandered until she reached the perimeter road, which followed the wall around the lower half of La Bendita. When she passed the back gate, she panicked. For the first time, a car with a guard was posted at the back gate. She circled the neighborhood and then rode past the back gate again. Nothing had changed. The guard was still there. She figured she'd better warn Jim.

She cycled to her house and picked up a handful of small pieces of gravel from her front yard that was landscaped in the southwestern style like all the yards in La Bendita. She cycled slowly past the Petersons' house and threw several pebbles at their front door. She picked up speed and cycled down the street and then back. She slowed as she cycled past the Petersons' house again. This time she threw several small stones at their front window. On her third pass, the garage door opened.

She jumped off her bike and guided it into the garage between a black Hummer and a gray Subaru Outback. The garage door closed immediately.

Jim stood inside his house with the house's door to the garage open. "We agreed you wouldn't stop here."

"Yes, unless there was an emergency."

"Which is?" Before she could answer, he added, "Be quiet. I don't want the neighbors to hear you."

She was annoyed that he was giving her orders but he was right. Nazi spies were everywhere. She whispered, "There are two police cars at the front gate."

"So what. We leave tomorrow night through the back gate."

"That's why I'm here." Jane figured her sleuthing would impress Jim. "There's a man in an unmarked car at the back gate. The reading light in the car was on, and the radio was blasting mariachi music."

"What did the policeman look like?"

"Young Hispanic."

Jim smirked slightly but did not interrupt her.

"You think the Nazis are on to us?"

"I doubt it. You'll have to divert his attention."

"How?"

"You know. The gun that Jean gave you today."

"I'm afraid to pick it up. She said it was loaded."

"Try not to be a coward."

Jane arched her back and her mouth dropped open, but she said nothing.

"Stay in the house tomorrow and get plenty of sleep. At ten tomorrow night, cycle down to the perimeter road and shoot off a round. Try not to be too close to the back of either the center or the clinic. Then cycle to the corner where Zinnia Avenue and the perimeter road meet. We'll be waiting for you in the Hummer. As soon as the police car leaves its post to investigate the shots, we'll be out through the back gate."

Jane's face twisted. "Don't know. Is that the best place to shoot off the rounds?"

"It's the most deserted area because a few unsold lots are there."

"Don't know. What if I can't get to you?"

"Don't worry. You've timed it. You can go on the perimeter road from the deserted spot to Zinnia Avenue in less than two minutes."

"Don't know. What if the police car doesn't move?"

"He'll move." Jim eyed Jane who was tinkering with her bicycle pedal. "Come on Jane. You can do it. Jean will visit you tomorrow afternoon to update you on last minute details." He looked at his watch. "Better go now."

Jane gulped. "See you tomorrow a little after ten."

The garage door rose and Jane darted out on her bicycle. The garage door closed.

CHAPTER 13: Saturday Night — Jim Peterson

Jim opened the cargo hold of his Hummer. He felt under the carpet and pulled a catch. A door to a compartment in one fender opened. The compartment was filled with bulging blue Gortex tote bags. He pulled out a revolver from between two bags and checked it. He pulled a second catch. The door to a compartment on the other side opened. This compartment was filled with more full bags but these were maroon. He smiled and carefully closed the compartments.

His wife joined him in the garage. Jean rubbed her fingers on his neck. "Who'd ever think we'd live in a place called 'the blessed' in Spanish? I mean La Bendita is such a schmaltzy name."

"Yeah, but this place has been good for us. This planned community with its big clubhouse and hokey name attracted mainly upper middle class, proper residents. The image we wanted."

"I think I fit into the stereotype perfectly with my proper little lady routine."

He slapped her rear lightly and pushed her into the house. "You could have fooled me."

He looked her up and down. "Why don't you show me your other side?"

Jean ignored him and continued with the previous conversation. "It wasn't easy, always talking about the wonderful perimeter wall and front gate. Hell, the walls can't even keep the coyotes out. But they sure make the streets, with all their stupid flower and tree names, so dead it's easy to spot anyone snooping around."

"Yeah, but I wouldn't have liked if it the walls were higher. Would have made me feel caged, like in prison. These walls were just decoration."

Jean frowned. "I was afraid we would have to leave five years ago when they proposed the center and the clinic."

"Me too." He steered his wife toward their bedroom. "But it worked because we knew how to handle Howie."

Jean unbuttoned her pink sweater and revealed a red lace bra. "Do you realize how many boring evenings we spent with Howie and Susan Steele because you wanted to learn every detail of what the HOA Board was planning and make sure Howie voted right."

"Thank God, he talks too much when he drinks."

Jean pulled down her matronly polyester beige slacks and revealed her red lace thong. "After you learned he had a gate pass to the back-emergency gate, you got impatient. It made me nervous the evening you spiked his and Susan's claret wine with GHB."

"Why? It's a standard product. Good old gamma-hydroxybutyrate delivers." Jim licked his lips as Jean shimmied out of her slacks.

"Yes, but I had to sit with them while you ran off and got your friends to copy the pass card."

"Jean, as I remember, you had to make the table look like we'd eaten a full meal so the Steeles wouldn't notice the loss of three hours."

Jean unbuttoned Jim's shirt, rubbed her hand on his chest, and cooed. "It was nerve racking."

"Yes, but I had to go all the way to Zuni Avenue on the south side of Albuquerque to get the pass card duplicated. Takes time."

Jean unzipped Jim's jeans. "You know one of our funniest moments in La Bendita may have been when you slipped back in the house and helped me wake Howie and Susan."

"Susan kept saying where did the time go?" said Jim. "And I don't remember eating."

"The egotistical bastard Howie claimed it was the best claret he ever tasted," said Jean as she whipped a bit of Jim's chest hair around her finger.

"What a fool. GHB isn't perfect. Like Susan, he should have sensed something wasn't right."

Jean looked at her husband tentatively. "Are we ready?"

He looked down at his jeans. "Sure looks like it."

"Not what I mean." She laughed as she finished tugging his jeans to the floor. She began to caress him.

"It's hard to concentrate on business."

Jean peeked up at him. "Try. What about tomorrow night?"

"You gave Jane the gun. The police car at the back entrance will respond. Then I'm out again unnoticed."

Jean stopped stroking him. "And if the police car doesn't move?"

"You know the answer." Jim looked at Jean. He grasped her shoulders and pushed her onto the bed. "No more questions."

CHAPTER 14: Days Five and Six of the Crisis— Cesar Pena, Aletha Bradley, Julia Chavez

Dulce looked into the tiny, light gray room designed to be an examination room, not a patient room with a bed. Cesar sat on a decrepit recliner reading *The Cat in the Hat* to Maria. She lay in a hospital crib with one of its barred sides down. The paint on the bars was chipped. University Hospital had gotten it out of warehouse storage when La Bendita was chosen as the site for the quarantine. The Penas' possessions lay on the floor.

"How are you?"

Cesar rose and almost stumbled on the pile on the floor as he left the room to talk to Dulce. "I think her fever is higher. She doesn't want to talk now. Can we up the antivirals? She can have my share."

"Not work that way. I take your vitals."

"I'm not the problem. Put your attention on Maria."

Dulce grabbed his arm and pushed him into a chair in the hall. In what seemed like one continuous fluid motion, she slapped a blood pressure cuff onto his arm, took his temperature, recorded notes on a file, and then shoved the clipboard into a plastic holder on the wall outside Maria's room. She eyed his face slowly. "Your BP is up. Not surprising. You need to eat. There's food in the first-floor break room. Pretty good tonight. Frito pie."

Cesar stared at her.

"Go."

Cesar ambled to the elevator.

Dulce was waiting for Cesar when he returned. "Go to the conference room. Dr. Gonzales is waiting."

Cesar heard the words he feared most during the next two minutes. "We're doing everything possible," and "We should know in twenty-four hours."

He returned to his daughter's room and finished reading *The Cat in the Hat* before he fell into a fitful sleep in the uncomfortable chair by

Maria's bed. Sometime around ten, Cesar heard a distant sound. He assumed it was fireworks but when he woke more fully and thought, he knew it was a gunshot probably near the rear of the clinic.

He raced down the hallway to windows in the lounge that faced the rear of the La Bendita property. At first, he saw nothing but trail lights from his third-floor view because the nearest street light on the perimeter wall was burned out. Then a police car raced into view and stopped. Next an ambulance appeared. Their headlights were focused on something at the edge of the street. It was placed on a stretcher and carried into the ambulance. The ambulance raced to the back door of the clinic.

Cesar checked on Maria. She was asleep.

He took the elevator to the first floor where an ambulance attendant greeted him. "Sorry man, but you've got to return to your room."

Cesar started to ask a question. The attendant interrupted, "Man, don't give me trouble. We've got enough already. Stay in your room." He shoved Cesar back on the elevator.

Cesar spent the rest of the long night watching a fevered Maria toss and turn.

Dulce appeared slightly before six the next morning. She ignored Cesar's questions about the gunshot, as she examined Maria. "No petechial hemorrhages."

"What?"

"Tiny bruises all over. Her ears and nose are clear, no blood. Her temperature down to hundred."

Cesar grabbed Dulce's arm.

She smiled for the first time. "Maria is getting better." She departed at her usual measured gait.

She returned less than five minutes later. "Julia bake these cookies for you and Maria on Saturday. The public health nurse deliver them to the ambulance crew, but they get busy and forget to drop them off at the clinic until now."

Cesar smiled. It felt good to be remembered by someone.

-/-/-

The night had been a long night for Aletha, too. She'd been wakened by Julia's call at five on Sunday morning. "Mama, it's time you come here. Don't forget to pick up hamburgers and fries at McDonald's." Julia hung up before Aletha could say anything.

Aletha was prepared. She had updated her will and appointed a conservator for her businesses during the last two days. She had also purchased toys, lots of kid-friendly foods, and gallons of disinfectants and cleaners. She had been too busy to visit friends, except two old ones — the Secretary of the New Mexico Department of Health and the Governor or New Mexico. She had reminded them both they would not hold their current positions without her political and financial support. They had pointed out she was seventy-two and the experimental antivirals weren't approved for use by someone of her age. A courier had delivered ten vials of the antiviral medications and syringes to her house late Saturday afternoon.

As Aletha raced down I-25 from Santa Fe to Julia's house in Riverview, she did not cry. She pulled off I-25 and stopped at a McDonald's on Route 550. One of her staff members had called ahead. Even though MacDonald's did not serve its lunch menu until ten-thirty, two Quarter Pounders, several orders of fries, a mocha latte, a regular coffee, and several breakfast burritos were ready for her. Aletha had noticed Julia purchased a McDonald's mocha latte and a breakfast burrito for herself many mornings. A tear slipped down her cheek when the clerk handed her the food. This might be the last food that she served Julia.

Aletha arrived at Julia's home thirty minutes before the public health nurse. Julia, Lalo, and Gabi ate breakfast while Aletha unpacked her car and parked it a block away. When the public health nurse arrived, she looked surprised to see Aletha but quickly turned her attention to Julia.

The ambulance arrived less than an hour later. Julia refused to be carried on a stretcher into the ambulance because she thought it would frighten the boys.

Even so, Lalo pounded the side of the vehicle as the ambulance crew helped Julia climb in. He began to scream over and over again. "You can't take my mother. She's mine."

Aletha tried to grab his hands to stop him from hitting the ambulance. Lalo then started to hit her until Julia began to sob. Gabi stood beside Aletha and held onto her jacket with one hand and his "blankie" with the other hand during the whole scene.

Aletha whispered into Lalo's ear. "It's time to be a man for your mother and Gabi. Give her a kiss. Be a man."

Lalo suddenly stood up straight and approached his mother. He kissed her cheek. "Get well." He ran into the house.

After Gabi kissed Julia, Aletha stood with Gabi and waved until the ambulance disappeared from view. The public health nurse led Aletha and Gabi back into the house and droned on about the rules of quarantine for thirty minutes.

As soon as she left, Aletha pulled out two new computer games for the boys. Neither boy was interested. Gabi wanted to be cuddled. Lalo stormed into his room and slammed the door.

-/-/-

Julia sobbed softly as the ambulance moved along. She recited, "Yea, though I walk through the valley of death," as she was transferred from the first ambulance to another at the gates of La Bendita.

Dulce greeted Julia at the emergency entrance of the clinic, rolled her in a wheelchair to the elevator, pushed her into a tiny gray room on the third floor, and tucked her into bed. "Better not call your kids until you rest some. I call your mother and say you arrive okay."

Cesar appeared. His unshaven face looked pale and he looked older than the last time Julia had seen him. "I saw Dulce roll you in. Sorry to see you here. Maria is still fevered, but they say she will survive." His lips trembled, and tears began to stream down his bleak face. After a minute he gave up any attempt to control his emotions and sobbed violently. He resumed his composure when Julia started to cry too.

"The cookies were good." He darted from Julia's room.

Dulce reappeared. "No more visitors." She plunged a needle into Julia's arm. "You need this. It makes you sleep."

CHAPTER 15: Sunday, Day Six of the Crisis — Chief Gil Andrews, Sergeant Chuy Bargas, Gil Again

Mercado Police Chief Gil Andrews pulled his unmarked car in back of one of the two squad cars parked at the front gate of La Bendita a few minutes after midnight on Sunday. Gil sat quietly and thought for a moment. He'd bragged to his wife when he took early retirement from the Albuquerque Police Department that he was through with night calls. He'd been wrong.

Gil heaved his heavy torso from the car and spoke to Sergeant Chuy Bargas. "Chuy, what we've got?"

"An apparent suicide attempt by the back wall of La Bendita," replied the sergeant, a trim man of about thirty-five with a full head of shiny black hair.

"Suicide attempt. Why'd you get me out of bed?"

"A problem. La Bendita is under quarantine. Once we go in, we're stuck there for a week. When he heard the gunshot, Juan rushed in."

"Damn young fool. He left the back gate unguarded and got himself sequestered in there."

"Yes, I stayed out and sent the ambulance crew already in La Bendita to assist him. They got the victim to the gate and another ambulance crew took her to University Hospital for surgery."

"Why didn't they take care of her here? They got six or seven docs in there and lots of nurses."

"No surgery suite. Well, not a major suite. No surgeons. The boss." He checked his notes. "Dr. Ellen Behren. She and Doc Gonzales argued a bit. Then she yelled into her phone and ordered the ambulance crew to take the victim to University Hospital."

"Did Juan get a statement from the victim?"

"You know Juan, he's green. He said the victim kept moaning, 'not work.' And he said the gun looked funny."

"Where's the gun?"

"At the scene."

"How much did Juan mishandle it already?"

"Good question. He says he put it back about where it fell."

Gil groaned.

"Juan has the scene blocked off. He and the ambulance crew are keeping gapers away. Pretty easy because there are only two. Seems most residents are afraid to leave their houses."

"They're scared of the flu."

Chuy gulped. "Here's the problem. We need to photograph the scene, send the gun to the crime lab for investigation, search the victim's home, and talk to witnesses or people who knew the victim. Juan's not up to it."

"You want to know who I want to sacrifice to do it?"

"Probably one can do it with Juan. The ambulance crew is good."

"Let me talk to this Ms. Behren."

"Better call her Dr. Behren."

"Mmm. I was briefed last Wednesday and Thursday on this quarantine business by state health officials, but I'm a bit fuzzy on details."

"One more thing. Doc Gonzales thinks this might be part of a bigger scheme. What he calls a 'prison break.' He wants us to check out the houses of several residents."

"I better call my old pal Doc first." After a pause, "Chuy you're going in and getting those photos and the gun."

Chuy grimaced.

"Try not to kill Juan for his mistakes. I don't want to have to send another guy in to investigate his murder." Gil chuckled at his own joke.

-/-/-

Chuy jogged to the scene of the reported gunshot with a camera and a couple key pieces of equipment needed for the investigation. The ambulance crew and Juan were there. The gawkers had left.

Chuy immediately sent the ambulance driver with the ambulance to the front gate to help Gil. He ignored Juan's constant jabbering as he photographed the scene. He put on gloves and picked up the mangled gun with tongs.

He'd seen a gun look like this before when a kid wedged a stone down the barrel before he fired it to see what would happen. Generally, any debris in a barrel was blasted out when the gun was fired but sometimes, actually rarely, this happened. The gun exploded.

J. L. Greger

He dusted the mangled gun for prints. There were prints at the end of the hilt with the thumb on one side and two fingers on the other side. Of course, the explosion had probably destroyed prints on the barrel and trigger.

He asked the ambulance crewmember still at the scene, not Juan, about the victim. Her injuries were severe but mainly in her right arm, shoulder, and leg, not in the gut or head.

"Looks like the victim tried to carry the gun and shoot it with her arm extended from her side. If she had held it normally, she would have sustained more injuries to her trunk. Being afraid of the gun may have saved her life."

The ambulance crewmember nodded and pointed to a knapsack next to a nearby desert willow bush. "Look at this."

Chuy photographed the backpack before he looked inside and found a few pieces of women's clothing, a cell phone, an address book, and a wallet. He checked the wallet for identification. "If this is the victim's, she was planning to leave La Bendita not to shoot herself."

Juan came out of his usual daze. "It's a suicide attempt, isn't it?"

"Don't think so."

Juan blinked his eyes. "A murder attempt? But who? They're all nice here. Did I ever tell you how nice?"

Chuy tuned out Juan's babbling again. He texted his conclusions to the Chief. Then he debated how to get the evidence to him. He knew Juan had touched everything he saw. The ambulance crewmember had been careful with the backpack. Chuy placed the gun and backpack into separate bags and handed them to the ambulance crewmember. "Deliver these to the Chief immediately. Then join me at Jane Lane's house."

Juan drove Chuy to Jane Lane's house. Chuy left Juan in the car and searched the house alone. He found nothing unusual except a typed note:

Can't stand this place anymore.

-/-/-

"Yes ma'am, that's all I need from you. But could your aides call these people." Gil rolled his eyes and held the phone at arm's length as he listened.

"Yes, right now. They were near the scene or live in houses near the scene of the shooting. Thanks."

He thought working a crime scene in a quarantine area was like being a blind man crossing a street with a cane and a dog. Actually worse — Dr. Ellen Behren was more like an attack dog than a service dog.

Gil saw an ambulance coming straight at him as he stood at the open gate. He was ready to jump aside when it stopped just short of an invisible quarantine line that separated La Bendita from the rest of the world.

The driver jumped out of the ambulance and approached Gil. "Chuy figured you'd need my help to rouse several residents."

Gil handed the man a list. "Dr. Behren, really her staff, are calling these folks. Can you bring them to the front gate? I can't…"

"No need to explain. The boss lady won't allow anyone who comes in here to leave. I'm stuck here." He looked at the list and departed.

Gil knew it would be hard to get people to talk freely with him when they were standing on the other side of an open gate with police cars blocking their exit. Then too, most folks weren't talkative when they were dragged from their beds in the middle of the night. He decided donuts, good donuts, and hot coffee might make them more talkative. His old friend Doc Gaspar Gonzales said he could get coffee but not donuts from the center.

Gil sent a patrolman in a squad car outside the gate for donuts. A few minutes later a van pulled up to the gate from within. Two young women jumped out and began to retrieve chairs, a coffee urn, and boxes from the back of the van. While they quickly set up a coffee station inside the gate, Gaspar climbed out of the van and ambled to the gate.

"Doc, I didn't expect you to deliver the coffee so fast."

"Sylvia runs a tight ship. Did Ellen cooperate?"

After Gil complained about Ellen, he plied Gaspar with questions about the victim.

Gaspar finished his response by saying, "I doubt Jane Lane had any real thoughts since the quarantine started. She just mouths Jim Peterson's words. It's Peterson you need to check out." Then Gaspar had sighed. "Make sure all residents put on gloves before they touch anything on the coffee service table. Although we don't think any of the residents on your list have been exposed to patients with the flu, don't allow them to mingle."

Gaspar and the coffee crew departed before ambulance driver began to deliver residents on Gil's list to the gate. All told stories consistent with Gaspar's comments. Jane had called the staff maintaining the quarantine "Nazis." She had bragged about driving in Jim Peterson's Hummer through the gate whether it was closed or open.

When the other ambulance crewmember delivered the gun to him, Gil interrupted the interviews to call a clerk at the state crime lab. The clerk had sounded groggy until Gil told him to get prepared to process a bloody gun that was potentially contaminated with deadly Philippine flu virus. The clerk had become hostile, and soon a pathologist came on line and demanded to talk to Dr. Behren. The gun properly tagged and bagged was rushed off to the state crime lab in a special container about an hour later.

At about three in the morning, Chuy pounded on the door of the Petersons' home while Gaspar and both members of the ambulance crew watched from their vehicles parked in front. Juan waited at the sidewalk. No one answered the Petersons' front door. As Chuy began to move toward the back of the house, the front door swung open.

Jean Peterson wore a black silk nightie and robe. She aimed a shotgun at Chuy.

Chuy identified himself quickly and asked her to lower the shotgun.

Jean Peterson blinked her heavily mascaraed eyelashes. "Oh my, so much commotion." Jean spoke in an artificially high-pitched whisper. "All these big strong men here."

She waved at Gaspar and giggled. "What are you doing here Doc?"

She winked at Juan and then turned to Chuy. "Why are you scaring a nice lady like me?"

"Lower the gun ma'am," ordered Chuy again. "We aren't trying to scare you but we need to talk to you and your husband."

As Jean placed the gun on the ground, she managed to give Chuy a full view of her breasts that were originally partially hidden under the sheer black silk.

He knew the view was not accidental. She wasn't acting like a "nice" lady. He suspected she was desperate to distract him. "I need to check your house and speak to your husband."

"Well officer, ladies don't let police enter their homes without warrants. You haven't explained why you're here. A lady like me can't be too careful."

Chuy picked up the gun. "Please step outside your house."

"Must I? I could catch the flu." She twisted her light silk robe more tightly around her body.

"Not from any of us. We're all immunized against the flu."

He motioned to Juan to watch Jean, sped to Doc Gonzales's car, gently laid the shotgun on the back seat, and then called Gil. "Chief, since we're under quarantine, as I understand it, I don't need a warrant." He explained the situation at the Petersons' house.

Gil agreed he could legally search the place without a warrant under the quarantine but asked Chuy to stall a bit while he called a number in the New Mexico Attorney General's Office. He had learned during the briefings on Thursday that the Attorney General's Office would man a hotline night and day for quarantine-related questions.

Chuy returned to face Jean. He decided he didn't need to frisk her. Nothing was hidden under the sheer nightie. "Ma'am, where's your husband?"

A man turned the corner and whistling sauntered toward the Petersons' house.

"Oh, there's my husband now." Jean waved her arm enthusiastically and the robe and the strap of the nightie slid from her left shoulder. "Jim likes to take little strolls when he can't sleep"

As Chuy walked toward the man, he noticed Juan staring at Jean with his mouth agape. "Sir, Mr. Peterson, put your hands in the air."

Jim Peterson lifted his arms. Chuy frisked him.

"Really Officer, can't a man take an evening stroll? The safest time to hike around this place during this epidemic is when no one else is out. I see you've scared my poor wife." Jim called to Jean. "Mother, is everything okay?"

Chuy noted that Jean immediately drew her black robe around herself more tightly, restricting Juan's view. However, Juan still stared at her like a schoolboy.

Chuy evaluated the situation. Juan was useless. He'd brought Gaspar and the ambulance crew along as witnesses but he couldn't ask them to do anything more than carry evidence back to Gil. He needed decent backup but Gil couldn't afford to sideline more men here.

Chuy guided Jim Peterson to the front seat of the ambulance and then nervously cleared his throat. "Mr. Peterson, under the terms of a quarantine, I have the right to search your house without a warrant. I'd prefer to have your permission."

The muscles in Jim's face tightened and he looked like he was ready to explode. Suddenly he whistled and his face relaxed. "I guess it's a matter of whether you report I cooperated or not?"

Chuy resisted the urge to gloat. He'd won only a small skirmish in the war with the Petersons. He tried not to smile as he nodded.

"Mother, let the police in."

Chuy leaned against Gaspar's car and whispered in Gaspar's ear. As soon as he stepped aside, Gaspar sped away. Chuy searched the house while Juan guarded or at least watched Jean at the front door.

One car was parked in the garage. Chuy thought a large vehicle must usually be parked in the empty spot. The living room was awash with family photos and decorated with overstuffed furniture like that in his parents' home. In contrast, the bedroom looked like swinging bachelor's pad with lots of mirrors, chrome, and purple and black satin sheets. No pictures of family.

"Nothing wrong, but odd," muttered Chuy as he took notes.

He opened the door to the front bedroom. It contained an ornately carved oak game table with chairs and a well-stocked bar. He opened the double doors to the library. It was empty except for a long table, two chairs, and a printer but no computer. "Too bad. I'd like to check out their computer."

He opened closets and drawers. He found two loaded handguns. Gun ownership was legal but he could confiscate anything suspicious under the emergency situation created by the quarantine. He put on plastic gloves and emptied the guns of their bullets, placed the guns and bullets in separate bags, and hid the bags in the bushes behind the house. He'd claim them later after he talked to Gil. No need to rile the Petersons now by making a big deal out of confiscating their guns.

When he emerged through the front door, Jean and Juan were still standing by the door. Jim Peterson called from the ambulance. "Well Officer, are you satisfied? My wife is getting chilly."

"Where's your other vehicle?"

Jim smiled. "For fun, Mother and I drove the Hummer around La Bendita earlier in the evening. I dropped her off, parked the car, and walked home. You'll find it on Zinnia Avenue. Mother changed into something cozy and was waiting for me when you arrived. No wonder you near scared her to death."

"Mind giving me the keys to the Hummer?"

Jim hesitated. "Does it matter if I do?"

Chuy smiled. Jim handed over the keys.

"Now what about your computer?" said Chuy.

"Oh, we took it in for repairs last Tuesday. Haven't been able to claim it yet with the quarantine."

Chuy thought Jim Peterson was one cool character. He wondered whether he could extract more information if he made him nervous enough to make a mistake. "Where's your claim ticket for the computer?"

Jim scratched his head. "Mother, do you know where I laid the claim slip for the computer repair?"

"Dear, if the stub's not in your wallet, you must have lost it." Jean smiled at Chuy.

"Where did you drop it off?"

"Not sure. Someplace around Cottonwood Mall. Mother, can you help me?"

Jean smiled at Jim. "How would I know? It's your computer."

"Fine," said Chuy, "We'll look through the phone book together and identify the place."

Jim stiffened. "Officer, is this necessary?"

"Afraid so."

Chuy stepped out of earshot of both Jim and Jean Peterson and called Gil. After a short discussion he instructed the ambulance crew and Juan to drive both Petersons to the front gate for a chat with Gil.

Chuy waited until the ambulance was out of sight before he retrieved the bagged guns and bullets. He paced down Willow Drive to the back of the clubhouse and then toward Zinnia Avenue. He doubted the Petersons would see him because Gil would grill them thoroughly even if an iron gate separated him from them. They wouldn't have a chance to turn around and look in his direction.

He spotted a black Hummer H1 and unlocked it. He looked under the front seat and patted down the cushions before he laid the bagged handguns and bullets on the front seat. He opened the glove compartment. It was empty except for the owner's manual. The car looked like it had just been detailed recently.

"Damn, this guy is too careful and too calm." He tapped the fenders, lifted the cargo liner in back, checked the storage compartment, and lifted the hood.

He called Gil. "I'd bet the car has secret compartments in the fenders but I couldn't find the catches. It was cleaned professionally recently, very recently."

CHAPTER 17: Day Six Continued — Dr. Gaspar Gonzales

Gaspar and Chuy trudged into the La Bendita clubhouse. "I figure you might as well listen to our daily update. And you can explain the details of the shooting better than I can."

Chuy gulped. "I'll try."

"This will help you understand how small the problems created by a misfiring gun in the hands of a neurotic woman are in comparison to the problems engendered by the flu. I, none of us, have ever seen anything like it. It's, it's like," Gaspar paused, thinking, "like the great flu epidemic of 1918."

Beads of sweat dripped down Gaspar's forehead and he wiped his bald head. He always carried a handkerchief in summer to wipe sweat away but during the last week he'd found his head dripped sweat even though the temperature was pleasant. He doubted the excessive sweating was a flu symptom because he'd been vaccinated. Just a sign of stress.

He pushed Chuy onto a wooden chair and sank into a comfortable overstuffed chair facing the table at which Ellen Behren sat. She was on the phone, as usual. Her hair looked stringy and her eyelids were puffy. Martin Bloom, a disheveled mess, was slumped in another overstuffed chair. Sylvia Otega looked the best of the lot. Her hair was clean and neat, but there were bags under her eyes.

Martin looked up. "How goes it?" He hung his head. "Stupid question in this valley of death."

Sylvia didn't look up as she made notes in a file.

Ellen gave a stiff, forced smile. "I asked Sara to listen in on our update today by phone. I thought we needed someone fresh to participate in the discussion." She looked at Chuy and continued. "She's a respected epidemiologist."

Gaspar interrupted, "Perhaps more importantly, Sara is a resident of La Bendita. Both Sylvia and I have found her to have good…" He searched for the right words.

Sylvia finished his sentence. "Intuition on the other residents."

Sara's voice boomed from the speakerphone. "Hey, that sounded like an obit. I'm not dead yet."

"Why isn't she quarantined here?" said Chuy.

"Long, boring story," replied Sara.

Ellen interrupted, "Sylvia, let's start with the patient tally."

"As of one today, five residents of the assisted living center remain symptom free."

"So, the total deaths?" Ellen picked up a pencil to take notes.

"Including the Mortons, one hundred and sixty-eight."

Chuy gulped in astonishment.

"One hundred and thirty-three were residents of the assisted living center." Sylvia wiped tears from her eyes. "I've lost almost one-half of my patients in four days." She broke down completely and sobbed. She regained her composure after a minute and spoke in a monotone. "Now I can give my nurses more time off because of the reduced patient load, but they're too depressed to sleep. Oh by the way, we need another refrigerated truck to store bodies."

Gaspar pursed his lips trying to think of a tactful way to ask his question. "Sylvia, I don't mean to trivialize the losses in the center, but what about the residents of the La Bendita community?"

Sylvia consulted her notes. "Twenty-nine out of two hundred and ninety-three of your residents have died. That's ten percent. Twelve yesterday. More than any other day so far for that group. Fifty-five more residents of the community are hospitalized."

Martin raised his head. "I don't think many critically ill patients are left. I think the worst is over for this wave of the flu." He lowered his head and seemed to go into a trance.

Sylvia was now completely in control of her emotions. "There's more. One more of my clerks and a janitor died today."

Martin came out of his stupor. "So, four of your unvaccinated staff members have died. How many weren't vaccinated two months ago?"

"Twenty-nine. Eleven developed flu symptoms so far."

"Do we know why some did better?"

Sara's voice boomed from the speaker. "You'll find that those working on the third floor of the center did better because they were exposed to the flu later than those working on the first and second floors. Thus, they got antivirals before they developed flu symptoms or at least before their flu symptoms were severe. I'll have more answers for you, once I get a few more pieces of info from the staff."

Ellen gave a rare smile. "Sara has several interesting leads to share with you."

Sara again boomed from the box. "I've been trying to identify what made the five who appear to be untouched by the flu special. One characteristic they share is all five had farm backgrounds. More specifically, all had handled hogs repeatedly. Four as farmers; one as a veterinarian. Only two had handled poultry much."

"Not so loud," said Gaspar.

Sara continued more softly. "I talked to several virologists in the CDC's Infectious Disease Control Unit. They referred me to a virologist from USDA. He's at the National Veterinary Services Lab in Ames, Iowa. Over the last twenty years he's acquired cultures of most of the known swine viruses in the world. He volunteered to analyze the blood samples from these five men to see whether their antibodies reacted with any of his swine viruses by inhibiting their growth in tissue cultures. He also will determine whether the men's blood samples have antibodies that react to the hemagglutinins on the various swine viruses."

"What are hemagglutinins?" asked Gaspar.

"Reactive proteins on the surfaces of viruses. Generally, most avian or swine viruses are not harmful to humans because their hemagglutinins do not bind to human cells. However, viruses mutate or change over time. Only small mutations in the hemagglutinin on a swine or avian virus can cause the virus to bind to human cells. Then they are contagious and dangerous in humans."

"I'm still confused," said Gaspar.

Martin replied before Sara could answer. "The field of immunology has gotten a lot more complicated since you were in medical school. We now know most us have antibodies, let's say partial defenses, against most common flu viruses. We may get sick but unless we have other weaknesses, like an impaired immune system, we survive. The Philippine flu virus is especially dangerous because it differs from H1N1 flu virus and other common human flu virus. Thus, most of us have no defenses against it."

"Okay. I get it. So far, we've only identified five men out of about three hundred residents at the center with some natural immunity to the Philippine flu." Gaspar paused. "Now let's get back to the lab tests. Why two assays?"

Sara responded, "Inhibition of growth of the viruses in tissue cultures is probably the best test for similarities among viruses but the hemagglutinin inhibition assay is faster."

Martin nodded in agreement. "When can we expect results?"

"Maybe partial results late tomorrow. Samples, that is blood and nasal swabs, from the five men, me, my sister, George Kent, and his wife were delivered to the Ames lab yesterday by nine in the morning."

"Why the last four?" asked Martin. "Other than you signed off on unrestricted usage of your samples."

"That too, but George, my sister and I grew up on Midwestern farms with hogs. Doris Kent didn't. Linda and I rarely handled the hogs when we were teens. George handled hogs daily as a teen-ager. Hence, we have graded exposure to hogs and potentially swine viruses. And this might answer one of our questions. George played poker with Marv a week ago on Monday night. The other three men who played poker with Marv are dead, so are their wives. Thus, we appear to have at least six men who appear to be immune to the Philippine flu out of all of La Bendita."

"Our first good lead." Martin smiled. "But that's a limited group. If those who handled hogs perhaps as long ago as the sixties and seventies are immune to the Philippine flu virus, that suggests a swine virus must have mutated to be contagious in chickens, the believed source of the Philippine flu in humans, sometime in the last fifty years. Do they know when this swine virus mutated to affect poultry?"

"I asked that question too. I was told the avian virus, thought to be the source of the Philippine flu, was first noted in poultry in the Philippines in the nineties."

"With this many people dying," blurted out Chuy. "Why do we care about this trivia?"

Sara replied quickly, "Because then we will be able to identify individuals who have a natural immunity to the flu with a few questions and a simple blood test for hemagglutinin cross-reactivity. And more importantly, it puts us in a position to develop a less dangerous vaccine than the current live attenuated vaccine to the Philippine flu, which must be sprayed into the nose."

Chuy muttered, "Do we really need another vaccine? All I got was the sniffles when I was vaccinated."

"You were lucky." Martin straightened in his chair and assumed his professorial tone of voice. "The live attenuated virus is fine for individuals with robust immune systems but it's too much for many. The lab developing the Philippine flu vaccine was in such a hurry they didn't weaken the virus much when they attenuated it in the lab. It's deadly if it gets out of the nasal passages into the lungs. Hence the reason it is sprayed into the nose not injected like most vaccines."

Sara added, "It sure inflamed my nasal passages and gave me one hell of a headache."

"So back to my original question?" said Chuy.

Martin replied, "Many with weakened immune systems, like cancer patients and the elderly in nursing homes, couldn't survive being vaccinated with the current vaccine for the Philippine flu. They need a safer vaccine."

"What will this guy in Ames do?" asked Chuy.

"If the immunologist in Ames identifies any swine virus that shares the unique part of the hemagglutinin peptide in the Philippine flu virus, we could luck out. Then scientists could make a vaccine that reacts to the swine virus. Evidently, they've been unable to make a safe vaccine from the avian virus so far. Of course, there will be problems, but a vaccine based on the swine flu is apt to be much safer than the current live attenuated vaccine to the Philippine flu."

"How long will it take?"

"Six months probably. It won't help us here, but could be important nationally and worldwide."

Ellen cleared her throat. "Now back to our situation here. Sylvia, what about your staff and their families?"

"Ten family members were transferred here yesterday after they developed fevers and coughing. All had received antivirals."

Martin looked at Gaspar. "How are they doing?"

Gaspar replied, "They should survive. Remember, only patients who received antivirals prior to the development of symptoms are sent to my clinic. They're also younger than your patients."

"Lucky dog." Martin slouched deeper into his chair. "I'd really like to be able to give antivirals to those over sixty-five. Then we might save a few."

"No," said Ellen. "There are not enough of the experimental antivirals. We need to save them for those who have a future, and that's not the elderly."

Sylvia gasped. "I hope you never administer any federal programs for the elderly."

"Sorry, but we're on a sinking ship here. You don't understand the big picture. I'm trying to save those whom I can here, but mainly I've got to prevent the flu from spreading to the rest of New Mexico. I have greater responsibilities than you."

"Ellen, don't act like the rest of us are children!" Martin yelled. "I'll be back when I've cooled down." He slammed the back door of the clubhouse as he left.

Ellen announced to Sara. "Better stay connected. He'll be back shortly." Then, as if nothing had happened, she turned her back on the others and spoke to one of her clerks.

Gaspar looked at Sylvia, who was sobbing. "We'll be back in a few minutes." He, Sylvia, and Chuy departed more slowly and less noisily than Martin.

CHAPTER 18: Day Six Continued — Sergeant Chuy Bargas

Ten minutes later, Sylvia, carrying a box of cookies and a stack of foam cups, led Chuy, carrying a small coffee urn, into the clubhouse. Martin and Gaspar trailed behind. Ellen intently studied her computer screen and ignored them until Sylvia set a cup of steaming coffee by Ellen's hand.

"Let's continue by talking more about the pool of people who have been exposed to the flu in the Albuquerque area." Ellen smiled triumphantly at Martin. "Sara, please repeat what you told me."

"We, that is the clinic clerks quarantined in their homes with young children and I, did our best to identify everyone exposed to La Bendita residents infected with the flu between last Monday and last Wednesday when the quarantine was initiated. However, we're bound to have missed some. Think about it. Every resident of La Bendita went on some sort of shopping trip or errand between last Monday and last Wednesday. They potentially," Sara emphasized the last word, "transmitted the flu viruses to hundreds, maybe thousands, of unnamed people. We have no way of knowing who they are. I'm afraid we identified only eighty-one nameable individuals."

Ellen nodded. "All these named contacts are quarantined in their homes and have been monitored daily by state and county health officials with the help of the police. Those younger than sixty-five are receiving antivirals. Ten aren't receiving antivirals because they're older than sixty-five. So far, eight have been sent to us with flu symptoms."

"The two over sixty-five who were sent to the center are in bad shape," noted Martin. "What about the rest?"

"They'll survive," said Gaspar.

Ellen pulled a page from one of her files. "The CDC and the New Mexico Department of Health recognized from the start the severe limitation of our quarantine, really any quarantine. They contacted all physicians, clinics, schools, and government offices last Thursday and began in-service training of staff at major local businesses on Friday.

They also drafted public health workers from other states to man phones."

Martin finally seemed to come out of his funk, opened his eyes, and asked, "What on?"

"On how to spot flu symptoms, what to do if you see someone cough, how to disinfect smooth surfaces, etc. They required all employees in grocery stores and pharmacies to wear plastic gloves and masks at all times. Public health nurses are visiting the schools. Public health officials are closing schools for at least a week if a child attending them comes down with the flu."

"Didn't that cause an uproar when schools were closed?" Sylvia took a sip of coffee.

"It was only the schools in Mercado and one middle school in Albuquerque. They, state health officials, released partial information to the parents and the press."

"What do you mean?"

"They mentioned broken water mains or asbestos at the schools or something like that. I wasn't given details."

"In other words, they lied. That will make people suspicious and probably will accomplish little," said Martin. "Is it even legal?"

Ellen sniffed. "Not my call. Probably yes under the Model State Emergency Health Powers Act and the surrounding legislation. As long as any action ultimately protects the public, it's okay."

"So much for individual's rights," said Martin.

"Back to my question about the school children," said Sylvia. "Did they quarantine all the families of children in the affected schools?"

"Not enough county and state health workers to quarantine them all. So far…"

Gaspar completed her sentence, "Only sick children of our staff have been sent to me. Thus, I doubt they identified anyone with the flu."

Sylvia's face relaxed a bit and she looked younger. "How did we luck out so?"

"We quarantined your staff and the residents of La Bendita before most showed flu symptoms. Well, within hours of showing symptoms," replied Ellen.

"And you were lucky." Martin again assumed a professorial tone. "Think what would have happened if the flu had struck three weeks later at Halloween. Trick-or-treaters would have spread it to everyone.

And we would have run out of antivirals to control the death rates even in those under fifty." He paused. "Imagine. They'd have to run lotteries to decide who got the antivirals."

Ellen sniffed. "Nothing so obvious."

"I don't want to talk about what-ifs," said Sylvia. "I want to understand our current situation. Why haven't we been hit by the news media? CNN is broadcasting hourly updates on the flu epidemic in El Paso."

"You have time to watch TV?" said Martin.

"It's on in the women's tent all night. We're all glad the media hasn't shown up here. But how did we luck out?"

"Everyone, well everyone in New Mexico law enforcement agencies and public health agencies, agreed it would be unfortunate if the press stormed the homes of those quarantined or came to the gates of La Bendita. Judges agreed, and the names and addresses of all those quarantined weren't released."

"But nothing keeps those quarantined from calling their neighbors, relatives, and friends."

"Agreed," said Ellen. "But I believe the state and county public health workers monitoring those quarantined must have done an exceptional job of creating trust in those exposed."

"They haven't had to work with Jim Peterson or Jane Lane," said Gaspar. "I'm surprised both of them haven't called the press. Guess that would be too logical. Of course, Jane can't now."

Ellen pointed at Chuy. "Now for a more trivial problem. A backfiring gun."

Chuy nervously cleared his throat and coughed. Everyone stared at him. "It's okay. I got the vaccination for the Philippine flu virus two months ago. I'm not sick, just nervous. Anyway, the shooting last night was not a suicide attempt, but someone tried to make it look like one. Someone with access to Ms. Lane's house."

Gaspar nudged Chuy. "Tell them about Peterson. I always knew the guy was trouble."

"We, the Chief and I, think Jim and Jean Peterson are involved in the shooting, but we can't prove it yet. They acted strangely last night and are reported to have been in frequent contact with Ms. Lane. We found similar partial fingerprints on the gun that Ms. Lane used and the shotgun that Jean Peterson pointed at me last night."

"So, you've got a match?' asked Martin.

"Not exactly."

"What?"

"The prints had no real ridges."

Ellen looked up from a file. "So, you have nothing."

"We have strong suspicions, but like I said no proof yet."

"And what do you mean they acted strangely? It'd be pretty hard to not act strangely if you were quarantined here," said Martin. "Imagine how bad it would be if they knew our death rates."

"Right." Chuy cleared his throat. "The Chief checked the Petersons' backgrounds. It seems they paid for their house in cash."

"Not strange at La Bendita," interrupted Sara. "Lots of us did."

"Right, but the Chief can't find any evidence the Petersons existed before six years ago when they moved here. No credit records. No driver's and marriage licenses. Nada." Chuy waited a few seconds for his audience to digest the new information. "I also confiscated several weapons last night."

"A number of the residents of La Bendita keep guns," said Sara. "I'm surprised one of our elderly residents hasn't shot a toe off as he or she shuffled along."

"She's not kidding," said Gaspar.

"Right, the shotgun and the loaded guns that I confiscated from the Petersons were registered. But when the forensic guys checked the car..."

Ellen sucked in her breath. "Can I assume you broke the quarantine by sending the car out, not by bringing men in?"

Chuy nodded. "They found a gun in a secret compartment in the Hummer. Its registration number was filed off. The Chief is checking ballistic records to see if this or any of the guns were used in crimes in the area."

"Get real." Ellen glared at Chuy.

"We are. Juan is watching the Petersons from next door, I believe it's the Benders' house. But I need your help. Have you ever noticed anything strange about the Petersons? Little things that seemed out of sync." Chuy noticed everyone was studying the floor.

Sara spoke first. "Jean Peterson always dresses and acts like, like a caricature of the perfect woman in the nineteen-fifties or early nineteen-sixties. You know, with her red hair in a neat French twist, no shorts, and ironed cotton blouses, not knit tops. She speaks in a breathy Marilyn Monroe-type whisper." She stopped. "I know that sounds catty on my part but I don't think we ever see the real person. Her outward persona is too..."

"Perfect," said Gaspar. "I mistakenly stopped by her house around eight one evening when I tried to drop off medications for the Benders. Herman was sick again. I was surprised, but pleasantly, when Jean answered the door. She had the Stones playing and she was dressed in black Spandex shorts and a low top. She seemed embarrassed. I didn't see why, she looked good. Great," he paused searching for words, "breasts."

"Right, she gave me a view last night. Anything about Mr. Peterson?"

Sylvia sat up straight. "He's just an annoying bantam with little worthwhile to say."

"Right." Chuy looked at his notes. "According to my records, only the police and emergency vehicles have access to the back gate of La Bendita. Right?"

"Sylvia and I have gate passes too." After a pause, Gaspar added, "We also made gate passes for the two other HOA Board members, Howie Steele and George Kent."

Sylvia cut him off. "I think I have a detail that might interest you. Several of my residents have reported a ghost regularly opens the back gate. They claim the gate sometimes opens in the middle of the night, and a big black vehicle without headlights glides through. Of course, none of my staff have seen the back gate used except by emergency vehicles."

Chuy thought this was the best tip he'd gotten. "Can you be more specific? Which residents? Can I talk to them?"

"Many of my residents aren't talking anymore." She wrinkled her brow and frowned. "The staff hear of sightings at least twice a month." After a long pause, she added, "Gerald Sands and, I think, Luis Thomas claim they've seen the 'black phantom.' That's what the residents call it."

"Are they dead?"

"No, they are two of the five who didn't get the flu. They would love to tell you about the 'black phantom.' Of course, Gerald has trouble with reality most days, but Luis is pretty lucid. I'll take you to see them after this meeting."

"Good."

"I guess we're done," said Ellen.

"Don't you want to hear about Jane Lane?" said Gaspar. "She lost her right hand and arm up to the elbow. She had a lot of shrapnel removed from her right shoulder, hip, and leg. She might lose the right leg but should survive. Gil will interview her when she becomes lucid. Considering Jane, it may be a while.”

Everyone stared at Chuy.

“No news yet.”

Sylvia Otega led Chuy through the front entrance of the center and around a corner to a room with a large, ivory masonry kiva fireplace in one corner and built-in masonry seating on two walls. Six heavy, Mexican-style game tables with matching chairs were centered in the room. The chair seats were upholstered with a bright Indian blanket fabric, as were the pillows on the built-in-seating. Three colorful Indian blankets hung on the wall.

“This is our game room.” When she noticed Chuy was gaping, she said, “It’s what Anglo interior decorators call a Mexican-style room. It’s not my taste, but the residents like it. Or used to like it.”

“They should. I didn’t know this place was so grand.”

“After listening to what has happened during the last week, it’s hard to believe, but this was an excellent facility for the elderly.” Sylvia sighed. “I called ahead. A nurse’s aide is bringing Mr. Sands and Mr. Thomas down to talk to you.”

Almost immediately, two wizened men and a young woman appeared.

“*Hola, Hola,*” yelled Luis Thomas as he wobbled into the room.

“He’s hard of hearing and compensates by being loud,” whispered Sylvia.

Gerald Sands shuffled silently after Luis. He straightened slightly and lifted his head as he entered the room.

The nurse’s aide brightened when she entered the room after the two men. “I forgot how pretty this room is.”

Luis grabbed her arm and tried to whisper in her ear but his words were clear to Chuy. “Why? Ask why?”

“The boys are awanting to know why the police want to talk to them.”

Luis jabbed her in the ribs. “They are also awanting to know about the shooting last night.”

Sylvia said, “That’s what Sergeant Bargas wants to talk about, too. He thinks you might have seen or heard something.”

When the two elderly men nodded in agreement, they looked like bobble toys.

The nurse's aide said, "Wow. Something to talk about besides the flu."

After brief introductions, Sylvia said, "You can stay in this room after Sergeant Bargas leaves if you wish." The nurse's aide flashed a wide grin. Sylvia was almost out the door when she said to the aide, "Why don't you and Ella round up the five or six residents who have recovered from the flu and our other three healthy residents and bring them down here for a bingo game. I'll have the kitchen send over cookies and coffee."

"Thank you, Ma'am. It's been bad here for a hound's age." She paused, "Well less than a week, but it seems like a hound's age." She ran from the room.

Chuy asked a question.

The men stared at him.

Chuy asked another question.

Gerald Sands droned in a soft, slow monotone. "I don't know why I'm alive. They say my wife died. They won't let me see her. My neighbors died. They won't let me see them. I don't know where they took them." He looked sadly at the floor. "All gone. All gone." He started to cry.

Chuy asked another question.

Gerald didn't seem to hear him. "I talk to a nice lady on the phone."

Luis interrupted, "Gerald knows Sara. She brings books and games to the center sometimes. And she brings Bug. He's everyone's favorite. You know he can dance on his hind legs." Luis poked Gerald gently.

Gerald continued as if he were a wind-up toy. "She asked me lots of questions about my childhood. About my past. She even asked what we raised on our farm."

Chuy tried again. "Have you seen anything strange at the back gate at night?"

Gerald seemed to look right through Chuy and continued as if Chuy weren't there. "My dad." Gerald smiled. "He had a little farm in Missouri. He kept a few head of cattle and a few pigs. My mom had lots of chickens, red chickens, Rhode Island Red chickens." Suddenly, he seemed to see Chuy for the first time. "Young man, what do you want?"

Luis replied before Chuy could answer. "Gerald, he has different questions than Sara. He wants to know about the black phantom."

Gerald nodded and appeared to be organizing his thoughts.

Luis turned to Chuy and yelled, "Gerald's the expert on the black phantom. He has an apartment on the third floor on the back side of the center. He can see the back gate from his living room window."

"My wife, she slept like a log." Gerald stopped and wiped his eyes. "I often can't sleep and sit at the window at night." Suddenly he spoke more rapidly and with more expression. "I see the ambulance go out and come in. Lots of light and noise. Every night I see a police car come in. A little light, no noise." He paused.

Chuy waited silently. He didn't want to interrupt Gerald's fragile concentration.

"Sometimes, sometimes, I see a big black vehicle. No light, no noise. It creeps out and in slowly."

Chuy waited at least a minute but Gerald appeared to be through talking. "How often do you see the black vehicle?"

Gerald contorted his face. "See it, see it not often. Tell other boys."

Chuy looked at Luis.

"He told a bunch of us about the black phantom. That's what we call it. About ten of us were on the lookout for it. We had to take turns. It never left before ten, and it always returned before daybreak."

"How often?"

"Mmm. Let's see. Once a month." Luis paused. "No, more often but not regular-like. I mean not on same day of the week."

"What did the black phantom look like?"

"Big, big," droned Gerald. "Like a tank in Korea."

Chuy wanted to scream hallelujah. Finally progress. A Hummer looked a bit like a tank with its small front windows. He fiddled with his laptop and found pictures on the web of a Hummer 1, a Cadillac Escalade, a Chevy Tahoe, and several smaller SUVs. "Any of these look like the black phantom?"

Both men studied the pictures. They quickly eliminated the SUVs as too small.

"It had small windows in the front like this one." Luis pointed to the picture of the Hummer. Gerald agreed.

Chuy was pleased. "Did you ever see who was in the vehicle? Was it a man? A man and a woman? Two men?"

"Dark, dark. See no one," responded Gerald. Luis sighed in agreement.

"I guess I'm done. You can play Bingo now." Chuy packed up his laptop. "Oh, by the way, do you remember the last time you saw the black phantom?"

Luis shook his head.

Gerald rasped, "I didn't sleep last night. It's lonely in my apartment without my girl." He paused and stared at Chuy. "I see black phantom go out."

Chuy felt as if someone had socked him in the gut. Juan had left the gate a little after ten last night. A replacement didn't arrive at the gate until almost four. "When?"

"It was dark." Gerald shrugged his shoulders and dropped his head to stare at his hands. He moaned, "Gone. All gone."

"Sir, did the black phantom come back before sunrise?"

"Gone. All gone."

Chuy decided the interview was over. He opened the door to the game room. The nurse's aide stood talking to a shrunken woman in a wheelchair. Another young woman, presumably Ella, was conversing with a gnarled man in a wheelchair. Five other elderly men and women stood nearby. Two stood with the help of walkers; two used canes; one stood unaided. As soon as they saw the door open, they surged forward.

"Now ladies and gentlemen, let's allow our guest to mosey out." The old people stopped in response to Ella's comment but did not move aside for Chuy to pass.

He didn't think Ella could have stopped them if the cookies had already been on the table. No wonder these folks had survived, they were tough.

One man noted Chuy's police uniform. "Someone die here, Officer?" He guffawed at the joke.

The others shuffled as fast as they could past Chuy.

Suddenly Chuy realized a rumor could soon spread around the center that he had asked about the black phantom. Jim and Jean Peterson might hear it. He thought a bit more. No resident of La Bendita would visit the center this week. Jane Lane was no longer circling on her bicycle and reporting all her sightings to everyone. He guessed even bad news had its bright side.

"I've got a few questions for you while you wait for the cookies."

"I'd rather have beer," said one shrunken wisp of a man.

Ella quickly replied, "I know you are parched as the desert, but you know the rules. No beer before four. Be good while I find those cookies."

Chuy learned nothing in the next five minutes except that everyone in the center had heard of the black phantom.

He wondered whether Juan saw any action at the Petersons'? He might as well enjoy the sunshine and stroll down and see. When Chuy knocked on the Benders' door, Juan didn't answer. He pulled out a passkey and unlocked the door. Juan was not in the house. He used his cell phone. "See any action at the Petersons'?"

Chuy frowned as Juan replied, "I'm in the bedroom of the Benders' house now watching the Petersons' house. No one's been out all day except Jim. He went up to the clubhouse to claim his mail and get food around noon."

Chuy did not allow emotion to change his voice tone. "Good." He stood for a moment in the Benders' empty bedroom and then hastily departed the house.

When he was a block away, he called Gil. "Chief, we got problems. Real problems."

CHAPTER 19: Day Six Continued — Sara

Sara tried to expand the database on the unvaccinated employees of the center and the clinic. The calls were difficult even though she asked only three questions. Those quarantined in their homes were eager to chat, but those working in La Bendita were too busy to answer questions civilly. Those who were patients had difficulty answering any questions.

As she interviewed staff, Chuy's question rebounded in her head: Anything strange about Jim Peterson? In the middle of an interview with a member of the dietary department, Sara suddenly remembered a specific conversation a few months after the Mortons moved in.

She debated with herself what to do and finally called Chief Gil Andrews. "This is Sara Almquist. I'm sorry to bother you, but I just remembered a detail that might help Chuy. It's about Jim Peterson."

"At last, I talk to Dr. Almquist. The boss lady Ellen Behren and old Doc Gonzales speak highly of you. What've ya got?"

"At this year's Fourth of July barbeque, Jim Peterson said everyone called Marv Morton 'String Bean' in high school." She was glad she couldn't see the police chief's face because now he was probably thinking she was a real kook. "After Jim's comment, Marv left the event quickly. He seemed nervous. He refused to participate in any discussion with or about Jim Peterson ever again, at least in my presence."

"No problem. I'll have a little chat with Marv."

"Only if you speak with the dead. He was the first flu victim."

"How about his wife?"

"Dead too, but there's a daughter. Ellen Behren will probably know how to contact her." Sara paused. "Maybe there's an easier way to get info. Marv showed me his picture in his high school yearbook once. The yearbook is probably still in the house. No viable viruses should remain on surfaces in the Mortons' house."

"I doubt Jim was called Peterson then."

"Yes, but Gaspar or I could look at yearbook pictures and pick Jim out. He has a pretty distinctive nose."

"No need. FBI computers can compare a current photo with hundreds of old pictures for key features in minutes."

"So, I didn't waste your time?"

"Not at all."

Sara returned to calling more of the center's employees and asking them the three standardized questions. She wished she could work on her beaded, white and ivory wall hanging. The reason she'd retired early was she was tired of epidemiology. She'd been working more than twelve hours a day on epidemiology this week and wanted a change of pace.

Sara forced herself to concentrate. Finally, she had data from all the unimmunized employees capable of responding to questions. She began to program statistical analyses.

The phone rang. "Dulce called me," said Aletha. "She said Julia spiked a fever this morning."

"I'm sure they're doing their best," replied Sara. "She received antivirals. Her prognosis is…"

"I didn't call to hear the usual pap," interrupted Aletha.

"Okay."

"Lalo is being a defiant brat again. He fights me on every detail, even refuses to take his antivirals."

"Will he talk to me?"

"Yes."

Sara could hear Aletha screaming "Lalo, come here" over and over again. Finally, Aletha spoke into the phone. "I'll drag him from his room."

About two minutes later Sara heard Lalo's whine. He was definitely pouting. "Granny said I had to talk to you."

"Well, I'm glad to talk to you. I missed you. I've been quarantined."

"Me too. All because of those stupid people in La Bendita."

"The people in La Bendita didn't want to get the flu, but they didn't take medicine like you're getting. So, they got very sick."

"Are you going to nag me like Granny?"

"Your grandmother loves you. We all know she's a nag when she's worried, and she's really worried now."

"I get that. But Mom took the medicine and still got sick."

"Lalo, you're a big boy. You've had science in school."

"Don't like science."

"Well, you know I'm a scientist, and I'm going to talk to you like a scientist."

"Do you have to?"

She thought it best to ignore his comment. "Flu viruses can take control of cells in your body and make you sick with the flu."

"What are viruses?"

"Mmm. Viruses are very, very tiny things. Smaller than germs. You can't even see them with a regular microscope. It takes special microscopes to see them."

"Okay."

"Well, if you take the medicine before the viruses take control of your cells, you won't get sick. Your mom took care of Maria and talked to Elena before she got sick. We think viruses were already controlling a few of the cells in your mom's body before she got the medicine. Remember how your mom did not let you see Elena or play with Maria?"

"Mom was real grouchy with Gabi and me when we tried to peek in to see Maria."

"Well, your Mom was smart. We don't think viruses were controlling any of the cells in your body before you got the medicine."

Lalo was silent.

"Make sense to you?"

"Sort of. Does that mean if I take the medicine, I won't get the flu?"

"Yes."

"Okay. Why didn't Granny tell me?"

"She forgot what a big boy you are now. You're not a baby like Gabi."

"Yeah, he just cries." After a long pause, he added, "Granny wants to talk to you now."

"Did it work?" whispered Aletha.

"Don't know. I tried."

She wanted to politely tell Aletha to back off, but knew she'd probably behave the same way if she were in Aletha's shoes. She decided politeness was irrelevant now. "Try not to smother him. He wants to be a big boy."

"He doesn't act like one. I'm feel so… so helpless. I'm used to being able to make things happen. Now all I can do is wait."

CHAPTER 20: Day Six Continued — Ellen Behren

Ellen sat in the main room of the La Bendita clubhouse with her two aides. She contemplated the vaulted wood ceiling. It was pine stained dark to look expensive and old. Fakey, like many things at La Bendita.

When she was appointed to head operations at La Bendita, she thought the assignment would make her career. Then reality struck. She'd be lucky if Martin Bloom and his crew saved half of the almost three hundred elderly in the center. Worse still, they all blamed her for their failures because she hadn't released the antivirals for use with the elderly. Of course, she'd be a hero if the flu hit the schools like it did in El Paso, because she'd have plenty of antivirals for kids and their parents. Ellen flicked on the TV in the main room of the clubhouse and watched the CNN hourly flu update from El Paso.

The CNN reporter explained how the first death attributed to the Philippine flu in El Paso had been a three-year-old in a day care center on the previous Monday. A picture of a little girl with big dark eyes and black hair tied in pigtails flashed on the screen. The reporter then stated that all but one child attending the day care center had died within three days. Then the flu had spread like lightning among children in the public school system in El Paso. There were sweeping shots of overcrowded pediatric wards and of closed schools.

A CDC official, someone only slightly more experienced than Ellen, was speaking now. "As of today, more than five hundred have died."

"Wow." Said the CNN reporter. "Aren't any medicines working?"

"Most died in the first four days. Then the CDC rushed in experimental antivirals last Thursday. Now we're saving eighty-five percent of our patients if," he emphasized the word if, "we see them before they start coughing."

"A big if," said the reporter.

A phone number flashed on the screen. Residents of El Paso were urged to call the number immediately if they or anyone in their family started to sneeze or cough.

Ellen thought the whole situation wasn't fair in many ways. First off, kids dying unexpectedly in El Paso made better news stories than old people dying faster than expected in La Bendita.

Second, the CDC had sent five staff members to El Paso two weeks ago when flu deaths were first reported in Juarez. They had mobilized the Texas Department of State Health Services by last Monday when the first reported flu death occurred. She, with three other CDC staff members, had to get the New Mexico Department of Health and the docs at the University Hospital up to snuff in basically one day last Wednesday. Of course, they couldn't have done it without Gaspar Gonzales. He wasn't a great physician but he knew everyone.

The third point really bugged her. The lead CDC official in El Paso was really stacking up points for future plum assignments. He had controlled media announcements on the flu in El Paso from the start. Here the governor's office controlled all interactions with the press while she did all the dirty work. She wasn't even allowed to talk to anyone outside her chain of command.

A ticker appeared at the bottom of the TV screen:
Officials estimate ten thousand people may be infected with the flu in El Paso.
The CNN reporter asked the CDC official hard questions. Finally, the CDC official admitted, "Attempts to isolate the sick have not been as effective in El Paso as we hoped." Another ticker appeared at the bottom of the screen:
Texas State Troopers block all roads to El Paso.

She probably should be glad she wasn't facing the press. Of course, she could brag about her prevention efforts — a perfect record. No one who was not under quarantine here, either in La Bendita or in a quarantined home, had come down with the flu.

Shots of the border between Mexico and the United States now flashed across the screen. The ticker at the bottom of the screen read:
Is an effective quarantine possible?

Ellen realized she'd been lucky in one way. The epidemic here started in a walled community.

One of her aides transferred a phone call from Gil. She listened quietly and said, "Damn, he ruined my record."

She called Gaspar. "Chief Gil Andrews says Lily called his office."

"Lily who?"

"He didn't give a last name. He called her a good-hearted working woman. She told him that she had nursed a sick friend for three days. I'm quoting what Chief Andrews claims she told him. 'Then he up and croaked. Will you come and get his body before it smells?' Her friend was Ricardo Vargas."

"Who's he?" said Gaspar.

"Remember there was a janitor at the clinic Elena Pena visited. He was the only named contact that we couldn't locate. Gil's men and the state police checked his home daily for the last three days."

"Oh yes, now I remember. The comments sound like the famous Lily of Mercado." Gaspar began to tell a story about Lily.

"You and Chief Andrews should trade stories about Lily someday. Now you've got to find housing for her. He figured Lily wouldn't submit to quarantine in her own house. The net result is the Mercado ambulance will deliver her to our front gate in about five minutes."

"Gil's right. I'll have to employ Lily or she won't stay here either. And there are only two things that Lily can do. I guess I'll pay her minimum wage to do routine cleaning around the clinic."

"Are you sure?"

"Don't think you want Lily to earn money the other way."

"Will you give her antivirals?"

"Yes, she's younger than sixty-five, though on a bad day she doesn't look it anymore. Will they deliver Vargas's body to us too?"

"No. Chief Andrews made the state lab take it."

"Too bad he couldn't make the state lab take Lily, too."

CHAPTER 21: Ellen's Interpretation of Sara's Data

Ellen perused Sara's new email and then reread it carefully.

First, Sara detailed how Marv Morton had contracted the flu. Marv and Marcia drove to El Paso a week ago Saturday to purchase chicken manure for their garden. The manure was probably from fighting cocks infected with the Philippine flu. Those who sold the manure to Marv probably had the flu and were from Juarez.

Second, Sara explained how Marv spread the flu to patients in the center. Marv mixed the manure with dirt and used it to pot plants on Sunday morning. He delivered the contaminated potted plants to all the nurses' stations on the first and second floors of the center on Sunday afternoon. A nurse remembered he was coughing as he delivered the plants. As he coughed and sneezed, he spread viruses over the counters and other furniture. Everyone who touched the counters or the potted plants in the six hours after their delivery was exposed to the flu virus.

Ellen skipped Sara's statistical analyses but noted her conclusions. Marv and his plants infected probably thirty to forty patients and unvaccinated staff directly. The number was sufficient so that as they coughed and infected others, flu symptoms developed rapidly in virtually all the patients on the first and second floors of the center. Thus, the patients on the third floor, which he did not visit, on average, developed symptoms almost a day later than those on the lower floors of the center.

Third, Sara described how the flu had been transmitted to residents of homes in La Bendita. Monday night Marv played poker with George Kent and three other men. All four men, when interviewed on Thursday, noted Marv coughed and sneezed a lot during the poker game. The aerosol from his sneezes spread viruses on the playing cards. Thus, all the poker players were exposed even if Marv did not cough on them directly. They spread the virus to their spouses. All the poker players and spouses, except George and his wife were dead now.

The next part of Sara's memo contained detailed line drawings, almost like family trees. They showed contacts by the poker players with other residents of La Bendita. Sara had used the transcripts of the interviews by the public health workers with residents from last Thursday to draw the diagrams. Ellen didn't find the complicated drawings interesting. However, Sara's conclusions were thorough. Eighty-four residents of homes in La Bendita were hospitalized with the flu. Sara demonstrated that seventy-nine of them had contact with the Mortons, the dead poker players and their wives, or others who became ill. She speculated one or more of the five remaining flu victims had visited the center before the quarantine and didn't sign in.

Ellen concluded she'd been lucky in one way. It was likely she could claim a scientific breakthrough before the El Paso group because of Sara's efforts.

Ellen called Sara to get direct answers on her interpretation of the lab data from the veterinary immunologist in Ames. She didn't bother to say hello. "Sara, tell me about the lab results from Ames."

Sara responded in kind without any chitchat. "Antibodies in the serum from our lucky five men and George Kent cross-reacted with hemagglutinins from two different swine flu viruses. One was rare; we haven't seen that type of flu in hogs in the U.S. since the early 1970s. The other pretty commonly causes flu in swine in the U.S."

"I understood that part. I got lost when you talked about hemagglutinin inhibition."

"Yeah, immunologists use too much jargon. Let's see if I can say it more simply than what I wrote to you. There is a protein on the surface of all flu viruses given the silly name of hemagglutinin. Mutations in this protein determine whether the virus is infectious to humans. For example, this protein on most swine viruses will not bind to cells in the trachea and lungs of humans. Hence, we aren't affected by the virus. However, our bodies will make antibodies to variants of the flu virus if we are exposed to enough of them. Then these antibodies kill the virus if we are exposed to the virus again."

"I'm not a child," said Ellen. "I know the basics."

Ellen noticed Sara's tone of voice didn't change and she plodded on with her explanation. "Scientists can estimate how much a person has been exposed to various flu viruses by measuring how much the proteins in his blood react with isolated hemagglutinins from various flu viruses. Anyway the scientist in Ames found the blood of the six men, who appear to be immune to the Philippine flu, reacted strongly with the hemagglutinin from a rare swine virus that hasn't been seen in the U.S. since the 1970s and more weakly with a common swine virus."

"Explain in practical terms."

"The hemagglutinin on the Philippine flu virus is pretty similar to that on the rare swine virus. Anyone exposed to that rare virus will be immune to the Philippine flu."

"Why did you include the mumbo jumbo on the other common swine virus?"

"Those with exposure to the common swine flu virus will probably be more resistant to the Philippine flu virus than most. Maybe only one-half of them will become sick if exposed to the Philippine flu, and their symptoms will probably, note I said probably, be less than those never exposed to the common swine flu virus."

"Why do I care?"

"I care because samples of my blood cross-reacted weakly with the more common swine virus. So, I had about a fifty percent chance of being immune to the Philippine flu even before I was vaccinated."

"I see your point. What about the others?"

"I analyzed the medical records and histories of the thirty-nine unvaccinated employees. Eight had a history of living on a farm that raised hogs, of working in a butcher shop or a veterinary clinic, or being married to a pig farmer. I hypothesized they would have antibodies to the common swine virus."

"And?"

"None of the eight with probable exposure to hogs died of the flu. The four of the eight who got the Philippine flu are recovering. The scientist at Ames confirmed my theory. He found the serum from the eight whom I identified as having been exposed to hogs cross-reacted weakly, like my blood sample, with the common swine virus. None cross-reacted with the rare swine virus. The serum of the other unvaccinated employees did not cross-react with the common or the rare swine viruses. Seventy percent of them were hospitalized with flu. Ten have died so far."

"What about the residents in the homes here?"

"The Ames lab hasn't analyzed their blood samples yet."

"You've been busy."

"Couldn't have done it without the clerks assigned to work at home because they had young children."

Ellen interrupted. "We could have gotten more work from them if they'd been separated from their families."

"Maybe not. Several of them had their whole families helping me comb the computerized transcripts of the interviews with La Bendita residents. They were bored and treated it as a puzzle."

"Oh." Ellen was alarmed. The clerks' families didn't have clearance to see the confidential data on patients and residents of La Bendita. Lecturing Sara on confidentiality would do no good at this point. Besides, her bosses at the CDC and potential bosses at FDA would be impressed by these new data. "I've got to go now."

Ellen forwarded Sara's email, including all the lab data and statistical analyses to the CDC under her own byline after she deleted Sara's name from the memo.

Then she noticed a new email. Sara wanted to send a manuscript on what she described as "our" work with the scientist at Ames to the CDC's *Morbidity and Mortality Weekly Report* and *Science* immediately. Sara thought it would interest those trying to develop a safer vaccine against the Philippine flu.

Ellen thought Sara's idea was a good one. As the co-author on an important paper with a retired scientist, Ellen would garner most of the credit for the discovery.

CHAPTER 22: Day Six Continued — Dr. Gaspar Gonzales

Gaspar and Chuy whispered as they walked to Ellen's table by the fireplace in the clubhouse. When Ellen didn't look away from her computer screen, Gaspar cleared his throat. "Ellen, please take this calmly."

"More bad news?" Ellen groaned.

"Do you remember our discussion about Jim and Jean Peterson today at our meeting?"

Ellen nodded. "Don't tell me there's been another shooting."

Gaspar said, "Not if we act now. I'll let Chuy explain."

"Right." Chuy swallowed hard as he eyed the glare on Ellen's face. "Today the Chief got a tip from Sara. She thought Marv Morton and Jim Peterson might have known each other in high school."

Gaspar interrupted, "Chuy found copies of Marv's old high school yearbooks in his house here in La Bendita. Gil contacted the FBI. They compared pictures in the yearbook to a photo of Jim Peterson with a fancy computer program."

Chuy interrupted, "To make a long story short. Peterson's real name is James Mazzone. He's from a bad family in a rough neighborhood in South Philadelphia. He's got a brother-in-law in prison for murder and a brother and a nephew with prison records. We suspect he's running drugs in Albuquerque."

Ellen straightened in her chair and rubbed her forehead with her fingers. "Why didn't you figure this out sooner?"

"Seems James Mazzone has virtually no police record and no military record. Never been charged with any crime. Philadelphia cops suspected him of crimes but never had enough evidence to charge him because they never located any witnesses left alive." Chuy licked his lips. "Now comes the real kicker. Juan Vigil, one of our Mercado police officers, was assigned to watch the Petersons. We just discovered he's in cahoots with them. Now we have to disarm Juan and isolate him from the Petersons before he gets hurt or hurts one of us. We need to do it without raising the Petersons' suspicions."

"The easiest way is to make Juan sick and bring him to the clinic," added Gaspar.

"Sorry guys, the Hippocratic oath and medical licensing boards."

"Don't be uptight. Look the other way while I do what has to be done — give him a little Ipecac."

Ellen frowned.

"You don't have to administer the Ipecac or tell Juan he might have the flu." Gaspar forced himself to smile at Ellen. "Just don't rat on me."

"Believe me, James Mazzone, if he's like the rest of his family, will kill me, Gaspar, you, or anyone who gets in his way. We've got to act fast." Chuy gulped. "The FBI bureau chief here in Albuquerque is concerned and is sending three agents disguised as a nurse and public health officials to help us. They'll be here soon."

Ellen glared at both men and then closed her eyes. "I'll say I had no visitors in the late afternoon while I worked on my report to the CDC."

Twenty minutes later Gaspar glanced at Chuy and muttered, "I'm ready to perform." He jumped out of the ambulance and charged into the Benders' house.

"Juan, I'm worried about you. One of the vaccinated nurses may have developed flu symptoms. We think one batch of the flu vaccine was defective. We checked. You were vaccinated with the same batch of vaccine."

Gaspar whipped out a digital, rapid-response thermometer and placed it on Juan's forehead. Despite Juan's protests, he forced him to drink a thick liquid. As soon as Juan drank the liquid, Gaspar turned away. He didn't look at Juan again until the ambulance driver and Chuy wheeled in a gurney from the ambulance. In less than a minute Juan was strapped to the gurney with his arms immobilized.

As Juan was loaded into the ambulance, Gaspar caught a glimpse of Jean Peterson at her front window. She was staring slack-jawed at the scene. "Chuy, I think we may have alarmed the neighbors. You may need to speak to them later."

"Yeah, sure. First, we take care of Juan."

As the ambulance moved toward the clinic, Juan moaned. "Doc, I don't feel good. My stomach."

Gaspar put a plastic bucket by Juan's face and lifted Juan's head slightly. Juan began to vomit and quickly filled the small bucket. Gaspar positioned another bucket by his face.

The ambulance rolled up to the back entrance of the clinic. "Juan, I see your nurse now." Chuy nodded to a tall blonde in scrubs.

Agent Rachel Jones took one look at Juan and rolled him to a room on the second floor of the clinic. Chuy and Gaspar had to run to keep up.

"Let's get comfy." Rachel winked at Juan. "I'll help you get into a hospital gown."

In less than a minute, she threw all Juan's clothes but his briefs into a box and handed his gun to Chuy. Chuy departed rapidly.

Gaspar checked Juan's blood pressure and then picked up the box containing Juan's clothes. "I'll leave you in the nurse's capable hands." He bolted from the room and raced down the hall to a small room where Chuy and two FBI agents waited behind a closed door.

"Doc, you gave an Academy Award-winning performance," said Chuy. "You would have scared the hell out of me."

"I did star in a play in high school, but it would never have worked if Juan wasn't naïve. No, let's be honest, he's dumb. So dumb he may not have realized Jim Peterson was a crook."

One FBI agent nodded. "We'll soon know the truth. Believe me, he'll talk to Rachel. She'll start all cuddly and sweet. If that doesn't work, she will be one mean mother."

Gaspar looked alarmed. "She won't hurt him, will she?"

Chuy snorted. "You can say that after making the poor bastard heave his heels off?"

"I gave him a medicine his mother might have given him." After a long pause, "If he had consumed a poison."

"Whatever, now comes the hard part. The Petersons are a lot smarter than Juan. We've got to convince them to come to the clubhouse for an interview about their potential health problems while these two guys check out the Petersons' and the Benders' houses, yards, and cars. I figure you guys need at least an hour."

Both FBI agents nodded their heads in agreement.

Chuy studied Gaspar who shook slightly. "Can you kill an hour?"

"No, but Sara can. I told her to be her most academic self and really explain every detail."

"Did you tell her about the Petersons?"

"Didn't have to. She's suspected them of being… How did she say it? Oh yes, he of 'being Machiavellian' and she of 'being a fake.' She also suggested we have another couple present at the interview."

"Who?"

"I chose carefully. Marian Crockett is under sixty-five and getting antivirals. Hank grew up on a farm. He's apt to have natural immunity against this flu if Sara's right. It's doubtful that we're risking their health. And most importantly, communicating with the Crocketts takes time. We have a lot of time to kill."

"Right, let's go."

"What if the Petersons pull guns on us? We can't disarm them the way we did Juan."

"I'm wearing a bug and a hidden gun on my leg." Chuy lifted his pant leg. "The FBI guys already installed bugs in the small meeting room in the clubhouse. The Chief has two guys in each squad car by the front gate. He'll pull up in another car as soon as we're in the clubhouse. Besides, I think I've found all their guns."

"Let's go before I lose my nerve."

Gaspar sat in the front seat of the police car and watched as Chuy knocked on the door of the Petersons' house. Chuy had a long conversation with Jean. After a couple of minutes Jim appeared. Jim's face reddened and his voice became louder and louder as he spoke to Chuy. Finally, Chuy escorted Jim and Jean Peterson to the back seat of the police car.

The Petersons and Chuy were silent during the ride to the clubhouse. Gaspar chattered about how he had gotten a local bakery to deliver donuts and cheese Danish rolls to the front gate every morning.

The Crocketts were already chatting with Sara by conference phone when the Petersons, Gaspar, and Chuy arrived at the clubhouse. Sara began with a detailed account about the six men who seemed to be resistant to the flu.

"I may seem as slow as molasses in winter to you, but I get the point." Hank Crockett rubbed his chin. "You're saying I might have a protein in my blood protecting me from the flu 'cause I was raised on a pig farm."

"Yes, but I need a blood sample to know for sure," said Sara.

"Why didn't you say that before you gave the science lesson? I trust you and Doc Gonzales. Where do I sign?"

"Great, now what about you other three. Did you ever work in a stock yard, a butcher shop, or a veterinary clinic? Maybe even as a summer job in high school?"

Gaspar noticed the Crocketts stared at the speakerphone, apparently concentrating on the questions. The Petersons eyed the far corners of the room. He hoped Jim or Jean didn't spot the bugs the FBI planted.

"Sara." Marian clutched Hank's arm. "Are you trying to say you need more of my blood? Doc took some on Saturday."

"No." Sara paused, "We need your permission to do an additional assay."

"Okay," said Marian.

Gaspar knew Sara was desperate to kill time. The form that the residents signed Saturday allowed for additional tests to screen for exposure to swine flus. Marian didn't need to sign another form.

"Jim? Jean?" said Sara. "Any contact with swine?"

Jim snorted. "I assume you don't mean the police. What's in it for me? Why would I let you have my blood to test your ideas?"

"Because public health officials won't let you leave La Bendita until they're sure that you don't have the flu."

"I was told we would be held here for one week. On Thursday afternoon, three days from now, I'm out of here." Jim puffed his chest and clenched his fists.

"Only if no new cases of flu develop among the residents of La Bendita."

"We'll see. No blood from me or Jean." Jim stared at the door.

Gaspar tried not to stare at the Petersons because he didn't want to rile Jim more. It wouldn't be pretty if Chuy had to use force to stop the Peterson's from leaving the clubhouse. Frankly, he didn't think Chuy could without using a gun. He could tell Chuy was worried too as he stared at his phone waiting for the FBI agents to call after they finished their search.

"Well, then there's the other experiment that we want to run,'" said Sara. "We'd like to vaccinate several of you who are over sixty-five against the Philippine flu and monitor the development of your antibody levels. So far no one…."

Gaspar felt like he couldn't breathe. Sara was going contradict what we told the Petersons to get them here. He knew Chuy should have let him tell Sara about the ruse. Gaspar cleared his throat nosily so no one could hear Sara's words. "What she means to say is that no one who has been vaccinated *properly* has developed severe flu symptoms."

"But Juan was vaccinated." Jean's voice was not her usual throaty whisper.

Gaspar prayed that Sara would listen to his explanation and not argue. "Appears one batch was defective. Poor Juan was vaccinated with

                                                    J. L. Greger

it." Gaspar gave a long sigh. "That's why he suddenly became sick, but we caught him before his symptoms became severe. Of course, he might have spread it to those he talked to during the last day or two."

Sara changed the topic slightly and talked about the problems of vaccine development. Gaspar was proud of himself. He'd informed Sara of the ruse and hopefully scared the Petersons, but probably not enough for them to admit that Juan had been in their house.

Jim growled after five minutes of Sara's explanation. "Enough. We don't want to be vaccinated if we have to give a blood sample first."

"Are you sure? The Philippine flu will be around for probably a year. It will come in waves. If you're vaccinated, you'll be protected."

"We're leaving." Jim stood and yanked Jean to her feet. Chuy also stood and planted himself in front of the door.

Gaspar knew Sara couldn't see the Petersons but she had to get their attention fast. "Sara, I know you didn't want to scare them, but it's time to tell them about the death toll here."

"Okay. Did you know half of the residents at the center have died of the flu already?"

Both Petersons gasped and stopped moving toward the door.

Hank coughed. "I'm thinking everyone would want to know that kind of information. Why weren't we told before?"

Marian squeaked, "Oh, God."

"What good would it do to scare the residents of La Bendita more than they're scared already?"

Jean whimpered.

Gaspar thought Sara had finally got the Petersons' attention. He escorted the Petersons back to their chairs. "Did you think this quarantine was a game? Why do you think I insisted you wear plastic gloves and masks at this meeting?"

Sara interrupted. "Gaspar and his nurses didn't work more than eighteen hours a day to keep you away from the center and each other for fun. Believe me, the last few days haven't been fun for him. He's been a nervous wreck."

Chuy spoke for the first time. "If Doc hadn't been bald to begin with, he'd be bald now. He must have wiped his head every two minutes for the last few days."

"Not that often." Gaspar studied the Petersons' faces. "A vaccination would protect you against the next wave of the flu. You're both over sixty-five. This proposed study is your best and really only reasonable choice at this point."

Jean squeezed her husband's hand.

Jim shoved his arm threateningly close to Gaspar. "Okay. Who takes our blood? How about the boss Dr. Behren."

Gaspar couldn't let Ellen be brought in after all the bluffing. She'd blow everything. "Ellen Behren has been a public health administrator for many years. She probably hasn't drawn a blood sample since her residency. I'd better do it."

Jim clenched his fists again. "How soon do we get the vaccinations?"

Gaspar knew the CDC human subjects committee had not approved any experimental use of the flu vaccine with those over sixty-five. Sara had bluffed, but he was also sure two or three doses of the vaccine would never be missed. He was about to get the vaccine when Sara came through.

"The lab has to check your blood first. If Doc Gonzales vaccinates you with a live flu virus while your immune systems are fighting off the flu, it could be lethal. And, of course, Marian can't be vaccinated while she's receiving antivirals. The vaccination wouldn't take."

Gaspar moseyed across the room. He brought back a tray with Vacutainer tubes, needles, swabs, cotton and alcohol. As he wiped Jim's arm with alcohol, he looked at Chuy who shook his head.

"Oh, I forgot to lay out bandages."

Gaspar sauntered to the next room, slammed several drawers open and shut, stayed there for a couple of minutes, before he emerged with a handful of bandages. "Had trouble finding them."

He scrubbed Jim's arm again with alcohol, drew the blood sample, slowly applied a bandage, selected a cotton swab with a long wooden handle and rubbed it around the inside of Jim's nose, and carefully placed the swab in a glass tube. He started the process with Jean.

Chuy's phone rang.

Gaspar relaxed and completed the collection process with Jean in less than thirty seconds. "Do you want the ambulance driver to drive you home or would you rather walk home?"

"Walk." Jim and Jean almost ran from the clubhouse.

"Now don't that beat all." said Marian. "You saved their lives. They didn't even say thank you. Hank and me were talking. We want you to know we appreciate your efforts."

Gaspar quickly drew a blood sample from Hank Crockett. Hank hugged his wife. They strolled home holding hands.

Chuy rushed to the front gate with the Petersons' samples.

Gaspar crumpled into a chair and sighed. "Sara, I don't know what I would have done to stall once I'd drawn Jean's blood."

"I know, and the worst is ahead. I think the Petersons were wise to us. Wonder what they'll do."

CHAPTER 23: Day Six Continued — Chief Gil Andrews

Gil was dog-tired. He hadn't been this weary since he retired from the Gang Unit of the Albuquerque Police Department. His throat was scratchy. His ears were ringing and his head ached. He wondered if he'd gotten the flu despite being vaccinated against it.

He swallowed hard. His throat was probably scratchy from talking so much to the state police, the state lab, and the Albuquerque Police Department. Then there was the Sandoval County Sheriff's Office, the state Bureau of Health Emergency Management, and not least of all Ellen Behren. This damn quarantine was a communications nightmare.

Gil sneezed violently as he read a text message from his secretary. The mayor had called again. He decided to delay his call to the mayor until he had something positive to say. Then he remembered that he'd forgotten to take his Zyrtec for his allergies this morning. No wonder his sinuses ached.

He tried to stretch his bulky frame within the confines of the squad car but couldn't. He had no one to blame but himself. He'd decided to listen to the feed from the bugs in the clubhouse at La Bendita's front gate because he thought Chuy and Doc might need him. If so, he was prepared to ignore the quarantine and rush in to save them.

Then too, this mess was partly his fault. He should have fired Juan months ago but dreaded writing all those stupid warning letters and keeping a file of all Juan's mistakes. It was easier to ignore Juan's incompetence. He never dreamed Juan would take a bribe.

A police officer from the other squad car leaned in over the open window on the passenger side of Gil's car. "Chuy is bringing out the blood samples. He says they need to be rushed to a lab. Doesn't seem like getting data for Sara's study is that important."

"It's not. There was unidentified blood found at the crime scene where a drug dealer was killed on Zuni in Albuquerque six months ago. The Albuquerque cops couldn't identify the source of the blood until we found a gun in the hidden compartment in Jim Peterson's Hummer."

"What are you talking about?"

That was another of his mistakes. He hadn't shared much with his staff since he'd come to doubt Juan. Time to start trusting them again. "The Albuquerque Police Lab thinks the bullets shot from one of Peterson's guns are matches for one found in a dead drug dealer six months ago. Now we'll see if his blood matches the unidentified blood at the crime scene, too."

"Why don't we arrest Peterson now?"

"He's not going anywhere as long as we monitor the gates. If we arrest him without the blood evidence, a lawyer could spring him in an hour or two. If we blocked his release then, we'd alert a lot of people about the quarantine. Could end up with a crowd of gawkers at this gate. Better to sit tight."

"I'll get the samples."

"First, put on a mask and plastic gloves. Wipe the tubes with alcohol. Follow procedure as you discard the gloves. Get the guys in the extra car to take it to the lab." Gil hated to sound like a schoolmarm but the procedures for handling samples from potential flu victims were complex.

After Chuy delivered the samples, he waited for Gil to amble to the front gate. "Chief, I think the Petersons might bolt tonight. Jim guessed we might use his blood sample for other purposes, I think. There's a reason he's never been arrested. He's smart and cool. So's his wife."

"Yeah, I agree."

"Right. How's Rachel doing with Juan?"

"Rachel read him his Miranda rights but convinced him that he didn't need a lawyer."

Chuy shook his head. "How?"

"Told him real men don't hide behind such details."

"Juan's slow, but not that slow."

Gil shifted his weight and tugged at his belt. "Rachel said she batted her eyelashes."

"He's stupider than I thought," said Chuy.

"No kidding."

Thirty minutes later, Gil remembered an important detail as he sat outside McDonald's eating a quarter pounder and fries. He called Chuy. "I forgot to tell you about Jane Lane. She's delirious and keeps moaning, 'Bet Jim and Howie left without me.' I figure Howie must be Howie Steele."

"Should I question Steele now?"

"Might be wise to talk to Gaspar first. A bee in my bonnet says Gaspar knows a lot about Steele."

Gil finished his meal and returned to his office to clean up paperwork. He'd almost cleared his desk when Chuy called.

"Chief, I might have new info."

"Spit it out."

"It's a hunch. I'd better tell you exactly what happened. Then you can draw your own conclusions."

"Okay."

"I asked Mr. Steele who had access to the back gate besides the police and fire departments. He said, 'It's me, Gaspar, George, and the bitch who runs the assisted living center.' Mrs. Steele jerked her head up when he referred to Sylvia Otega as a bitch. I figured she knew something more because of the way she glared at him. Then she went to the kitchen for coffee. I wanted to speak to her alone, so I asked to use the bathroom, which in these models, is just off the kitchen."

"And?"

"As I came out of the bathroom, I saw Mr. Steele grab his wife's arm. She yanked her arm loose and handed him a cup of coffee. He stared at her for thirty seconds before he returned to his chair in the living room. As he grumbled about 'the little woman,' I saw Mrs. Steele pick up a pen and start to write on a napkin. I thought it strange until I realized the message might be for me. I kept Mr. Steele talking. No wonder Doc calls him a toad. Besides being boring, he had no neck and his eyes bulge."

Gil wished Chuy would speed up the story but guessed Chuy wanted to impart the feeling of the conversation as well as the facts.

"Mrs. Steele brought me a cup of coffee with the special napkin. I quickly ended the conversation and stuffed the napkin in my pocket. As soon as I got to the car, I studied the napkin."

Gil tried to keep any impatience out of his voice. "What does the napkin say?"

"Her writing's shaky, but I think it says: Petersons drugged us long ago. Took and returned H's gate card. H plans to escape with JP tonight."

"You did good. We've got a witness now who can say the Petersons had a way out of the back gate. I wonder if she can explain 'long ago.' Those gang killings occurred about six months ago."

"But will she cross Howie?"

"Mmm, leave that to me. You'd better help Rachel now. She wants you to be the bad cop."

Gil was ready to turn off the lights in his office when the phone rang. "Chief, you should know," said the ambulance driver, "Doc asked us to take him to another home. The Crocketts told him no one had answered the phone for the last day. We found the woman dead. Her husband was quietly sitting by her body and stroking her hand."

"What'd Doc say?"

"He asked the old guy why he didn't call for help."

"And?"

"The old man smiled. 'Dunno. My old gal and I've been together for fifty-three years next June. She went off color yesterday. I didn't want her to be alone at the end. Isn't right.' Doc cried. First time, I've seen him break down with a patient."

"I know Doc can't take much more."

"Guess he liked this old couple. Said the old woman did a lot for patients in the center. Said she probably visited there last weekend without signing in and forgot to tell the interviewers."

"Mmm. Wives are often selective in what they remember."

CHAPTER 24: Sunday Night — Sergeant Chuy Bargas

"Juan," said Rachel Jones in a throaty whisper. "Are you scared? You should be. Let me help you before Chuy arrives. He's angry with you."

Chuy recognized his clue and noisily slammed open the door to the small room. "Where's the stupid bastard?" He yanked a chair from the corner and threw it next to Juan. He slid into the chair and crammed his face next to Juan's. "Stupid, you've blown your job." His spit spattered Juan's face. "You've also blown any deal with Jim Peterson."

"Jim, he'll protect me. He's a good guy."

"Fat chance. He'll want you dead. You won't last one day on the street."

Juan blinked his eyes several times.

"We've already created your cover. The Petersons saw you carried out on a stretcher from the Benders' house. I mentioned to them you must have the flu because you were vomiting."

"*Vómito mucho.*"

"I'll tell the Petersons. Hell, Doc Gonzales can let it slip you died. They'll believe it and won't come after you."

Juan looked confused.

Rachel touched his arm lightly. "It'll work."

Juan sat with his head hanging down for at least a minute. His eyes shifted to study Chuy, and then he ogled Rachel. "Okay."

"Tell me all you know about the Petersons."

Juan sat silently.

"Don't be stupid. If you don't talk, the Chief will tell Peterson you ratted on him. You know, make Jim Peterson good and mad."

"About a year ago." Juan bit his lip. "I... I saw the Petersons' Hummer go through the back gate about midnight. I was driving along the back of the center's parking lot." He sat silently for thirty seconds.

Rachel stroked Juan's shoulder. "Be smart. Keep going,"

"I went and parked the squad car on Zinnia Avenue about a block from the back gate." He smiled. "I checked. I couldn't see the squad car when I stood at the gate." He hung his head again. "I waited.

The gate opened about three. When his Hummer went by, I pulled in behind it."

"Good job. Keep talking," said Rachel.

"Mr. Peterson got out of the Hummer. He called me 'Officer.' No one else does. He said, 'You caught me red handed. Us men need a break from the old ball and chain. Don't get me wrong, Jean's a good wife.' He winked. 'Sometimes I need a bit of Latina hot blood.' I was surprised."

"You're doing great." Rachel whispered.

"Mr. Peterson said, 'Officer, couldn't we keep this between us men.' I said this gate was for emergency use. He winked and said, 'Seeing Consuelo seemed like an emergency to me.' He reached in his pocket. He pulled out a roll of bills and peeled off two hundred-dollar bills. He handed them to me, returned to his Hummer, and drove to his house."

"What did you do?"

Juan opened his mouth and blinked.

"What did you do with the money?"

"Put it in my pocket. It was a gift."

"Did Peterson ever again give you money or gifts?"

"Tell him everything," Rachel rubbed Juan's shoulder.

"He stopped me when I circled through La Bendita a week later. We talked about our favorite entertainers. After that he stopped me once in a while. He gave me tickets to a concert by Dwight Yoakam at Route 66 Casino, good tequila at Christmas." He paused and thought. "Things like that."

"Did you see him leave or enter through the back gate again?"

"Yeah, I tried to circle through La Bendita around midnight every night that I was on patrol. He went out about once a month by the back gate." Juan paused again and furrowed his brow. "No. more often."

The interrogation continued for more than an hour, with occasional breaks when Rachel and Chuy conferred in the hallway. Neither Rachel nor Chuy could fathom why Juan had destroyed his career for a few, rather paltry, gifts from Jim Peterson. Both found it humorous the way Juan seemed to delight in Rachel's flirtations.

At last, in the middle of a question, Chuy had a brainstorm. Jean was kind of old, but she knew how to strut her stuff. "Did you ever see Jean?"

"I felt sorry for Jean. I went to see her."

Chuy smirked. "Did you make her?"

Juan stared at Chuy like a deer caught in headlights. "It's not like that."

Chuy probed more and soon was convinced Juan had waited for Jim's Hummer to leave almost every night. When Jim left through the back gate, Juan drove his car to the clubhouse parking lot and slunk to the Petersons' house and spent time with Jean Peterson in her bedroom or at least in bedroom activities.

The interrogation continued until Chuy and Rachel were convinced that Juan could yield no more clues.

Dulce handed a copy of *Horton Hears A Who* to Cesar. "Aletha give it to the public health worker last night to give to Maria."

"Good, I'm tired of reading *The Cat in the Hat*." Cesar rose from the chair at the side of Maria's bed and led Dulce into the hallway. "How's Julia? I haven't heard any coughs from her room in the last two hours."

"Not good. Doctor Gonzales put her on a ventilator. Her fever better break soon."

"Would it help if I got the boys on the phone? They could read to her."

"It might get her mama off me. Aletha Bradley calls almost every hour." Dulce handed him a disposable mask, plastic gloves, and a paper gown. She sighed as she waddled away.

Cesar returned to Maria's room. His daughter had her thumb in her mouth and was snoring. She was a totally different child than on Sunday before her fever broke. He picked up his phone and left quietly. He took off his protective paraphernalia and donned the set Dulce gave him before he called Aletha Bradley.

"Mrs. Bradley, this is Cesar. I think Julia would like to hear Lalo's and Gabi's voices. Could they read a story to her? I'll put my phone on speakerphone mode."

He paused and listened to Aletha. "You'd better warn the boys that Julia won't talk to them." He saw no reason to tell her Julia was sedated so she wouldn't pull the ventilator tube out of mouth. "Are the boys ready?"

He put the phone on speakerphone mode and entered Julia's room. He held back a gasp. Julia had little bruises all over her neck, blood trickled from her nose, and her hair was matted with dry blood.

Lalo began to read poem.

Gabi screamed after a minute. "It's my turn now."

Lalo replied, "You can't read. You're a baby."

"Can too." Gabi proceeded to read, really to recite, *The Cat in the Hat.*

Cesar thought Julia started to breathe more rapidly. He rubbed the back of her hand.

After several minutes Aletha spoke. "Julia, this is your mama. Lalo, Gabi, and I love you and want you back. Fight. Fight hard to live."

A moment later Lalo began to read again.

Gaspar entered the room. "Aletha, this is Dr. Gonzales. I'll call you after I examine Julia. We're doing everything we can."

Cesar checked his phone. The line was dead.

"Julia's spirit appreciates hearing her sons. She thanks you." Dulce guided Cesar from the room. "Dispose of your gown, gloves, and mask right away." She pointed down the hall to a large box. As she entered Julia's room, she added, "Lunch good today — burritos. You better hurry. The nurses and doctors in the center are not busy today, and they are," she emphasized the next words, "hungry like a patient after his fever breaks."

Cesar sauntered to the break room on the first floor of the clinic. One of the nurses in the clinic introduced him to a medical resident and three nurses who had worked in the center.

"Are your patients getting better now?" Cesar asked the resident as he wolfed down a burrito.

The medical resident replied without swallowing his mouthful of food first. "Nah, mainly they're dead."

A nurse spoke. "Dave, don't be an ass. He has family in the clinic. He's scared enough."

Dave stopped chewing his food. "Okay, I exaggerated. About half survived."

The nurse tried to change the subject. "Five of the center's residents never got sick. We call them the lucky five. They went around and visited the other patients yesterday. About thirty others have recovered, but they're still a little weak."

"Yes, like my Maria. Doc Gonzales says she'll be running and playing soon, but my neighbor Julia looks bad."

"Did she get antivirals?" asked Dave.

"Yes."

"Before she had flu symptoms?"

"Yes."

"She'll make it," Dave bit off more burrito. "Probably."

Cesar stared at Dave.

A nurse said, "She's probably forty years younger than most of our patients in the center. A real advantage."

"My wife Elena, she died." Then in the brightly lit break room filled with people he'd just met, Cesar began to sob.

Another nurse stopped drinking her coffee, stood, and hugged Cesar. "Let it all out. We've all had to do it here. Everything has happened quickly. The patients just became numbers. The smart-ass eating the burrito cried for hours on Friday and again yesterday."

Dave snorted. "So did you, and you too." He pointed at two nurses. "That's why we were transferred from the center to the clinic, actually outreach."

"What's outreach?" asked Cesar.

"Dr. Ellen Behren, the boss lady, says the quarantine can be lifted on Thursday if no one new develops flu symptoms. She assigned four of us to go house to house in La Bendita. We're to examine and interview everyone again and take a blood sample, if we haven't already gotten blood from them."

"That's good?" Cesar scrutinized Dave's face for more information.

"Yeah, sounds good. But those who show the slightest flu symptoms will be sent to the center." Dave shook his head. "Poor devils."

Cesar shook his head. "Is the flu epidemic over?"

"Nah." Dave took a sip of his coffee. "Just this wave. Hopefully, the next wave won't be in the Albuquerque area. I don't want to repeat the last week ever again."

Cesar stared at the resident. "Many died. All for nothing."

Dave shook his head. "Not true. We, or I should say the mysterious epidemiologist Sara, learned a lot with the help of a scientist in Ames, Iowa. He proved Sara's guesses were right."

"Like what?"

"The five lucky guys and one resident in the La Bendita community have antibodies."

"What are antibodies?"

Dave thought a second. "A type of protein that helps us fight off diseases. The lucky guys all have a special antibodies that makes them resistant to the Philippine flu."

"Why is that important?"

"As of today, the CDC, really a lot of labs, will try to make a vaccine based on their special antibodies. It will be safer to give to kids and old people."

A nurse added, "If we had the vaccine two months ago, we could have saved most of those who died."

"How long?" asked Cesar.

Dave didn't bother to stop chewing his burrito. "How long what?"

"How long until the new vaccine is ready?"

"At least six months."

"So, this, this," Cesar searched for the best word, "disaster could occur over and over again for the next six months."

"Well, not quite as bad. Dr. Bloom and the mysterious Sara convinced the CDC and FDA to use antivirals with a wider range of patients. They showed that the experimental antivirals helped the majority of patients younger than sixty-five if they got the antivirals fast enough. And the side effects were less than expected, but they didn't get a chance to test the experimental antivirals with patients older than sixty-five."

Dave stopped and turned pale. "Now that they proved the effectiveness of the new antivirals, everyone will want them. There could be a shortage and the situation here could become common during the next six months."

Cesar sipped his coffee for several minutes and ignored the animated babble among the nurses and Dave. Finally, he nudged Dave. "Why do you call Sara mysterious?"

"None of us have seen her. She's holed up at her sister's house. Cranking out proposals, human consent forms, and stats like a machine."

As Cesar got off the elevator on the third floor, he saw Doc Gonzales talk to Dulce and then rush away. Dulce grabbed Cesar's arm. "He's upset about Julia. Her fever not break. Her mother wants to be with her."

Sara hummed as she wove on her loom Tuesday morning. She had already completed analyses of data from La Bendita, at least as much as was needed now, and was determined to have the wall hanging for the auction completed by Friday. Bug seemed to sense Sara's mood. Instead of sleeping at her feet, he was licking his favorite toy, a stuffed pink poodle.

The phone rang.

"He's gone!"

Sara recognized the previous screech as coming from Aletha. "Who's gone?"

"Lalo."

"Define gone."

"I found this note on his bed five minutes ago. It said, 'Mom needs me. Tell Sara I'll use our secret path.' What does that mean?"

"I'm not sure. Probably once he gets out of Riverview, he'll go along the flood control channel and then down a sandy path to a low point in the wall to La Bendita, but he might wander into the savanna and bosque. Have you called the police?"

"No, he'll hide from them because he doesn't want to be brought home. He wants to be with his mother." Aletha gasped. "Gaspar says Julia is weak, very weak now."

"I know this doesn't help, but I'm sorry." Sara waited while Aletha cried. "I suspect you didn't call for sympathy. What did you and Gaspar cook up?"

"Always direct. That's what I like about you. Gaspar told me you were unofficially still quarantined, but blood tests proved you didn't have the flu."

"So?"

"He said he'd make sure Ellen didn't file police charges against you for breaking the quarantine."

"I think I know what's coming. Spit it out."

"Lalo trusts you. He won't hide from you. You know the way, well probably, that he'll take to enter La Bendita." She took a breath. "Find Lalo before he gets into La Bendita."

"What if he's already in?"

"Stay with him. Gaspar said the quarantine will probably be lifted on late Thursday or Friday."

"There's a lot of ifs before that occurs."

"Please, I'd go but I don't know this secret path. Gabi needs me. Gaspar says I might be too old for the antivirals I've been taking to do much good. And you have a house to stay in at La Bendita."

Sara reached down and rubbed Bug behind his ears. She knew if she was exposed to the flu, she probably wouldn't develop symptoms because she'd been vaccinated and had some natural immunity. And if she did, the symptoms should be mild. She felt sorry for Lalo, even if he was a brat. She also knew Aletha was right. "Okay, Aletha. I'll look for him along the path I mentioned, but I might miss him."

"Not if you hurry."

"I'll try but it will take me thirty minutes to drive to La Bendita."

Sara gave Bug one of his favorite dental bones and threw items into a knapsack. She called Linda as she drove. As expected, Linda didn't like her plan.

Sara parked in front of Wal-Mart, walked across its lot and through several construction sites, and climbed down a concrete abutment of the flood control channel. No one was in the channel. In one sense, she was glad. She'd always told Lalo to only cross the channel at locations lined by concrete abutments because she was afraid the mud and sand in the natural part of the channel could contain quick sand. There was only mud and sand in the channel between the concrete, where she stood, and the next abutment, where she usually crossed to the savanna.

"Lalo, Lalo. It's Sara," she called repeatedly.

She climbed up the concrete abutment on the other side of the channel and hiked along the gravel road toward the low point in the perimeter wall of La Bendita at the end of Marigold Lane. She looked over the wall. Lalo wasn't in sight.

She sat in the shade of the wall and called Aletha. "Haven't seen him yet."

"What if you don't find him? He'll be alone all night."

"Aletha, if I don't find him by two, have Gaspar alert the police. Remind Gaspar about Peterson."

"What. What haven't you told me?"

Too late, Sara realized she'd given Aletha too much information. "Remind Gaspar that Peterson might know about this low point in the wall. Lalo and I don't want to be in his way."

"He's my grandson."

"Please do what I ask. I'll go to the savanna and then the bosque." Sara disconnected before Aletha could respond.

Sara looked for small shoe prints in the sand near the wall. She didn't know why. She was no Daniel Boone. She looked behind every shrub big enough to hide a small eight-year-old boy as she wandered along the sandy path to the back-emergency exit. She spied a lone police vehicle parked in front of the gate. She doubted Lalo would try to slip past the police car to enter La Bendita at the gate. Accordingly, she clambered into the flood control channel. The blazing sun overhead seemed hotter when she was in the concrete channel and she quickly climbed out into the savanna. She enjoyed the shade of two cottonwood trees as she scrutinized the bushes for motion.

She called Gaspar. "We need to talk."

"That would be nice, but I'm in quarantine and can't accept any dinner invitations."

Gaspar must not be alone. His gibberish was probably a hint. "Gaspar, I can't find Lalo in the savanna or near the wall. I think I'd better look in the bosque. Could you meet me at the low point of the wall at two?"

"I'd like to."

"Do you know where the low point in the wall is?"

"No, tell me how it'll be."

"Gaspar, are you trying to make this call sound like a conversation with a girlfriend? I guess that's one way to avoid questions. Are you with Ellen now?"

"Yes, dear."

"With Chuy?"

"Yes, dear that would be nice."

"You have to tell Chuy and Chief Andrews by two that we need their help if I don't find Lalo."

"Yes dear. What about those directions you were going to give me? I may want to use them when I get out of here."

"Go down Marigold Lane. Near the end on the left along the perimeter wall, you'll see the low spot. There's an engineering shack near the low spot in the wall."

"Thanks, dear. I'll talk to you later."

After the call, Sara tramped around the savanna. She doubted she'd find Lalo but she slogged on. Over and over again she yelled, "Lalo, it's Sara. Lalo, I can get you to your mom." Sara used her farm voice, the one she used as teenager to yell over the noise of the tractor when she called her father to dinner.

She saw something move in a clump of rabbitbrush at the base of a large gnarled cottonwood tree near the edge of the savanna with the bosque. "Damn, I almost never run into a coyote in the bosque. Guess I did this time." She studied the moving object. Not a coyote. Too small to be an adult, probably a child wearing a bit of blue. Probably Lalo and he didn't want her to find him. She knew Lalo could outrun her.

She stopped yelling and moved like a prowling cat toward the clump of rabbitbrush. She stopped about twenty feet from the shrubs. Lalo was lying on his side. He seemed to be digging in the debris at the foot of the cottonwood tree. She stepped closer. He stopped digging when he heard her.

She wanted to scream but kept her composure. "Lalo, did you hurt yourself?"

He pointed to his ankle but didn't look at Sara.

"Why didn't you go into La Bendita at the low point in the wall?"

"I almost did, but I saw a man and a woman in La Bendita looking at the wall. I didn't want them to see me. I went to the channel, but soon I heard their voices. I ran to the savanna. They saw me."

"Are you sure?"

"They waved at me. The man yelled, 'Hey kid.' I ran because he didn't sound friendly."

"Did they follow you?"

"No, I think they went back to La Bendita."

"What did they look like?"

"Like adults."

Sara sighed. Lalo could be a real pistol sometimes. "Was the man bald?"

Lalo thought for several seconds. "No."

"Did the man or the woman have gray hair?"

Lalo squinched his face. "The man did. The woman had red hair."

Sara gulped. She looked at her watch. It was one-twenty. "When did you fall?"

"When I heard you yelling, I started to run again. My foot got caught. I was afraid you'd take me back to Granny."

"So, you were going to lie here and hope I didn't see you?"

Lalo looked down probably to avoid her gaze.

"How did you plan to get out of here?"

Lalo shrugged his shoulders and tugged on his blue cap.

"Can you walk?" Sara knelt by his side. "Yell, if it hurts." Sara proceeded to press on Lalo's left knee and then lower leg. Lalo made no sound. When she pressed on his ankle and foot, he whimpered a bit. As Sara helped Lalo sit up, she noted the palms of his hands, his elbows, and his knees were bleeding. "I'll grab you under both arms and lift you. Let's see if you can stand. It will hurt some." Lalo was heavier than he looked but soon he was standing.

"How does it feel?"

Lalo bit his lip. "Okay."

"I'm pretty sure you didn't break your leg. Not sure about the bones in your foot or ankle. Try to take a step."

Lalo winced but hobbled several steps with Sara's help.

"You're a brave boy. I think it's a sprain. I'll try to bandage it."

"With what?"

"Good question." She opened her knapsack. "I've got a flashlight, water, and duct tape. What do you have?"

"My Cub Scout scarf and cap."

"Good. We'll wrap your ankle with your scarf. Then I'll wrap the tape over the top and up your leg a bit."

"Like we learned in Cub Scouts."

"Yeah."

Lalo gave Sara advice as she bandaged his ankle. He stood up and took a couple of steps. "I can do it."

Sara called Gaspar. "I found him."

"That's wonderful sweetheart."

"Lalo sprained his ankle in the bosque. If we're not at the low spot in the wall by two, look for us on the savanna or in the channel. Bring Chuy. Lalo spotted a man with gray hair and a woman with red hair at the low point of the wall about an hour ago."

"No."

"They saw him and followed him a bit. He thinks they went back to La Bendita."

"I understand dear."

CHAPTER 27: Day Seven Continued — Sergeant Chuy Bargas

One of Ellen's assistants summoned Chuy to appear at the clubhouse for another meeting at twelve-thirty on Tuesday afternoon. When he arrived, Ellen seemed agitated. One moment she rhapsodized about her big success — the identification of the factor that had protected five residents of the center against the flu. The next moment she ranted about a CDC decision that she considered to be an affront to her leadership.

All the while, Martin repeated over and over again, "I told you so."

Gaspar, as usual, wiped his bald head regularly as Sylvia calmly explained the situation to Chuy. Officials in Washington, D.C. and Santa Fe had decided the quarantine couldn't be lifted until there was a twenty-four-hour period with no flu-related deaths in La Bendita.

Chuy thought about his problem while he waited for Ellen to calm down. She wouldn't like his plans for getting Juan out of La Bendita.

His reverie was interrupted. "Chuy, Chuy, we're waiting for your report." Ellen glared at him. Gaspar, Martin, and Sylvia eyed him suspiciously, but more kindly than Ellen.

"Er, er. Juan Vigil took bribes from the Petersons and hid the fact that Jim Peterson, aka Jim Mazzone, regularly used the back-emergency gate of La Bendita late at night. The Chief wants to protect Juan Vigil from the Petersons."

Ellen frowned. "But Juan can't leave. The quarantine."

"It shouldn't be a problem," said Gaspar. "Juan's vaccinated against the flu. So are all the FBI agents. It'll sort of be a house quarantine at the FBI lock up after they take him out of here. Besides, if he stays, we risk potential violence."

Ellen frowned. "Don't let your imagination work overtime."

"Ma'am, Doc's not imagining," replied Chuy. "Juan ratted on Peterson. Peterson will want to finish his business with Juan before he escapes tonight."

Ellen stared first at Chuy and then Gaspar. "What have you forgotten to tell me?"

Sweat beaded up on Gaspar's head.

Chuy cleared his throat. "Susan Steele thinks the Petersons and Howie Steele will try to escape from La Bendita tonight. The Chief suspects Howie will have an accident when he tries to escape."

"What about Juan?"

"The Chief thinks he'll have an accident too." Everyone stared at Chuy. "Dead men can't testify. Peterson avoided arrests over the years by taking care of details."

"What about the patients who talked to you?" asked Sylvia. "They could testify they'd seen the Hummer leave at night many times."

"Peterson doesn't know about them. I don't think they'll ever have to testify, because no one thinks they'd do well on the stand. That's why Rachel Jones and I worked so hard on Juan. And we have an easy way to get Juan out of La Bendita. Jean Peterson saw him carried from the Benders' house on a gurney. We…"

"What do you mean we?" asked Ellen.

"Doc and me."

Ellen glared at Gaspar. "What are you two planning for an encore?"

"The FBI guys, disguised as state public health workers, will visit Jean and Jim," said Gaspar. "They'll tell them that Juan died and they're documenting Jim's and Jean's exposure to Juan."

Chuy interrupted, "While Jim and Jean are occupied, the other agent, Rachel Jones, and I will transfer Juan to an ambulance. The FBI will keep Juan in protective custody until the FBI with the Chief's help builds cases against the Petersons."

"What do you have on Jim Peterson?" asked Ellen.

"Bribery of a police officer. Suspicions of murder but not enough evidence yet. A lawyer could spring him in hours," said Chuy.

"So, the quarantine is a legal way to detain the Petersons." Martin chuckled. "Glad it works to someone's advantage. I know I shouldn't ask, but what do you have on Jean Peterson?"

"Not much. Bribing a police officer, that is, Juan," stated Chuy.

"Mrs. Perfect?" gasped Sylvia. "What type of bribe?"

"Sex for his silence. But he'll try to protect her and say they were friends."

"This is getting interesting." Martin straightened in his chair. "Now what about the planned escape by the Petersons you mentioned?"

J. L. Greger

Before Chuy could answer, Gaspar got a phone call. This was the third call during the meeting. Gaspar went to the corner and paced. He could be heard saying repeatedly, "Yes dear" and "Sweetheart."

Martin smirked. "There's more activity here than I thought. Isn't he a widower?"

Sylvia, who had been craning her neck to hear Gaspar's conversation, replied, "He is and has two grown sons. I've never before heard him call anyone dear or sweetheart."

Gaspar returned to his seat. "Sorry for the interruption. What did I miss?"

Martin winked. "Nothing here, but sounds like you're missing a lot from Sweetheart."

Chuy avoided looking at Gaspar because he was afraid he would snicker. He noticed Martin and Sylvia were less polite. They sat with big smiles on their faces and stared as Gaspar licked his lips and muttered, "Aletha… Aletha Bradley keeps… Aletha Bradley keeps calling."

"Who's Aletha Bradley?" asked Ellen.

"One of the wealthiest, most powerful widows in New Mexico. She's an art dealer and entrepreneur. Owns half, well perhaps a quarter, of Canyon Road in Santa Fe." Sylvia winked at Gaspar. "I'm impressed, but she's a little old for you, isn't she?"

"No, you've got it wrong. She's the mother of one of my flu patients, Julia Chavez. Julia's fever hasn't broken yet. Aletha calls every hour." He wiped his brow. "I call her Dear and Sweetheart because it annoys her slightly and then she talks less."

Chuy suspected Gaspar was trying to hide the truth from the group and thought this was not Gaspar's best performance.

As soon as the meeting ended, Gaspar dragged Chuy to his car and sped toward Marigold Lane. "Sara and Lalo are waiting for us at a low spot in the wall."

"Why's Sara here? Who's Lalo?"

"Lalo is Julia Chavez's 's eight-year-old son. He ran away from his grandmother Aletha to see his mother. Sara found him."

"Why didn't you tell Ellen?"

"She would have ordered Gil to take Lalo home, and I can't fault the boy for running away from Aletha. I would too. Besides, I think he might be the only one who can give Julia the will to live but we don't have much time. She's holding on by a strand."

"Why didn't the grandmother look for Lalo?"

"She's caring for Gabi, Julia's other boy. And Sara was more apt to succeed."

"So why do you need me?"

"Lalo's hurt. Sara and I may need help getting him over the wall. There's one more little detail. Lalo saw Jim and Jean Peterson about an hour ago on the path outside the wall."

Chuy wanted scream: What's wrong with you? How could he consider the Petersons' escape a little detail? His hands shook as he punched buttons on his phone. "Chief, the Petersons have escaped. They went over the wall about an hour ago."

"No. No. Listen to me," yelled Gaspar. "Lalo thinks the Peterson's went back into La Bendita."

"Wait Chief. Doc says they went back in."

Chuy listened to Gil for thirty seconds. "Chief, I don't want to be rude but shut up. It seems Gaspar, Sara, and a patient's mother hatched a weird plan. I don't know the details yet. Can you call the FBI guys posing as state health officials to check whether the Petersons are home? I should have more info in five minutes."

Gaspar jerked the car to a stop at an engineering shack. As he lumbered toward the La Bendita perimeter wall, a blonde, athletically-built woman climbed over the wall. A dark-haired boy tried to throw his leg over the wall but couldn't kick high enough, and the woman pulled on the boy's right shoulder to hoist him over the wall. Gaspar tugged on the boy's other shoulder.

Chuy figured the kid would have two dislocated shoulders by the time they were through. He ran to the wall, lifted the boy, and laid him on the ground.

The blonde extended her hand. "Hi, I'm Sara. You must be Chuy." She knelt and tapped the boy's arm. "And this run-away is Lalo."

Chuy stared at Sara. He'd expected the woman running all the complicated statistics to be gray-haired and fat. Gaspar eyed the woman almost affectionately as he awkwardly knelt to inspect the boy's ankle.

"Doc, move aside, I'll carry the boy to the car before one of the homeowners sees us."

Less than five minutes later, Gaspar shooed the ambulance crew aside when the group entered the clinic and took the elevator to the third floor. When the elevator door opened, Dulce stood in the way with her arms akimbo. "Doctor Gonzales, what are you doing?"

"I don't care if this is not consistent with the rules about quarantine. I have a little boy who wants to see his mother. And she needs him."

Dulce acquiesced.

Soon Lalo, sheathed in protective paper gear, was holding Julia's hand in his gloved hands. His dark eyes blinked back tears behind goggles, as he repeated over and over. "Mom, talk to me." Otherwise the room was silent except for the noise from the ventilator.

The scene was touching, but Chuy had other concerns. He ordered Dulce to notify Rachel Jones to get Juan ready to leave. He called the two other FBI agents. "Yeah, it's strange that they returned. I'll let Doc Gonzales explain details."

Chuy handed the phone to Gaspar. "You created the confusion. You can explain it to two irate FBI agents. Rachel and I will get Juan out of here before Peterson comes for him."

Chuy motioned for Sara to follow him. "Ma'am, I think Peterson will try to kill the kid if he learns he's here. The building is already in lock down mode, but keep the door closed until Rachel or I return. And tell Doc to fill in Ellen. She'll be steamed. Doc tricked her into believing he was talking to a girlfriend this afternoon when he took your calls."

Five minutes later, the ambulance crew transferred a "corpse" from their vehicle to a waiting ambulance. A red-faced Chief Gil Andrews stood at the open front gate gesticulating wildly. Chuy stood inside the front gate with his head lowered.

"You tell Doc, no more secrets," raged Gil. "Before Peterson makes his break tonight, I figure he will try to eliminate at least three loose ends."

Chuy shrugged his shoulders. "What if we arrested Peterson now?"

"Nothing will hold up in court until we have the blood analyses."

"Should we put the Steeles in protective custody?"

"No, Howie Steele hasn't admitted anything." Gil stopped stomping like an enraged bull. "Besides, he'd try to warn Peterson."

"What about Mrs. Steele? She gave us evidence."

"Probably should get her away from her fool husband."

"One problem." Chuy looked at Gil cautiously. "Doesn't look like the boss lady will win the battle to get us out of here on Thursday. People in Washington want La Bendita to stay quarantined until there is a twenty-four period with no deaths."

"Damn."

"Chief, Sara should show you where she found the kid. And where the kid saw the Petersons."

"Is the old lady up to it?"

"Oh, I think she'll surprise you."

Gil spoke into his phone. "Doc, get ready to move Sara and the kid out. Now." He listened for a minute. "What do you mean the kid won't go? He's a kid, make him."

Gil's face changed. "Oh, you think he's the mother's last chance."

His face was beet red when he ended the call. "Damn. I've got to talk to the boss lady again. She'll lecture me about her quarantine. Guess I'll lecture her. Bullets kill faster than flu, and we'll see bullets tonight."

"I don't know, Chief. The FBI and I think we've found all of Peterson's guns."

"You heard Doc's comments. At least a dozen people at La Bendita own guns."

CHAPTER 28: Day Seven Continued — Dulce Akee, Sara

Dulce had covered Lalo's body, arms, and legs with adult-sized paper protective clothing. She had placed a paper cap over his hair and made him wear a mask, gloves, and goggles. He looked like a green haystack.

He raised his capped head from Julia's shoulder every couple of minutes and whispered, "Mom, talk to me," or "Mom, I love you." As his dark eyes blinked back tears, he laid his head back on her shoulder and rubbed her arm again.

Sara was also covered in paper protective gear but she was too active to look like a haystack. She paced while she talked on her phone to Aletha, Ellen, Aletha again, and Gil. As she paced three steps in one direction, then three steps back in the tiny room, she avoided looking at Julia and Lalo. Finally, she composed a list of items that she needed or at least wanted.

Dulce studied the list that Sara handed her, shook her head, and waddled down the hall to Gaspar's office. She lowered herself onto a chair in front of Gaspar's desk.

"Little boy is good for mother. Hope Dr. Behren not find out. Against quarantine rule." She cocked her head. "Sara's not good. Too nervous."

"She's worried."

"So's the boy, but he sits still." Dulce unfolded and then refolded the paper in her hand.

"You know Sara is always busy. Chuy ordered Sara to stay in the room. She can't do much there."

Dulce handed Sara's list to Gaspar. "Do you want me to round up all these items?"

Gaspar scanned the wrinkled list. He punched buttons on his phone and announced, "Send up three or four sandwiches, a carton or two of milk, and several diet sodas to my office ASAP. We're hungry up here and can't spare the time to scavenge in the break room."

He punched numbers into his phone. "Ellen, do you have an extra laptop that Sara could use?" He paused and listened. "How do I know what for? She's pacing like a caged leopard in the zoo. Chuy ordered her to stay in Julia's room." He held the phone away from his face and groaned. "It's either a computer or a sedative. I think we may need her energy later." He smiled triumphantly.

"I'll send an aide over for the laptop and a couple of novels from the clubhouse library." Dulce departed before he could issue further orders.

Thirty minutes, later Chuy found Lalo still in full protective gear, except his mask dangled around his neck. He was nibbling a sandwich while he kept one hand on his mother's arm. He wanted to ask whether removing a mask to eat was allowed in rooms with such an ill patient but decided that Gaspar and Dulce had given up on trying to control Lalo. In the corner Sara was tinkering with a laptop computer. She eagerly followed Chuy to Gaspar's office.

"Are you claustrophobic?" asked Chuy as he closed the door to Gaspar's office.

"Yes, but I'm fine in small rooms like this."

"Not what I meant," countered Chuy. "We'd liked to wrap you like a corpse and take you out in the ambulance."

"I'm under quarantine now. I can't go anywhere."

"The Chief doesn't care. He wants you to show him where you found Lalo, where Lalo saw the Petersons, and generally give him the layout of this area."

"Why the disguise?"

"The Chief thinks it is better if no one sees you. So does the boss lady. She doesn't want residents to get the idea it's easy to get in or out of here."

Gasper added, "The natives are restless."

"Can it be only a loose sheet over me? Will this be quick or will it take…"

Gaspar interrupted, "She's saying she's very claustrophobic."

Sara frowned. "What about Lalo?"

"Rachel will stay outside his room." Chuy focused on Gaspar. "Doc, could Dulce visit him every few minutes?"

After Gaspar agreed, Sara jumped to her feet. "Let's go."

"Whoa, I've got to get a gurney." Chuy stopped before he left the room. "Hey, while you're waiting, make a list of all La Bendita households that have or might have guns."

After ten minutes Sara heard the clatter of a gurney as it was rolled on the ceramic tile floor of the hallway. Then something heavy slammed into the doorjamb and the door flew open.

"Something's wrong with it," said Chuy as he tried to maneuver the gurney into the small office. "It's impossible to steer, but it was the only one available. Doc, can you load her on it and make her look like a body ready for shipping?"

"It's not every day I get to tuck Sara in." Gaspar winked. "Take you shoes off. Lie with your feet here." He swaddled Sara in sheets and strapped her in. He tucked her shoes and a sheet of paper under her arms and laid a sheet across her face and body.

The ride to the elevator was bumpy and jerky. It got worse when the ambulance crew took over from Chuy. Sara thought she might smash into the driver's seat when they slammed the gurney into the ambulance. She fought the urge to scream when they tipped the gurney slightly to one side as they jerked it out of the ambulance after it screeched to a stop at the front gate. She heard a raspy voice instruct the crew of the second ambulance waiting outside the front gate to handle the gurney gently. Someone heavy climbed into the ambulance and the door slammed shut.

Sara smiled when Chief Gil Andrews pulled the sheet from her face.

He gaped at her. "You're not what I expected. Doc told me you were claustrophobic."

Sara giggled. "The wild ride on the gurney was kinda cloak and dagger. Now I know why bodies are strapped to the gurney. I almost fell off several times. Guess no one told the first crew about my disguise."

Sara regained her composure when Gil loosened the straps to the gurney. She sat up. "Well Chief, what can I do for you?"

"Call me Gil." He handed her a policeman's cap and jacket and signaled to the ambulance driver to move. "We'll transfer to an FBI vehicle once we're out of view of La Bendita. I don't like to sit in the back of an ambulance. Uncomfortable."

Sara handed Gil a folded sheet of paper.

"What's this?"

"Gaspar's and my list of potential gun owners in La Bendita. We're sure ten household have guns. They're starred."

Gil scanned the list. He recognized the names of four of the starred households —Peterson, Bender, Crockett, and Steele. "We've searched the Petersons' and Benders' houses for guns already."

"The Crocketts dislike Jim Peterson. They'd never give him their hunting guns or for that matter let him in their house. Howie Steele is another story."

"Mmm."

Gil had a muffled conversation with the FBI driver after the transfer to an all-wheel-drive SUV. He turned to Sara, "Let's focus on what the boy saw."

She gave directions to the driver on where to park the SUV and then led the men along the little-used sandy path. First she pointed out the spot near the perimeter wall where Lalo said he'd seen the couple assumed to be the Petersons. Next she guided them across the channel at the concrete abutment to the savanna. Finally she pointed toward the spot at the edge of the bosque where she'd found Lalo.

The agent shook his head as he scanned the savanna and bosque. "Plenty of spots to hide. Almost impossible to guard at night."

"Yeah, but we've got to try. I want two men stationed in the engineering shack and two men in those cottonwoods." Gil pointed to two cottonwoods in the savanna near concrete abutment that they had used to cross the flood control channel. "And two in the cottonwoods by the gate from La Bendita into the bosque. Get the Sandoval County Sheriff to loan us the men."

"What type of equipment will they need?"

"Night-hunting lights and goggles. The sheriff will know what to send."

The agent began to make calls on his phone as he hurried to the SUV. Gil and Sara followed at a more leisurely pace.

"Sara, what do you know about Susan Steele?"

"Let's see. She doesn't come to many activities without Howie. No games like bridge, mahjongg, or dominoes. No clubs." Sara shrugged. "Not much."

"Who's her best friend?"

"Goldie, her golden retriever. She seldom goes anywhere without him. He's a good dog."

"Not a dog, a person."

"I don't know." Sara pursed her lips. "I don't even know much gossip about her except one silly piece."

"Let's hear it."

"Susan said Howie goes online to watch the action on their credit cards when she shops. If he thinks she's spending too much, he puts a hold on her card."

Gil's face remained blank.

"It seemed strange to me, but then so did Susan's response. She said she buys most items by paying partially in cash and partially with her charge card. That way Howie doesn't know how much she spends."

"It sounds like a strained marriage."

"That's putting it mildly."

"What else?"

Sara's frown turned to a smile. "She and Howie have no children together but she has a son by a previous marriage."

"Name?"

"Don't know."

"Does he live locally?"

"Don't think so." Sara expected Gil to groan. He didn't. Instead he punched buttons on his phone and gave orders and then listened.

When he disconnected, he said, "Your friend Jane is going to survive."

"I'm glad. She's zany at times, almost like Lucy in the old comedy show, but she means well."

Gil frowned and scratched his chin. "Is she a reliable source of info on the residents of La Bendita?"

"Probably not but she thinks she knows more about every resident than anyone else."

They sauntered the rest way of the way to the SUV silently. As Sara climbed into the back seat, she said, "Whatever you tell Howie will be relayed to Jim Peterson in minutes."

"I know." Gil began to hum.

Sara interrupted his humming. "Could we skip the corpse routine on my return? Could I wear this cap to hide my hair and the police jacket? If Chuy met me at the front gate, people would assume I was another police officer assigned to La Bendita."

"Suppose so." He pressed the buttons on his cell phone and barked orders.

"Gil, what else I can do for you?"

"Call Jane Lane. Pump her for information on what happened on Monday night. Albuquerque Police are sure she's hiding something about the misfiring gun. She might say more to you."

Sara pulled on the cap's brim and fiddled a bit with her hair. "I know you don't need advice from me, but here's what I always told my graduate students. When you've got a knotty problem, think out of the box."

"Sounds like academic nonsense."

"That's nicer than what my students said. Try to think like the Petersons. They know you're watching the front and back gates. They're smart. I bet they find a different exit."

"Like what?"

"I don't know. Maybe the bosque gate. They're in good condition, especially Jim. Bet he could get over the wall in lots of places besides the low spot I showed you. With all your experience, you'll have better ideas. But think outside the box and worry less about the gates."

"Hmmf."

Sara felt sorry for Gil. She suspected he was drowning in advice. Most of it probably useless. She hoped hers was not.

CHAPTER 29: Day Seven Continued — Howie Steele, Susan Steele, Chief Gil Andrews

Howie Steele hung up the phone. "Your loser son sent you a package. The cops at the gate accepted it and want you to come and get it. It's marked perishable."

"It was nice of my son to think of us. Do you want to walk over with me?"

Howie looked askance at his wife. "Why would I want to help you claim a present from your son? The jerk probably sent chocolate candy because he knows I can't eat it. Damn diabetes. Besides, Jim might call."

"I'll take Goldie."

"Try not to screw up this simple errand."

Howie called Jim Peterson as soon as the door closed behind Susan. "Are we still on for tonight at ten?" He scanned the ceiling as he listened.

"Did anyone see you check out the path to Wal-Mart?"

He listened a second or two. "No, good. Will we be able to climb up the embankment along the channel at night?" At first, he licked his lips. Then he lowered his head and listened quietly.

"Oh, but I thought." He sank onto a kitchen chair. "I thought we'd meet at the engineering shack and go over the wall together." He listened for another minute. "You want me to go to the channel on my own and wait for you at Wal-Mart." He listened for a moment and added indignantly, "Of course, I can do it."

"Have you told Jean about our plan?" His glance circled his kitchen as he listened. "Ah-ha, I suppose Jean is different. I haven't told Susan because she's too dumb to understand they won't lift the quarantine until we're all dead. I'm afraid she'll slow me down."

He thought he heard a noise, a squeak, from the patio. When he finished his call, he opened the vertical blinds in front of the open patio door to the kitchen. No one was there. He whistled as he moved about the house and collected a flashlight, a handgun, and a change of clothes. He stuffed everything into a tote bag and slid it under his bed.

-/-/-

A breathless Susan and a panting Goldie arrived at the front gate. "Have you," Susan squeaked, "have you a package for me?"

The policeman at the gate didn't look up from his clipboard. "Name?"

"Susan Steele."

The policeman eyed Susan and punched a button. "Chief, she's here."

Susan was surprised when two men approached her from different directions. A man she did not recognize sauntered from the front porch of the clubhouse to stand in back of her. At the same time Chief Gil Andrews of the Mercado Police climbed from his car on the other side of the gate and lumbered toward her carrying a package wrapped in a distinctive red and white striped paper.

"Howie was right. My son sent Buffet's candy." Her glances darted back and forth between the two men.

"Mrs. Steele?"

Susan jumped back a bit when Gil spoke.

"Can I call you Susan?"

"Uh-huh."

"I've got a package from your son."

He motioned her to the pedestrian gate and opened it. The other man silently followed her like a shadow. Susan felt trapped between them. Gil stood two feet in front of her and the other man almost tramped on Goldie's tail as he nudged closer behind her.

"Ma'am, your son is concerned. Let me rephrase. We're concerned. We think your husband might be giving you a hard time."

Susan avoided looking at Gil and began to fiddle with Goldie's collar.

"Sometimes we men don't appreciate our wives. And some men say or do some pretty unkind things."

She tightened her grip on Goldie's leash and commanded, "Stand." Goldie's tail thumped the FBI agent as they turned to go home.

"Wait. This quarantine is really getting on people's nerves." Gil spit on the ground. "Hell, it's getting on my nerves. Anyway, a few people are trash talking. You know, stupid stuff."

He motioned to the other man, who had finally taken several steps back. "This FBI agent and Chuy heard a few people talking about trying to escape from La Bendita."

Susan peeked at Gil and then the FBI agent but averted her gaze to avoid their probing eyes.

"The boss lady, I mean, Dr. Ellen Behren, plans to lift the quarantine here as soon as possible. Trying to escape here tonight seems kind of foolish. Look what happened to Jane Lane."

Susan's jerked her head up when Jane's name was mentioned. "How is she? Jim told Howie she's a goner."

"Quite the contrary. She's going to make it. Granted without a right hand and arm because someone gave her a gun rigged to misfire. Someone wanted her dead." He paused and peered at Susan. "I think you might know who would want her dead."

Susan felt heat creep up her neck towards her ears and cheeks. She hoped the police officers didn't notice.

"I suppose you don't want to rat on anyone, but you need to know the facts. The registration number had been scratched off the gun that Jane tried to use. We found other incomplete fingerprints on it besides hers." The Chief eyed Susan for at least a minute. "Who would give her a rigged gun? Would the Petersons give her such a gun?"

Susan bit her lip.

"Susan, we need your help. Jane's been talking. She remembers she took Goldie back to your house before her accident." Gil bent down and petted Goldie who was now sitting at Susan's side. "Good boy. We know you don't go anywhere without your mistress. How did you wander down to Jane's house? Can you tell me, boy?"

"Okay." Susan's hands shook as she bent slightly and ran her fingers through Goldie's fur. "I was at her house. I… I… I'm ashamed. I heard Howie talk on the phone to Jim and heard Jane's name a couple of times. They planned to meet at the back gate. I went to talk to Jane because Howie wouldn't tell me anything."

She knelt and buried her face in the golden locks on the dog's neck. "Like Howie says, I'm stupid. I couldn't ring her doorbell and ask her what was happening. Instead I looked in her bedroom window. I saw her pack a backpack, like Howie just did."

Gil gently rubbed Susan's shoulder with his right hand as he held the package with his left. "There, there. What else have you seen and heard?"

"He called Jim as I was leaving to get the package. I hid by the open door and listened. He plans to leave tonight." She lifted her head and sniffed. Tears trickled down her cheek. "He… he might not take me." Susan began to rock back and forth on her knees as she convulsed into bawling. "I… I… I've tried to be a good wife. Not fair. I don't mean to mess things up."

"I know he doesn't appreciate you." Gil gently raised Susan's downturned face from Goldie's mane with his hand. He stepped back.

"What else did you hear? Think hard."

Susan stood and wiped her face with her sleeve. "They'll leave tonight."

"When?"

"At ten."

"Where?"

"In the channel. Howie has to get over the wall alone."

"What else?" Gil smiled encouragingly at Susan.

"Something about the engineering shack."

"And?"

Susan couldn't remember any more details and shook her head no.

"Do you want to go home? You don't have to. We can find you a safe place to stay here in La Bendita until the quarantine is lifted. Then your son says you can stay with him."

Susan trembled as she whispered, "Howie will be angry."

"Does it matter? He's making a foolish choice to trust Jim Peterson. You would be making a foolish choice to go with him. It could be dangerous."

"Howie packed his gun."

Both men sucked in their breath.

"Where would you take me that is safe? Goldie has to come because I don't go anywhere without Goldie."

"This agent can take you and Goldie to a room in the clinic. The room's been all scrubbed up, nice and clean. He'll stay with you."

Susan frowned.

"We can find a woman to stay with you."

Suddenly, she started to hyperventilate. "Howie will look for me."

"We'll tell him you got sick at the gate and we moved you to the center because we think you have the flu."

Panic spread through her. She stepped backwards. "I'm not sick. You said you were taking me to the clinic. Howie was right. You aren't telling us the truth. We're all going to die here."

"No." Gil choked. "You can call your son. He'll tell you that we're telling Howie the wrong building as a precaution, so he can't find you." Gil handed the package to Susan.

The FBI agent clasped Susan's arm and guided her to a waiting car before she had a chance to protest. Goldie jumped in beside her. He whisked them away to the clinic.

-/-/-

"Susan Steele almost bolted on me." After he filled Chuy in on all the details, Gil muttered, "Can't see why the Petersons returned to La Bendita this afternoon. If they merely wanted to escape, they would have kept on going then." Gil slouched into the seat of his squad car and adjusted his phone.

"Right. Maybe they were scouting a path for someone else." Chuy paused. "But I don't think they'd do that for Howie Steele."

"More likely, he's a loose end they want to eliminate." Gil began mutter. "Think out of the box. Think out of the box."

"What are you saying, Chief?"

Gil spoke clearly. "I've got it. I think they plan to lure Howie to the channel where it will be easy for someone Peterson hired to pick him off with a rifle."

"So, Peterson hopes the noise from the gunshots will draw our attention while he and his wife slip out unnoticed in the opposite direction. Maybe the bosque gate?"

Gil hummed two lines of *Wichita Lineman*. "Chuy, we don't have it quite right. Wonder whether six of the sheriff's deputies on lookout around the perimeter tonight is enough."

"Chief, I'm thin in here, too. Rachel is in the clinic with Susan Steele, Sara, and Lalo. The other two FBI guys are busy watching the Petersons. I'm watching Howie Steele and backing up the others."

"I know my backup behind the front and back gates won't be enough, especially if Peterson tries something fancy." Gil began to hum again.

"Chief, how am I supposed to protect Howie Steele? I doubt he'll believe me if I tell him about the Petersons."

"Good question."

"He's a sitting duck."

"He deserves to be. We'll keep him in the dark for a while."

Jim Peterson zipped his large backpack closed. He tapped his fingers on the counter as he watched his wife pack a small backpack.

"I've talked so much about Jim Junior and his kids." She motioned to the pictures on the living room wall. "I've almost begun to think they're real."

"Necessary cover. Stopped a lot of gossip. But our cover's blown. Cops have watched us constantly for the last couple of days." He paused for moment. "Too bad the stupid bastard Juan got sick and died."

"He's not dead. Those public health guys who stopped by an hour ago to tell us he was dead didn't seem right. They wanted to know about our contacts with Juan all right, but not because they were afraid we might catch the flu from him."

"What do you mean, Jean?"

"Did you see their shoes? Black, polished, with leather soles. All the ones who came last Thursday and earlier today to survey us wore soft-soled shoes, usually walking shoes. And mainly in white."

"Mmm. That's what I like about you. You see everything."

"That's all?"

He wrapped an arm over her shoulder and nuzzled her neck. "You know what I mean."

She unwrapped his arm. "Not now. We've got work to do."

She parted the drapes in the living room enough to peer through. "Such a dull view, like the Benders." She scrutinized the one window on the taupe stucco wall facing her. "Bet those fake public health workers are in the Benders' house now watching us."

"They can't see anything." He tapped a large lidded, green Tupperware bowl sitting in the middle of the kitchen counter. "And they can't hear anything either."

"Oh, I don't know about that." Jean pouted her red lips and blew Jim a kiss in Marilyn Monroe-fashion.

"How did you get so sassy? Putting an iPod playing "Tomorrow" and other show tunes from the eighties into this…"

"Salad crisper."

"With the three bugs I found. Serves the cops right for planting them while we were up to the clubhouse listening to know-it-all Sara. Stupid trick." He put an arm on her shoulder and let his fingers drift down her front.

"Not now. Do you think that the dumb pig Juan talked?"

"He wouldn't have much to say. He could say that I used an emergency gate. Against La Bendita's rules, but no crime. We, especially you," Jim winked at his wife, "gave him a few favors." He nuzzled his wife again, and she pushed him aside.

"They might call them bribes and get suspicious."

"They were suspicious already," said Jim. "Time to get to work."

Jean rummaged through the kitchen cabinets. Jim strolled to the garage and returned with a pile of newspapers that he spread over the granite counter of the kitchen island before he returned to the garage. When he came back to the kitchen with a can, he found an assortment of glass bottles covered much of the counter.

"This is all the bottles I could find. Will it be enough?"

He twisted the lid off the rusty can, put a tin funnel on top of the first bottle, and poured in a clear liquid. "It really won't take many if my pitching arm is good and no one notices the fires at first. With luck, we'll eliminate a couple loose ends and leave unnoticed in the confusion."

"Where do you think they stashed Juan?" Jean began to tear a bed sheet into pieces.

"Clinic or center. Bet Susan Steele is there, too." The acrid odor of the fluid now filled the room. "Wish we could open a window but it might alert our neighbors."

"What if we can't get to Jane's car?"

Jim stopped filling the bottles. "We'll use the Benders' car. I can hot-wire it."

"Pigs might be on the lookout for the Benders' car. Funny, how nothing is supposed to leave this place under the quarantine but they managed to get our Hummer out, or hid it well. I guess we could use our Subaru."

"No, I'll douse it so it burns well. Don't worry. We'll get to Jane's car. Don't want to waste all your good work casing out Jane's house when you delivered the gun and then getting her keys." Jim shook his head. "But you always had light hands."

"One of my many professional skills." She began to wad the rags into the necks of the bottles.

"The way you sand papered your fingertips over the years. I always figured it was an old wives' tale."

"But I really don't have identifiable fingerprints anymore."

Both continued to work. "I've tried to figure who was the most annoying: Howie the toad, Jane the motor mouth, or Sara the know-it-all," said Jim.

"Howie."

Jim looked surprised. "I thought you'd say Jane."

"She made a good decoy on Sunday night while you talked to your guys. She also had another useful trait. She was so afraid of losing things that she displayed all her keys on a giant corkboard. That's how I got her car keys when I left her suicide note. I already had the house key."

Jim turned and planted a kiss on Jean's forehead. "You've done good work this week, but I think your best work was stalling the pompous Mercado cop while I got back to the house. What made you think to change into your working clothes?"

"Experience. But the pig didn't seem to notice."

"His loss." Jim patted his wife's seat. "You know the pigs have all our guns now, even the Benders' gun I hid in back."

Jean smiled. "But not the Benders' other handgun and ammo I removed on Sunday morning. They're stashed in Jane's car under the front seat."

"Good move."

"I wish the kid hadn't seen us this afternoon."

"Yeah, it puts my man in danger if the kid talks to the right people." He stood silently for a minute.

"Kids that age like secrets," said Jean. "Bet he doesn't tell his parents anything."

"Still, I wish I knew where the kid came from. Did you get a good look at him?"

"Another dark-haired brat. He doesn't live here. Probably a kid from Riverview. Even if he talks, what does he have to say?"

"Yeah, he's not a problem like Juan, Howie, and Susan."

Jean grabbed her husband's arm. "I had a terrible thought. What if Jane talked before she died? Or worse still, what if she survived?"

"Couldn't have. I rigged the gun. It would have destroyed anything within three feet of the barrel."

"But what if?"

"Stop worrying." Jim filled the last bottle.

"Why did they post her death and those of other residents who died of flu on the door to the clubhouse today?"

"So?"

"But not before today." Jean stuffed a rag into the neck of the last bottle.

"Howie asked Gaspar Gonzales repeatedly for reports on the status of sick residents. Gonzales claimed he was too busy."

"What changed today?" Jean put the filled bottles into shoeboxes and slid them into the cabinet under the center island of the kitchen.

"Probably because Sara talked too much when we were at the clubhouse yesterday."

Jean drummed her manicured red fingernails on the counter. "Bet a few of those listed as dead are holed up in the center or the clinic. This whole quarantine could be a trick to find us."

"Don't go paranoid on me. I've seen them haul bodies into the refrigerated meat trucks behind the center when I was on scouting trips. The nurses and medical resident who went door-to-door surveying residents early today, before those fake ones, looked like hell."

"They did look like the nurses and docs in New York City after nine-eleven."

"Yeah, shell shocked. I think people really are dying of the flu." Jim looked at his watch. "We've got time to kill before we go."

Jean laughed and unbuttoned Jim's shirt. She twirled a ringlet of his gray chest hair around her finger and leisurely glided her hand down to his zipper. She giggled and sashayed into the bedroom. "A little romp always relaxes you."

CHAPTER 31: Chief Gil Andrews Prepares for Monday Night

Gil sat in a squad car in front of front gate as the sun neared the horizon on Monday. He hummed as he reviewed his preparations for the evening.

He thought he had adequate manpower. Well, he hoped so. George Soto, the chief of the FBI field office in Albuquerque, had sent in two more agents to monitor the Petersons — mainly sit in the Benders' house and stare at the Petersons' house. The two FBI agents posing as state health officials patrolled the center and clinic under FBI Agent Rachel Jones's direction. At the last minute, Soto had sent over one more FBI agent to circulate around La Bendita with Chuy.

Four state police officers waited in two cars at the back gate of La Bendita. Two more sat in a car parked at the front gate. Three officers from the Mercado Police Department and Gil waited in two cars at the front gate. For extra insurance, two state police officers in an unmarked car circulated around Riverview. Unfortunately, the front gate area looked like a parking lot. He hoped the state police cars at the back gate were less conspicuous.

Then he thought about another problem. What if the Petersons didn't make their move tonight? He'd have wasted the time of a lot of officers and agents. The head of the state police and county sheriff would be annoyed but would understand. George Soto of the FBI would never let him forget it. All he could do now was hope he'd guessed right. Besides they were all tired of waiting for the Petersons to act.

Then there was another minor problem — Ellen. When he'd told Ellen about all the FBI agents posted within La Bendita, she'd announced that none could leave La Bendita until she lifted the quarantine. She'd called George Soto, who for once kept his cool. He told Gil, "I'm not getting into a pissing contest with a woman."

The witnesses were a major concern because no past witness against Peterson had ever survived. The FBI had announced Jane Lane's death in the *Albuquerque Journal* today. Then the U.S. Marshal Service had her admitted to Lovelace Women's Hospital under an alias and had an officer with the Witness Protection Program pose as her attentive husband. He wished Susan Steele and Lalo had accepted the U.S. Marshal Service's offer to protect them outside La Bendita. Then they wouldn't be his problem. Although everyone else thought Jim and Jean couldn't mount a raid on the clinic, he wasn't sure.

Gil shifted his weight to be more comfortable in the squad car. When this was over, he'd try to convince the mayor of Mercado to invest in a van for the police department. A Cadillac Escalade would be nice. He knew if this went badly, he'd be lucky to keep his job.

He thought he was prepared but the knot in his stomach said otherwise. Jim Peterson, aka Mazzone, hadn't avoided arrest for over thirty years by being stupid or predictable. The FBI suspected he had committed at least four murders starting when he was a teenager in New Jersey. However, he had left no witnesses or evidence of his activities behind except burnt bodies. He was believed to have been involved in drug trafficking for at least twenty years but with no arrests. Gil knew why the bastard George Soto had cooperated with him. Soto planned to take all the credit for clearing up a string of murders when Peterson was arrested.

Gil got out of the car to stretch his legs. He paced among the cars parked at the front gate and hummed *Rhinestone Cowboy*.

He knew anyone inside La Bendita could be turned into a hostage tonight. If he had his druthers and no quarantine, he'd have evacuated most of the residents of La Bendita already. Gil had made Ellen, Sylvia, and Gaspar promise they would restrict all their personnel to the clinic, center, and housing quarters tonight. No one was to go for a walk. Gaspar had promptly requested discs of two recent movies to show. "Good old Doc."

"What are you muttering about, Chief?" called one of his officers in the other squad car guarding the front gate.

Gil shook his head and hummed *Rhinestone Cowboy* again.

The officer turned to his woman partner. "The Chief hums and paces when he's upset. This week he's hummed constantly."

The woman stopped texting. "No kidding. I'm tired of the Chief's renditions of Glen Campbell's songs. Even my mother doesn't go back that far. At least, we've got the easiest assignment. No one will try to escape through the front gate tonight."

Gil pretended he didn't hear them.

CHAPTER 32: Monday Night — Marian Crockett, Chief Gil Andrews

The ten o'clock news was on. Marian Crockett watched her husband Hank open the sliding glass door to their patio, as he did every night, and step into their back yard. He peered over the low, stuccoed back wall into his neighbors' yards and into the bosque.

"Mother, come here."

"Now, Hank, you know I got my pajamas on."

"Doesn't matter. Get out here."

Marian Crockett padded out of the house in pink fluffy slippers and pink baby doll pajamas. She adjusted the pink hairnet that swathed her hair as she stared at her husband. "You look like one of those cranes at Bosque del Apache. Standing on one foot and craning your neck."

"Do you see it?"

"What?"

"A flicker from a house on Aster Lane."

"No." Marian moved closer to her husband and craned her neck, too. "Oh wait, I do. What would do that?"

"Fire. I'll call nine-one-one."

"Will they come with this quarantine?"

"They'd better." Marian changed clothes as Hank made the call.

"What did they say?" Marian adjusted her light blue polyester, pull-up slacks.

"They'd notify both the police and the fire departments. We'd better take a look-see."

"Figured you'd say that. I'm fixin' to take our flashlights and a cell phone." Marian gasped when Hank opened the front door. She saw a flickering light coming from the rear of Jane Lane's house.

"Call nine-one-one," ordered Hank. "Tell 'em this is no accident."

"Hank, I'm scared."

"You stay here and watch while I go down to Jane's house." He stopped when he heard the sound of a rifle shot and then another from the north, most likely in the flood control channel. "I'd better get our Old Betsy." He re-emerged from his house carrying a loaded shotgun. He handed it to Marian. "Mother, shoot anyone who tries to come near our house 'less they do some explaining."

Marian paced in front of their house as she watched Hank. "Darn man's enjoying this." Behind him, the fire at Jane Lane's house was now a blaze. She hoped the fire truck arrived soon.

Hank waved his arms and shouted but she couldn't understand what he said. Finally, she realized he was pointing behind her. She turned to face the bosque. Curls of smoke rose from behind the perimeter wall that faced the bosque. She turned back toward Hank. He was sprinting toward her.

"Wake the neighbors." He ran by her toward a neighbor's house.

"You do that. I'll drive to the gate and get the attention of the police." She ran inside the house, opened the garage door, laid the shotgun on the passenger side of the front seat of their car, and backed out. The wheels squealed as she accelerated down Willow Drive blasting her horn.

The gate was open. Cars and police were everywhere. A state police car was parked at one side of the gate. Chief Gil Andrews sat in a Mercado Police squad car on the other side of the gate. A second Mercado Police car was behind Gil's squad car. Two Mercado Police officers stood two feet outside the gate with loaded guns aimed at her.

Marian waved her arms as she leapt from her car. "You got it wrong. Jane Lane's house on Willow Drive is on fire. And one on Aster Lane."

Both officers lowered their guns. Gil ambled toward her. "Fire trucks are coming. It'll be all right."

"No, it won't. The bosque's on fire, too." She pointed at the wall. "Look between those two houses at the wall." Flicks of yellow and orange had replaced the curl of smoke.

Gil punched a button on his phone. "Get out all fire trucks to La Bendita! Forget the quarantine! The bosque and two houses are burning. It's arson. The arsonists are at large. Both gates will be open. I need a dozen more officers."

Gil punched another button on his phone. He got no reply. He punched another button. "Chuy, check the Benders' house. Take backup. I got no reply from the FBI agents in the Benders' house."

He turned to his officers. "Contact those at the back gate, Agent Jones, and the three field posts. Tell them to be on the alert for arsonists. It's probably more than just the Petersons."

He yelled to the woman officer in the other a squad car, "Update the FBI. Send one of the state police cars at the back gate to the clinic." Finally, he turned to Marian. "Ma'am, where's your husband?"

"He's waking up neighbors. So was I. Why do you think I was honking the horn? I got to get home and wet down my walls. Someone should wet the perimeter walls, too."

"Ma'am, I don't think you should go back until my officers secure the area." He motioned to the officers in the second Mercado Police car to pull up.

"I'll be all right. I've got Old Betsy."

Gil ignored the quarantine, paced to her car, and looked into her front seat. He saw the shotgun. "Can you use it?"

"Sure can." She jumped in and threw her car into reverse. The car lurched backwards.

"Don't use it on anyone," he delayed a second and winked, "but the Petersons."

Marian blared her horn as she barreled down Willow Drive.

-/-/-

Gil signaled to the male and female officers in the second Mercado Police squad car. "Go with her and keep the crowd under control." They rushed off with their siren blaring.

Gil thought he heard more rifle shots in the distance, but he couldn't be sure with all the sirens wailing. Besides, he had other problems. "Where's the damn fire trucks?" fumed Gil as he pushed more buttons and roared orders. "They're supposed to respond in three minutes."

He heard sirens blaring and saw rotating red lights. Two Rio Rancho fire trucks sped through the front gate and down Willow Drive to the perimeter wall. At times like this, he was glad the fire departments in Mercado, Rio Rancho, and Albuquerque had cooperative agreements. All received notice simultaneously of major emergencies in the Mercado area and responded.

He flagged down the Rio Rancho ambulance following the fire trucks. "Until we know of injuries, you stay here. Besides, this is supposed to be a quarantine area and we've got an ambulance crew inside." The driver pulled aside.

Three more fire trucks from Rio Rancho raced through the front gate and down Willow Drive to Jane Lane's house. Three trucks from Mercado entered through the back gate and sped down Aster Lane.

Gil breathed a sigh of relief. His phone rang. He listened for ten seconds.

"Doc, say it again slowly." He suspended all his motions, even that required for breathing, as he listened.

He waved for the Rio Rancho ambulance to pull up. "Fires at the loading docks to the clinic and center. Get two of your hose trucks on Willow Drive over to the center. The burning houses are empty. The clinic and center are full of people. Many mighty sick. And the air intake and electrical controls for those buildings are at their loading docks. Fires on the docks can wreak havoc fast." The Rio Rancho ambulance moved like a torpedo toward the center.

Gil yelled to the deputy in his squad car, "Get Mercado to send their last fire truck to the clinic and to move one truck from Aster Labe to the clinic. Call Albuquerque Fire Department. Tell them we've got all Mercado's trucks in action and need more help. Get Albuquerque Police to send more backup."

Gil motioned to the officers in both state police cars now at the front gate. "Doc says a patient saw someone throw fire bombs of some sort at the clinic and then the center. I already sent an ambulance to the center. You circle around the clinic." He slapped the side of the first car. The second state police car, which until two minutes before had been idling in nearby Riverview, pulled up. "You circle around the tents and clubhouse."

As the state police cars roared away, Gil's officer yelled, "Agent Jones said she has one FBI agent with a rifle at a third-floor window of the clinic. One at the fire at the loading dock of the center. She's at the loading dock of the clinic near the first fire. She already gave the command to shoot any arsonist on sight. She needs backup."

"Tell her help is on the way." Gil paced three steps to the gate, turned, strode back three steps to his car, turned, and repeated the process again and again. He was too agitated to even hum.

After what seemed forever, but really was only two minutes, Gil noticed responses to his commands. First, two of the Rio Rancho fire trucks that had been at the fire at Jane Lane's house sped past him toward the clinic. Less than a minutes later, one of the Mercado fire trucks that had been at the house fire on Aster Lane arrived at the center. He heard the sirens of the last Mercado fire truck as it swung in the back gate toward the fire at the center. But no vehicles from the FBI or Albuquerque Police were in sight.

He punched buttons on his phone again. Before he could speak, he heard the distant sound of a rifle from the north. Then another shot. He had just decided both shots were in or near the channel when he heard a blast from the opposite direction — to the south near the bosque gate. "We've got open warfare here. Arsonists have started fires in at least four buildings and the bosque. I've heard rifle shots in two directions." Four more rifle shots echoed in the background as he strode back and forth and listened to someone in the state police headquarters.

Two more fire trucks from Rio Rancho whizzed by him through the front gate and turned down Willow Drive to the perimeter wall. Less than ten seconds later, two more fire trucks and an ambulance from Albuquerque entered the back gates and headed to the perimeter wall abutting the bosque.

The air had a bitter taste and irritated his sinuses. He felt tears run down his cheeks as he repeated the message from the dispatcher at the Albuquerque Fire Department. "Two trucks entered the bosque's fire lane. A helicopter is loading up to spray the scene." He didn't know whether the tears were caused by physical or emotional irritation.

He listened as the officer in the lone Mercado squad car by the front gate relayed a message from Chuy. "Tell Chuy not to be a hero. Keep the line to him open to monitor his progress."

Gil answered his phone. Three cars from the Sandoval County Sheriff's Office were approaching the back gate. "Sheriff, have one go to 724 Willow Drive. Sergeant Chuy Bargas is in charge at the site. Agents may be down. One should go the ambulance entrance of the clinic. FBI agent Jones is in charge. The other should come to me at the front gate."

His chest hurt, really ached. He controlled his panic and stopped and thought. It was the right side, probably heartburn. He knew he was too old for this much excitement. Hell, Mercado wasn't prepared for much more than a fender bender. This was a rampage. He'd warned the mayor that he needed more resources.

He heard rifle shots, again in two, no three directions, and punched buttons on a walkie-talkie. "Field Post One, are those your shots?" He listened for twenty seconds as a sheriff's deputy positioned by the bosque gate spoke. He popped an antacid in his mouth. "So, your partner clipped one and went in pursuit." Gil chewed his antacid. "How close is the fire?" He listened. "Don't be a hero. Break cover if it gets closer."

Gil punched more buttons. "Field Post Two, are those your shots?" He listened for ten seconds to one of the sheriff's deputies, posted at the engineering shack at the low point in the wall on Marigold Lane before he began to pace. "Okay, you saw Howie Steele climb over the wall and followed him. He was in the channel and fell when shots were fired."

He called Field Post Three stationed in the savanna. They had observed movement near them in the grass. He heard an exchange of fire before they broke contact with him.

Gil paced as he recalled Field Post Two. A sheriff's deputy informed him that Howie Steele was crawling up the channel embankment. Gil listened for another five seconds. "Check on the men at Field Post Three first." Gil suspected he'd lost men already at the Benders' house and at Field Post Three. "Bring in Howie Steele if you can without wasting manpower."

He marched back to his squad car and yanked open the door.

"Chuy broke contact with me," said his officer.

CHAPTER 33: Monday Night Continued — Cesar Pena, Sara, Cesar Again

"Why can't I go see Lalo and Julia?" Maria's voice got higher and more piercing when she whined. It was almost in the range where Cesar needed earplugs.

After the fifth rendition, Cesar was eager to escape. "Stay in your room and play with your doll while I check."

Cesar knocked on the door of Julia's room. Sara quickly appeared and let him peek in. He gasped. Julia's sunken eyes and cheeks made her head look like a skull with a thin coating of waxy flesh. At least all the dried blood he'd seen earlier had been wiped from her hair and face. Lalo's dark hair and face were almost invisible under the goggles, mask, and paper cap, which was at least three sizes too big for him. He was pressed against her shoulder with his small, gloved hand on Julia's hand.

"Mom, talk to me. Try harder, Mom."

Sara stepped outside the room. "Lalo's done this for hours. He seems to think he can will Julia to live. I got him to eat a part of a sandwich about two hours ago. He needs a break, but he won't listen to me. And Aletha's threats over the phone only strengthen his resolve."

"Is there any hope?"

Sara shook her head. "Gaspar gives her less than a twenty percent chance now. Her chances will be nil if the fever doesn't break soon."

"Maria wants to see Lalo. I talked to Doctor Gonzales. He said Maria could visit Lalo since Maria had the flu, and Lalo and I are on antivirals."

"Good. Somehow Dulce and I will get Lalo to the lounge. Maybe you could round up pop and snacks from the first-floor break room and bring them up to the third-floor lounge."

Cesar nodded.

-/-/-

Sara returned in time to see Lalo plead with his mother again. She placed her hand on Lalo's head. "Maria wants to see you. And she's bringing pop and snacks. It will be fun."

"Can't."

"I talked to Dulce. She's bringing a stretcher on a gurney into this room. Then you can lie on the gurney but keep your hand on your Mother's arm. I think it will be more comfortable. Would you like that?" Sara didn't wait for an answer. "You must go to the corner lounge area with Maria while Dulce works here."

Lalo looked up. His brown eyes were filled with tears. "Mom needs me."

"I know. I'll hold her hand while Dulce rearranges the room. Dulce will get you when the room is ready."

Lalo wiped tears from his eyes.

"Don't worry, I won't let go of her hand." Sara put her hand on Julia's hand.

"I'm hungry, and I want to see Maria. She was sick like Mom but she got better." He limped to the door. At the doorway, he appeared to brush away tears from his eyes and sighed. "Mom, I love you. Wait for me to get back."

Dulce, who was waiting at the door, removed Lalo's protective paper outerwear and bustled Lalo down the hall to the lounge. Sara could hear Maria's yelp of glee when she saw Lalo. Dulce reappeared with a gurney and rearranged the room. Sara, true to her promise, continued to stroke Julia's hand.

"Boy needs time away from his mother. I wait a while before I get him." Dulce left.

Dulce guided Lalo into the room ten minutes later. This time he was covered with yellow protective gear including yellow booties over his socks. She lowered the gurney so Lalo could climb on, cranked the gurney up to be level with Julia's bed, slid the gurney next to the bed, and locked the hand break.

"Now one big bed."

Lalo smiled, rolled over, and grabbed his mother's hand. "Miss me, Mom? I'm back." He planted a kiss on her shoulder. Julia emitted a noise that was a combination of groan and gurgle. It was the first noise she had made in five hours.

"She missed me." Lalo buried his head in her shoulder.

Dulce monitored Julia's vitals and rushed from the room.

Julia made the same strange noise again.

Lalo crawled onto his knees and leaned close to Julia's face. His lips covered by a paper mask were a few inches from tubing coming out of Julia's mouth and into the ventilator. "I'm here, Mom. Talk to me."

The gurney creaked and swayed. Sara gasped. "Lalo, be careful you'll fall."

Julia's arm moved. Next her legs started to jerk. Soon all her limbs were flailing. She seemed to be attempting to remove the sheet covering her.

Sara glanced at Cesar who stood in the doorway with Maria. "Get Dulce. And take Maria."

"No," screamed Maria. "I want to see."

-/-/-

Cesar, clinging to the screaming, kicking child, fled down the hall. He was so preoccupied with Maria's tantrum he ran into Gaspar. The usually placid Dulce ignored the incident and hustled to Julia's room.

"Julia's moving her arms and legs and moaning," shouted Cesar even though Gaspar was next to him.

"Yes, Dulce thought she was about to regain consciousness. Gaspar stared at Dulce. "That nurse moves like an old donkey most of the time but if she gets in the mood, she's a regular jackrabbit." Gaspar hurried forward with Cesar straggling behind him.

When Gaspar reached the open doorway, he assessed the situation. Julia was pulling at the tube in her mouth with one hand and gagging. Sara was pulling Lalo from Julia's other arm while he screamed, "Mom, I'm here. Don't leave me."

The usually patient Dulce was yelling, "Julia, calm down." She reached for Julia's free arm but missed. Julia's flailing arm hit Dulce in the jaw. Dulce stiffened and finally caught Julia's arm. "Julia, stop it." Dulce enunciated every word clearly. "Or Lalo has to go. Julia, I mean it. Stop it."

Everyone in the room, including Julia, stopped.

No one, except Gaspar, had heard Dulce before when she assumed command. Gaspar took a deep breath. "Now you know the real Dulce." He rushed over to Julia and placed his stethoscope on her chest. Then he pulled the dislodged tubing from Julia's mouth and rolled the ventilator machine away from the bed while Dulce restrained Julia's arms.

During the whole process, Lalo murmured, "Mom, I love you. Hold on for me."

J. L. Greger

When Dulce and Gaspar finally stepped back, Julia hoarsely croaked, "Aao."

"She said my name," screamed Lalo. Sara could not constrain him. He threw himself across Julia's chest.

Julia croaked, "Eard Aao." She tried to hug him.

"Enough," said Dulce. "Dr. Gonzales, I'll handle everything if you take the young man for a walk." She glared at Cesar and Maria. "Take his friends too."

She pointed at Sara. "Get another nurse to help me."

She started to pull at sheets and bustle about Julia. When she noticed no one had moved, she put her hands akimbo. "Go."

CHAPTER 34: Monday Night Continued — Cesar Pena, an FBI agent

Cesar looked at the calm night sky out the window in the lounge. Then he looked at the two bouncing children at his feet and gulped. "Let's count stars in the sky while we wait."

Maria began to count loudly.

Lalo groaned. "It's not fair. I want to be with Mom. I don't want to count stupid stars."

"I know counting stars is for girls. Let us men see whether anything is moving on the ground below. You've got a good spot. You can see the delivery docks and emergency entrances for this building and for the center next door."

Cesar began to collect the plastic cups, paper plates, and food that were scattered around the lounge. Maria counted to ten twice. He thought good for her age. By the time she started again, he had neatened the lounge and the wastepaper basket was overflowing.

"I see something," yelled Lalo. "Look, it's a car without headlights."

Cesar ambled to the window.

"Look, someone threw something at this building."

Cesar gaped at the scene. Lalo was right.

Maria jumped up and down. "Daddy, it's sparkling like a star. It's pretty."

Cesar gulped.

"There's another one. And another one," screamed Maria.

Cesar craned his neck and looked down at the ambulance entrance to the clinic. Three lights burned on the concrete delivery landing at the back entrance. Two open dumpsters were a few feet away from two of the fires. The ambulance was close to the third fire.

"Stay here." Cesar ran toward the nurses' station.

"Fire! Fire at the loading dock!"

The nurse, who had been slumped over a clipboard, straightened immediately, and punched buttons on a phone. "What else?"

"Someone in a car lobbed three lit objects at this building. All appeared to land on the loading dock." He felt a small tug on his sleeve.

"Daddy, they threw four more stars. It's pretty."

"So, seven lit, I guess you'd say, bombs hit the loading dock of this building."

The nurse proceeded to follow hospital procedures and buzzed several numbers. A siren blared and red lights flashed along the hallway. Nurses scurried into rooms. All patients who could stand or could sit in wheelchairs were lined up in the hallway.

Cesar felt another tug on his sleeve. "Lalo says the car is throwing lights at the center too."

Gaspar appeared while Cesar was answering the duty nurse's questions. Gaspar listened to the nurse for about ten seconds and called Gil Andrews. He alternated between listening to Gil and giving quick orders to the nurse, "Update Rachel Jones," "Warn Sylvia Otega," and "Call Ellen Behren."

Cesar grabbed Maria's hand and led her toward the window where Lalo stood. A man rushed toward them and ordered them to move. Cesar complied, but Lalo ignored him.

The man smashed a sledgehammer against the window. The glass splintered. He continued to wield the sledgehammer until all the major shards of glass had fallen to the ground three floors below. Cesar backed further from the window when he saw flames shoot upward toward the window. Lalo moved closer to get a better view. The man knelt and aimed a rifle though the open window.

"Daddy, I'm afraid."

Cesar picked Maria up.

Lalo spoke to the man with the rifle. "It's blue."

"I don't see it."

The man turned and eyed Cesar. "Who are you?"

"Cesar, who are you?"

"FBI. Stay at this window. Yell, if you see the blue car again." The agent stood. "Where'd I find a woman called Sara?"

Cesar motioned toward Julia's room. Before the agent could move, Lalo grabbed his pants leg. "I'll show you." Lalo pulled the agent along the hallway. All the while Maria emitted a high-pitched howl.

"God, I hate her screams," muttered Cesar. At first, he tried to comfort her by hugging and kissing her. It was to no avail. He put her on a chair, handed her a cookie, and stared at the scene below.

A fire truck spewed water at the loading dock of the clinic. The dumpsters were aflame and sparks shot upward.

He looked over at the center. Plumes of flames and smoke spewed from the dumpsters. Occasionally a sizeable piece of flaming debris shot through the air from the dumpsters toward the refrigerator truck parked at the dock. Two fire truck sprayed the loading dock with water but weren't containing the fires. He looked closer and yelled, "Something burning is stuck to the roof of the refrigerator truck."

No one on the third floor heard him or at least paid any attention to him.

A man opened a door of the cab to the refrigerator truck parked by the center and stood on the seat leaning out from the truck. The man swept a broom across the truck's roof. He didn't reach the flames. He tried again and this time the broom nudged the flames. He hefted the broom and swung it in a wider arc. A flaming object was swept to the ground. A woman ran up and unfurled something like a doubled up blanket, across the burning object. She stomped on the blanket.

Meanwhile a second man flipped a blanket over the flames on the truck cab. Someone handed him another blanket and then another. He flipped each over the flames. Flames were replaced by gray smoke.

Members of the group cheered as the first man jumped into the cab. The truck lurched backward and then sped away from the loading dock.

Lalo reappeared and stationed himself in front of the window. After a minute he pulled Cesar's arm. "See it?"

"What?"

"Look to the right. Not at the dock. Something near those two trees over there. It's moving."

Cesar squinted in the direction Lalo indicated but saw nothing.

Lalo ran to the FBI agent and dragged him to the window. "There's something moving beyond the first tree by the wall."

The FBI agent glanced quickly at the wall. "Don't see anything moving. I'll look later."

The FBI agent marched to the nurses' station and announced, "I want Cesar." He pointed to Cesar with his right hand. "To lead all of you." He motioned with his left hand to the patients lined up in the hallway. "Down those stairs." He nodded to stairs at the other end of the hallway. "Those stairs lead to the front of the building."

Cesar, dragging Maria, pushed past several patients, who were barely able to hobble with the help of aides, to the stairway entrance.

Aides wrapped children in blankets and picked them up from wheelchairs. Two aides had formed a chair with their arms. A nurse positioned a stooped man into the arm chair. Gaspar Gonzales rushed toward the doorway.

"Let Doc through," yelled the FBI agent. "He'll lead people from the second floor down the stairs."

The agent yelled above the noise in the hallway. "Listen up everybody. Join hands. Cesar will be number one through the door. Yell the next number as you go through the door." He pointed to Dave Sedley, who stumbled out of one of the rooms with a child. "And that man will be the last one in the queue. Now go."

Cesar looked behind him. He did not see Lalo or Sara. "Where's Lalo?"

Maria smiled coyly. Cesar wanted to shake her. "Where's Lalo?" Maria looked at the shoes. "Tell me young lady."

Maria sucked her thumb and mumbled, "He went down the stairs." She pointed to a door on the other side of the corridor. Cesar blanched. The stairway led to the loading dock.

"What's the holdup?" bellowed the agent.

"Lalo's missing."

The agent stared at Cesar. "Who?"

"Lalo, the boy who saw the blue car. He may have gone down the back stairs."

"Damn kid." The agent yelled to Cesar, "Go. I'll find him."

Cesar picked up Maria and put her on his shoulder and opened the door to the front stairwell. He grabbed the hand of an aide carrying a child and yelled, "One and two." Then the sirens of another fire truck began to blare.

The aide managed to yell over the ruckus, "Three and four." She grabbed the hand of a recovering teenager swathed in a white hospital blanket, who grasped the hand of another child wrapped in a blanket.

As the group headed down the stairs, the FBI agent yelled, "Hold on to each other after you leave the building. Wait at the front of the building until the police give you directions."

-/-/-

The FBI agent scanned the emptying hallway and dashed into Julia's room. He said to Sara, "Find the kid. He ran down the back stairway."

Sara dropped Julia's hand, straightened up, and looked around the room. "God, it's obvious I'm not used to young boys." She almost slammed into the agent as she raced to the back stairwell.

Dulce marched to the window where the FBI agent now scanned not only the streets and bushes but also the roofs of homes. When Dulce approached him, he didn't look at her. "How many?"

"Eighteen patients and staff leave this floor. Doctor Gonzales and thirteen more leave the second floor."

"What about Susan Steele?"

"She's with Doctor Gonzales."

"The kid?"

"Sara is looking for Lalo."

The FBI agent continued to stare out the window. "Good. How many left inside?"

"Four patients on two floors. We can't move them. We have fewer critical patients than the center because all our patients received antivirals. Most young."

"Whatever." The agent continued to stare out the window. "In total, how many are now on the second and third floors?"

"Three aides and me stay with four patients."

"Is that everybody?"

Dulce pointed to the back stairs leading to the ambulance entrance. "No, two run down the back stairs."

"I forgot about the kid."

He fumbled with his phone. "Rachel, sent thirty-two out the front. Eight left in the building. Location of two unknown: a kid named Lalo and Sara." He listened for a few seconds.

"Damn. The kid was the witness who saw the Petersons this afternoon. I'll send Dulce." He paused and squinted. "Wait, I think I see something."

He threw the phone to Dulce and grabbed his rifle. He fired two shots and grimaced. He grabbed the phone from Dulce who now fixed an annoyed stare on him.

"I saw something on the wall almost three hundred yards south of the clinic. It fell to the other side when I fired shots. I think I hit it."

As he listened to Rachel, he muttered, "But… but the order was to shoot any arsonist on sight. The only other movement I've seen was fire trucks. The kid saw a blue car throwing firebombs. I assumed the movement was due to an arsonist on foot." He disconnected and noticed Dulce's stony stare.

"I'm supposed to see whether I shot a house cat, a flowerpot, or someone escaping. Rachel bets I hit a house cat."

"I think a cat, too. You men have no sense with your guns."

CHAPTER 35: Monday Night Continued — Sergeant Chuy Bargas, FBI Agent Steve

The unmarked cruiser moved from the parking lot by the center and crept slowly to the back lot of the clinic. The two occupants had heard a nine-one-one call on their scanner, then another. Now they were looking for any signs of fire or movement near the two largest buildings at La Bendita.

"Steve, sorry the Chief ripped you a new one back there." Chuy observed the FBI agent seated next to him in the car. He probably was no younger than Chuy but still had a boyish, well-scrubbed appearance.

Chuy couldn't say the truth. Chief Gil Andrews disliked the uppity George Soto and was always grouchy when the chief of the FBI office in Albuquerque was mentioned. Instead he said, "This situation has made the Chief a little edgy. You can't blame him. He's sitting at the front gate of La Bendita like a clay pigeon waiting for the next shot."

Steve peered into the darkness. "I don't see any signs of fire here. The house fires might be accidental."

Another nine-one-one call went out. This time for fires in the bosque. "It's arson," said Chuy. "Bet we have more than one torch."

Gil's voice squawked over the car audio system. "Chuy, check the Benders' house. Take backup."

Steve snickered. "They were probably taking a leak." His laughter stopped when Gil added that he couldn't get a response from the two FBI agents in the house even though the phone rang repeatedly.

Steve called Rachel. "You're losing our backup. Better post your guys high. Look for more than one arsonist."

Chuy raced toward Willow Drive without his siren blaring because he didn't want to rile the neighbors. He turned onto Willow Drive. The street was a whirlwind of activity. The neighbors were riled.

A Mercado Police squad car was parked two houses down from the blaze at Jane Lane's house. The officers had strung yellow tape to keep bystanders away from the house. Firemen pulling hoses were jumping out of two fire trucks with blaring sirens. Lights were on in

                                          J. L. Greger

every occupied house. Most residents weren't gawking at Jane's house. They were spraying water onto their own houses or onto the wall facing the bosque. Other fire truck sirens could be heard in the distance.

"Great, we'll never see a torch in this crowd. I can hardly get around all the traffic." Chuy turned on his flashing lights.

"The worst may be ahead," said Steve. "Why don't you let me out now? I'll get positioned at the Benders' back door before you open the front door."

Chuy stopped the car and beckoned to Hank Crockett. Steve nonchalantly departed the car. Chuy waited until Hank was close by. "Seen anything strange tonight at the Benders' or Petersons'?"

"No."

"Seen either Peterson?"

"No, just as well. Chief Andrews told Mother not to shoot anyone but the Petersons. She's told everyone." He pointed to his wife standing on an aluminum ladder propped against their house and spraying the tile roof with water. "Half of this crowd would shoot the Petersons on sight now." He wiped his sweaty brow. "But why would they set the fires?"

"That's what we want to know. Make sure that no one approaches the Benders' or Petersons' houses in the next few minutes." Chuy started to pull the car away. He stopped. "And if you see either or both of the Petersons, get out of their way and call this number." He handed Hank a card with Gil's number printed on it. "And, if I don't come out in five minutes from the Benders' house, call the number."

"I'll keep an eye on you."

Chuy noted a pungent odor as he got out of the squad car. He heard engine roars and sirens as more fire trucks zoomed onto the street. He saw Steve slip behind the Benders' house as he approached the front.

The front door of the Benders' house was unlocked. Chuy swung the door open. It smelled like a roast had been left in the oven too long. No, it wasn't that pleasant.

Steve yelled as he slid open the Benders' unlocked patio door into the kitchen. Chuy checked the door to the garage. The garage was dark. He flicked the light on. The Benders' car was missing. He moved down the hall toward Steve who had checked out the pantry closet in the kitchen and stood with his gun pointed at the master bedroom suite.

Chuy checked all the rooms as he passed them in the hall. The front bedroom was as the Benders had left it. Three days of men making pit stops as they watched the Petersons' house had taken a heavy toll on the front bathroom. It stunk, but no one was in it. The living room and kitchen were empty. Chuy gulped and felt the door to the master bedroom suite. It wasn't hot but a wisp of smoke leaked from under the door. Steve stepped aside when Chuy cautiously opened the door.

Both men gagged. The room was smoky. One FBI agent lay on the bed. His throat had been slit. The once blue cotton quilt on the bed was now an ugly mixture of various shades of red with areas of blue peeking through. The blood-soaked bed smoldered. The other FBI agent was strapped to a chair nearby. His head drooped over his chest but did not hide the sticks of dynamite that were taped to his chest. Chuy stepped into the bathroom and checked the closets. No one else was there.

He called Gil. "One, probably two, FBI men dead. Dynamite strapped to one. Bed on fire. We need bomb experts fast. Get more police in here to clear everyone away in case the bomb blows."

Steve stepped across the room and felt the neck of his colleague in the chair. He shook his head.

Chuy spoke into his phone. "Both men confirmed dead." He listened for a moment and then looked at Steve. "The Chief says to wet down the bed to keep the fire from spreading."

As Steve left the room, Chuy asked. "With what?" He listened a few second and said, "With a garden hose. We'll try." Chuy opened a window and yelled to Steve.

Steve quickly placed a dripping garden hose through the open window. "Lucky I almost tripped over it by the bushes when I came in the back of the house."

Chuy laid the nozzle on the mattress. The room became grayer and the stench of burning flesh, mainly blood, became more intense.

Chuy went to the kitchen and rifled through a utility drawer and pulled out two hammers. He stepped out on the patio and handed a hammer to Steve. "Now we do the same at the Petersons' house. I go in the front. You take the back. This door will be locked, give me sixty extra seconds."

"Understood."

Chuy ran out the front door of the Benders' house and almost bumped into Hank Crockett. "Get back. There's a bomb."

"No one's come out of the Petersons' while you were in the Benders' house." Hank stepped back to the street while Chuy raced to the Petersons' front door. Rifle shots could be heard in the distance.

Chuy rang the doorbell and announced, "Police." He broke the front window with a hammer after waiting less than a minute. Steve broke a window in the back almost simultaneously.

Chuy smelled an acrid odor. Like the smell of liquor, but not the same. Before he could say gasoline, he heard a loud noise at the back of the house. Windows exploded. Chuy darted to the back yard. Flames were hurtling from two windows. Steve lay on the ground moaning.

"How bad you hurt?"

Steve looked up at Chuy and panted. "I got the wind knocked out of me when the kitchen window exploded. Should have guessed this house would be booby-trapped, too." Steve sat up slowly.

Chuy heard the roar of approaching fire trucks. "Guess I'd better direct the fire crew in while you catch your breath."

Chuy rushed to the front of the Petersons' fire-engulfed house and directed firemen to the back of the Benders' house.

-/-/-

Steve stiffly crawled to his knees as three firemen rushed onto the patio of the Benders' house. "You the bomb squad?"

One fireman, encased in thick gear and a large helmet, moved his head up and down. Steve assumed that meant yes. "Yell when it's safe to enter."

Steve limped to the front of the house. It wasn't easy. Every muscle in his body ached. He brushed glass chards from his jacket. His right shoulder felt numb. He reached inside his jacket to feel the spot. His left hand was red when he pulled it out.

The smell of smoke, the sound of sirens, and the flashing red lights of fire trucks seemed to spin around him. He felt himself whirling too as he watched fire crews direct streams of water at the houses.

A car pulled up. Two sheriff's deputies jumped out and ran toward him.

He motioned to the Benders' house. "Guess Chuy and I were lucky. The two inside weren't." He'd been in the FBI for eight years but this was the first time he knew the victims. His wife and he had gone to barbeques and Christmas parties at their houses.

Steve noticed the deputies' stares. He looked down. The sleeve of his jacket was turning red. He stopped wobbling and crumpled to the ground. He heard one of them on the radio, "Ambulance now. Another agent down."

CHAPTER 36: Monday Night Continued — Rookie Sheriff's Deputy

"Rookie, think of it as like deer hunting. You're even sitting in a deer blind in a tree," whispered a hefty, middle-aged sheriff's deputy into his walkie-talkie while he stared intently at the bosque gate at the rear of La Bendita.

His leaner and twenty years younger partner in a tree fifty feet away replied, "Yeah, only these are two-legged deer." He slowly swept his gaze along the south perimeter wall of La Bendita using his night vision goggles. He stopped and squinted. "Look over at those cottonwood stumps."

"Where? Remember I'm on the ground and behind a blind."

"To the west. By the south wall five hundred feet up. Hard to see with these goggles." He pulled out his infrared binoculars.

After thirty seconds the first deputy whispered into his walkie-talkie, "Nothing there. You're just spooked. Worst part of this assignment is we'll probably sit here all night and see nothing."

"The worst would be to catch someone."

"Better stop talking. We don't want to alert our prey."

The young deputy adjusted his infrared binoculars and focused on the distant cluster of cottonwood stumps. Tall stalks of grass near the stumps swayed. More than they would if they were rustled by the wind. An animal emitting heat was moving from the stumps southward toward a clump of scraggly wild olive trees surrounded by rabbitbrush. It was too big to be a jackrabbit or even a coyote. He readjusted the heavy infrared binoculars. He was sure.

He signaled his partner and focused his searchlight on the rabbitbrush. He flicked on the searchlight and yelled, "Police. Get your hands up or we'll shoot."

The older deputy shot into the rabbitbrush, but too late. The man in the bushes stood, threw a lit object to his left deeper into the bosque, and ran toward a fire lane almost three-quarters of a mile away to the west. The older deputy fired another shot, then another, and another while his partner kept the searchlight directed on the runner.

The younger deputy noticed the runner's stride changed after the third shot. He was limping. "Think you winged him."

The older deputy stopped shooting and trotted after the man. The inexperienced deputy continued to focus the searchlight on the runner until he disappeared.

The young deputy was about to shove his searchlight into a sling on the left side of his perch, when he noted a speck of light in the cottonwood stumps where the runner had started. He didn't need an infrared filter on his binoculars to see the light. He turned a bit. There was a flicker of light coming from the stand of wild olive trees and rabbitbrush, too.

"Fire in the bosque!" The young deputy screamed it over and over. After thirty seconds he realized no one heard him. He gulped and radioed in a Code Red and thus alerted the Rio Rancho, Mercado, and Albuquerque fire departments. Then he used his walkie-talkie to describe the situation to Chief Gil Andrews at the front gate of La Bendita.

Five minutes later his partner radioed him. "Bastard got away." He gasped for breath. "Figured he'd go west toward the fire lane. He veered south into the bosque."

The rookie deputy managed to talk, not scream, about the fires in the bosque.

The older deputy groaned, "I might as well stay by the fire lane to direct the fire trucks. Our cover's blown. You should come down."

"Chief Andrews said to stay here at Field Post One and watch the gate unless the fire gets out of control." He did not add that Chief Andrews guessed the Petersons might make a run for it through the gate because they expected the escaped arsonist to have drawn off all guards at the gate.

The young deputy readjusted his goggles and slowly slid a rifle from a sling on the right side of the perch. He aimed his rifle at the gate and scanned the wall.

Soon he saw La Bendita residents spray water from their garden hoses into the blaze by the wall. Their efforts did not slow the spread of the flames from the clump of cottonwood stumps to the nearby grass. He was amazed how fast the flames zipped across the grass. Another group of cottonwood stumps and debris ignited and flamed. Now the clump of wild olive trees and rabbitbrush in which the arsonist had hidden emitted more than occasional streaks of light. They were smoldering and sent out a pungent smoke, which made him sneeze repeatedly. Bits of fiery embers leaped onto the grass and lit more fires.

A fire truck in La Bendita started to spray a heavy stream of water over the wall and onto the first blaze about two minutes later. It only slowed the spread of flames into the grass from the first blaze.

Two firemen in heavy protective gear tumbled over the wall. They dragged a second hose and sprayed the wild olive trees and the rabbitbrush. Two more firemen climbed over the wall and dragged a third hose toward the second clump of cottonwood stumps. A fourth team rolled over the wall. Water gushed in all directions. Slowly smoke and steam replaced the flames.

The young deputy radioed Chief Andrews. The firemen had missed a fourth blaze in the bosque where the arsonist's last flare had ignited.

In the west he saw four fire trucks with red lights swirling. Abruptly two turned around. Two continued toward La Bendita's front gate. All kept their sirens blaring.

The older deputy's voice blasted in the rookie deputy's ear, "Get your flood light directed at the new blaze farthest into the bosque. They'll send men in from La Bendita while the two trucks that I diverted use the fire lane into the bosque."

The young deputy put his rifle back into the sling on the right side of the perch and directed the searchlight at the fourth blaze. Every so often he glanced at the gate while he manned the searchlight.

Shortly, at least five more men in heavy fire gear climbed over the La Bendita perimeter wall. They lumbered past the men who were directing water at the smoldering clump of wild olive trees and rabbitbrush and the still flickering cottonwood stumps. The new fire fighters did not drag hoses. They yelled into walkie-talkies as they moved toward the fourth blaze.

The young deputy noted his floodlight was wobbling more now because his arms ached from directing the beam toward the blaze for so long. Eventually he heard the buzz, then the roar of a helicopter. It dropped to hover about six hundred feet to the southwest of his perch. The firemen no longer needed his searchlight. The helicopter had a stronger searchlight. He turned his off and placed it in the sling on the left side of his perch. He adjusted his binoculars.

The rookie thought about how easily the firemen had climbed over the wall. He began to monitor the perimeter wall not only near the fires but also at the gate. He turned one hundred and eighty degrees and scanned the wall that he had ignored until now. He knew his task was impossible as he'd tried to watch the wall in both directions.

His attention was drawn back to the blaze in the bosque when the helicopter discharged a flood of dirty river water and swung away. Some dribbled on him. Most of it landed as intended. Steam rose from the ground. He peered through the steam and thought the flames were lower. He hoped he'd be out of this tree before the next load of water was dropped. Then he heard two fire trucks approach the blaze. The fire lane in the bosque must have been overgrown and difficult to drive.

He felt like an owl as he constantly turned his head to scan not only the wall in both directions from the gate but also to examine trees for sparks. He spied a movement as he looked through his infrared binocular. A lump was emitting heat in the ditch. It was to the east, the part of the wall that he had ignored initially. The "live lump" split into two small "live lumps." Both lumps moved away from him following the wall toward the corner where the wall bent northward toward Field Post Three. He was ready to call Chief Andrews when the "lumps" bounded out of the ditch. They were coyotes.

He continued to scan the wall. Another heat-emitting lump appeared in the ditch by the turn in the wall not far from where he saw the coyotes. It was bigger than the last lump and moved slowly. He adjusted his goggles and slid his rifle out of the sling. It was two lumps. The lumps didn't move like coyotes.

He picked up his walkie-talkie and radioed Chief Andrews. "Chief, I may have sighted two individuals in the ditch by the wall about two hundred feet to the northeast of me and the bosque gate. They're moving slowly." He listened to Gil for a few seconds.

"I'm alone. My partner is at the fire lane." He listened again.

"Plenty of firemen between me and the road. No one behind me to keep them from running south into the bosque." He listened again.

"I'm not a good shot. This is my first night-tracking mission. Don't know if I can manage the searchlight and my rifle." He juggled equipment and listened, finally he said, "Sure hope someone gets here real soon." He focused the searchlight and then aimed his rifle at one of the lumps and pulled the trigger. Before he could pull the trigger again, his searchlight had toppled to the ground.

CHAPTER 37: Monday Night Continued — Sara

"Lalo, come back here."

Sara stood at the top of the stairs on the third floor of the clinic and listened to Lalo's steps reverberate on the concrete steps. Lalo was still running down the stairs. Sara sighed and followed more slowly.

"Lalo, there's no need to run."

She stopped and listened. Lalo was almost to the first floor. She wondered how he'd done it. The stairwell was hot. "Oh my God." She screamed, "Don't open the door!"

"Why?"

"There's a fire on the other side of the door. When you open the door, the air from the stairwell could fan the fire."

Lalo stopped. Sara staggered onto the first-floor landing with Lalo. She placed her hand on the door that led to the loading dock at the back of the clinic. It was hot and the smoke in the stairwell tickled her throat.

She pulled at the door to the first-floor corridor. It was locked or at least jammed shut. "No way out but up." She tried to keep the sound of fear from her voice as she grabbed Lalo's hand.

She must not have disguised the situation from Lalo. He gave her a wide-eyed look, not of innocence but of fear. He gulped and bound up the stairs dragging her. He gave her a few seconds to pant after he yanked open the door to the second floor. Then he sprinted through the empty hallways of the second floor pulling Sara. She wondered how a child who injured his leg this afternoon could run so fast but she was grateful.

They emerged at the front of the clinic. Staff were busy seating patients on chairs dragged from the clinic's lobby. Search lights from the police cars gave the scene a garish look while police paced around the edge of the crowd focusing their guns into shadowy areas.

Lalo had no interest in the scene and tried to pull Sara toward the wall behind the building. She took two steps and then planted her feet firmly. The effect was the same as when she snapped the leash on Bug when he was being willful. Lalo spun around. The stress on her arm was a lot more with Lalo than with Bug.

She glared at him. "Before we go on, you've got some explaining to do. Why did you run away? Your mom needs you."

Lalo stared at her in apparent surprise. "She needs Dulce now, not me. The police need my help to find who started the fires. How about the lady who owned the blue car?"

"No, she's in the hospital." Sara frowned. "Maybe someone who borrowed her car."

"You mean stole it."

"Okay, what's your plan?"

"I saw something near that tree when I was upstairs." Lalo pointed southeast of the back of the building. "It was moving toward the wall."

Sara shook her head. "Why didn't you tell the FBI guy?"

"I did. He couldn't see it." Lalo looked down and scuffed his shoe in the gravel. When he looked he up, he smiled. "But he promised to look again at the spot."

Sara spied Gaspar. He was seating patients in patio chairs at the front of the building.

"No." Lalo grabbed Sara's other hand to keep her from waving to Gaspar. "He'll slow us down."

"We have to tell someone before we wander off. Besides, we shouldn't go far as long as the blue car is circling around."

"Okay." Lalo looked around and pointed to the FBI agent who had befriended him earlier. "Tell him."

The agent ran toward them. "Hey kid, what are you doing?"

Lalo pointed toward the wall. "Helping you. I know I saw something move toward the wall between those two cottonwood trees. I'm going to check it out."

"Not by yourself." The agent fumbled with his phone. "Witness Lalo and Sara found." He listened for a minute but never took his eyes off Lalo. "So, they found the blue car. Empty. Rachel, I'm going to check out the spot where Lalo and I saw movement. We'll need a searchlight. Can you send a car by?"

The agent turned to Lalo. "You led me on quite a chase. It was smart of you not to go out the back door."

Lalo looked up at Sara. "She's a good guide but slow. She found me in the bosque too."

The agent for the first time really looked at Sara. "Oh, you're the one everyone talks about, the statistics whiz. You gave us the cover to check the Petersons' house."

"That's me."

The agent stooped to be at eye level with Lalo. "I saw something on the wall too. I shot at it, but my boss says it was a cat. Let's prove her wrong."

The three of them left the raucous scene of pulsating fire trucks, frenzied firemen, and frightened patients and headed for two cottonwood trees near the wall. Sara felt the pounding in her head decrease as the noise level fell.

When they reached the wall, the agent turned to Sara. "Little Mister Detective and I are going to crawl along the wall with a flashlight and look for evidence. You stay on the path. When the car gets here, have them focus their searchlight on us."

Soon a state police car pulled up and two officers set up their searchlight. The light swept the wall. A red stain dripped from the top of the wall almost to the ground. It was about ten feet farther to the south than Lalo and the FBI agent had searched so far.

The two state police officers took one glance at the stain on the wall and began to work. The blond officer carried a satchel toward the stain and proceeded to pull out vials and test plates. The dark-haired state police officer lugged a ladder, a portable searchlight, and other equipment to the wall. He talked to the FBI agent.

Sara decided it was time to get Lalo out of the way. She grabbed his hand and dragged him to a spot near where the car was parked. "Why don't you and I stand here and watch for a while."

"I'd rather climb over the wall."

"I'm sure you would, but I think the police should go first." She didn't want Lalo to see a cat with its guts hanging out or, less likely, one of her neighbors bleeding.

The dark-haired state police officer handed the searchlight to the FBI agent who carried it over the wall. The blond officer scraped a bit of the red substance from the wall and put it in a vial. He sprayed luminol on part of the remaining stain and stared at the luminescence. "Probably blood."

"No kidding," said the dark-haired officer. "I think our FBI agent may be a good marksman, but he hasn't done much tracking."

"Asti, you'd better join him before he messes up your clues," said the blond officer to the dark-haired officer. "I can take care of the sample processing."

Asti strapped on infrared night goggles and climbed over the wall while the blond officer put more of the red substance into another vial and shook it.

The blond officer yelled, "Asti, preliminary test suggests it's human blood. I'm going to get a camera and take a few shots of the wall, but I'll be done here soon. I'll take the kid and the lady back to the clinic area."

CHAPTER 38: Monday Night Continued — State Police Officer Asti

Asti studied the scene on the other side of the wall. Field Post One was less than a half-mile ahead to the north and around a bend in the perimeter wall. Field Post Three was less than a half-mile behind him to the south. The portable spotlight sat on the sandy path but was focused on the ditch by the wall about where the stain was on the other side. The weeds in the area were flattened and bloodied. The FBI agent crawled on his knees in the midst of the stained weeds destroying all evidence.

Asti shook his head. No use examining that area. From now on, he'd try to stay a few steps ahead of the FBI agent, because there would be nothing to see once the agent trampled an area. He picked up the portable spotlight and shone it on the sandy path as he paced along. He paused and knelt. "Blood on the path and more activity in the sand. Whatever you hit moved from the grass to the path here because it was easier going."

The FBI agent dashed to the spot and squatted. He looked back and forth between the spot and the wall. "Don't see how an animal could lose so much blood at that site and so little blood here."

"My partner said the blood was human. I'd guess he, or could be a she, tied a tourniquet around the wound to slow bleeding."

"I'll call Chief Gil Andrews."

Asti scanned the trail with infrared binoculars and then directed the spotlight to an area about fifty feet ahead on the trail, where the sand seemed particularly disturbed, and paced toward it. On closer examination he noticed blood, actually quite a bit.

The FBI agent sprinted to join him at the spot.

"A load was readjusted here. Must have been two people. One carrying the other." He looked at the agent. "What did the Chief say?"

"The sheriff's deputies at Field Post Three think no one went by their station except one sniper who came from the Wal-Mart area. So, we're going in the right direction."

"I heard they shot at a sniper. Did they clip him?"

"Evidently not."

Asti tracked the trail of the wounded couple down the path for the next fifteen minutes. It was hard in the dark even with all his special equipment. The FBI agent trailed behind and called in Asti's progress. The agent always said "our" progress but Asti wasn't concerned. He'd worked with Chief Gil Andrews before. The Chief would know who in this operation was doing the tracking and who was just talking.

Asti handed the spotlight to the agent. "Stay here." Asti left the trail and began to examine the ditch by the wall. The agent focused the portable searchlight on the ditch near where Asti stood.

"Swing the light down the wall to near the bend. See how the brush is flattened right before the bend in the wall." Asti pointed toward a stand of bushes. "They musta known about Field Post One somehow. Better call Field Post One."

"Why?"

"Don't want anyone to shoot us when we turn the bend."

"No need. The rookie officer at Field Post One is waiting for us. His partner shot and then ran after an arsonist."

"So?"

"The rookie saw someone, probably two, in the ditch just past the turn in the wall. He shot in their direction. When he heard another shot, he accidentally knocked most of his equipment to the ground. Chief Andrews told him to sit still and wait for us."

"Why didn't the Chief tell us sooner?"

"He did, but I told him we couldn't track any faster."

"You told him wrong. I could have moved a lot faster if I knew the probable suspects had been sited up ahead. Stay ten feet behind me." Asti stalked to the bend in the wall and yelled, "We're turning the corner now. Don't shoot."

A voice about two-hundred, fifty feet ahead and in a tree replied, "About time."

Asti edged forward around the bend and moved slowly forward in the two-foot high grass. He stopped and pointed at a blob five feet ahead. The FBI agent, who had just turned the corner, focused the searchlight to where Asti pointed.

"What is it?" The FBI agent ignored Asti's directions and tramped through the weeds to where Asti now stood. "Oh, my God!"

Asti bent over the body and nudged it. "Got a hole in the shoulder." He looked up at the FBI agent. "Expect you did that."

"And the rookie deputy at Field Post One did the head shot?"

Asti's jaw dropped. He squinted at the FBI agent. "This your first body? The shot came from close range and from a hand gun, not a rifle."

The FBI agent turned ashen. "We were told Jim Peterson was never arrested because he left no witnesses to finger him, but this was his wife."

CHAPTER 39: Tuesday, Day Eight of the Crisis – Sara

"Blood dripped down the wall, like in a scary movie." Lalo waved his arms as he told his mother of his adventures.

Julia didn't lift her head from the pillow and her face was ashen but a respirator mask no longer covered her face. She grabbed Sara's hand and whispered, "Thank you."

Lalo watched the gesture. "Sara found me today twice but she wouldn't let me track the bad guys."

Dulce stomped into the room and injected Lalo with his antivirals. "Enough story. It's past midnight. Your Mom needs to sleep. You do too."

As Sara and Lalo ambled past the clubhouse, Sara saw a young woman with her hair swept back into a ponytail leaning against the clubhouse wall and smoking. She recognized the woman as a nurse's aide in the center.

"Sara, what are you doing here?"

"This rascal." Sara held up Lalo's arm. "Decided to break into La Bendita to see his mom this, well I guess yesterday, afternoon. He had a few problems." Sara noted the bags under the aide's eyes. "How's this week been for you?"

"I'd stopped smoking for six months. This week I started smoking again."

"Just knowing you can't leave is frustrating. And eating school cafeteria-type meals gets old," said Sara.

The aide blew a smoke ring. "The food's good, if you're not watching your weight. Sleeping in a tent and waiting in line for a shower are for the birds, but the worst part is being surrounded by death constantly."

Sara nodded.

"It gives me goosebumps to think of one woman who lived on Aster Lane. She grabbed the arm of anyone who made the mistake of being within a few feet of her bed. Each time she pleaded, 'Let me die in my own house.' Finally, she was too weak to grab anybody's arm, but kept chanting, 'Home. Home.' It was eerie."

Sara misted up. "How did you get transferred to the clubhouse?"

"I worked in the center until so many died they didn't need me."

"This must be better."

"In some ways. The boss likes to keep two staff members on duty twenty-four seven. So, there's three shifts of us. I drew the graveyard shift."

"Tough."

"Not really, I'm a night person." The aide studied the concrete walk but looked up when she heard a rapping sound on the front glass doors of the clubhouse. A bedraggled middle-aged woman in a gray, wrinkled pantsuit was alternately knocking on the glass and pointing at the aide. Once she had the aide's attention, she glared and stalked away from the door.

"Guess my break is over. Boss lady wants me to get back to work." The aide snuffed out her cigarette and sauntered into the clubhouse.

Sara dragged herself along Willow Drive while Lalo skipped and hopped down the street. Lights were on in many houses even though it was now one in the morning. A fire truck still stood in front of Jane Lane's house. The front window and door of the house were smashed in. Sara was too tired to wander farther down the street to the Benders' and Petersons' houses. Besides, she didn't need to see any more destruction or smell any more smoke.

She dropped her keys twice as she tried to open her own front door and wipe her nose at the same time. The door to her house finally swung open.

The house stunk. It was musty and smoky at the same time. She wanted to cry, but she didn't have the energy to really sob.

CHAPTER 40: Ellen Behren Reviews Her Day

Ellen looked at the clock. It was eight on Tuesday morning. She began to review the major events of the last eighteen hours.

-/-/-

It had begun when Chief Gil Andrews posted law enforcement agents of every ilk all around La Bendita and everyone had said, "Aye. Aye."

Gaspar and Sylvia had put their staffs on high alert late yesterday afternoon at Gil's request. Ellen had reluctantly called her bosses at the CDC and officials in the state health department but told them "nothing will come of this police feeding frenzy."

She had gone to bed at ten. A little before eleven she was awakened with news of the fires. When she learned swarms of lawmen and firemen had entered La Bendita, she reminded Chief Andrews and Bureau Chief George Soto of the FBI that no one could leave La Bendita, even if they were vaccinated, until she lifted the quarantine.

Ten minutes later Sylvia warned her that she couldn't house and feed all the fire and police staff until Thursday afternoon or whenever the quarantine was to be lifted. Around midnight the State Fire Marshal, and then at twelve-fifteen the Secretary of the New Mexico Department of Public Safety, warned her the state would be "helpless to act on any other emergencies" if fire and law enforcement officers were not released from La Bendita as soon as the emergency was over.

She'd called the Deputy Director of the CDC to seek support but received none. The Deputy Director listened to her for a minute. "Don't be a martinet. Worry only about those who aren't vaccinated against the flu. Work with law enforcement officers."

Accordingly, Ellen ordered two clerks to check the health records of all the emergency personnel, both law enforcement officers and firemen, who'd entered La Bendita. They determined all the emergency public safety personnel had been vaccinated against the Philippine flu except the volunteers in the Mercado Fire Department.

Ellen then announced all the emergency personnel who'd been vaccinated could leave La Bendita, but they must report in daily for the next four days to be checked for flu symptoms. State health officials agreed reluctantly to do the check-ins at three police stations and two firehouses. Gaspar called the daily check-ins "overkill."

At two in the morning, Ellen ordered the ten unvaccinated Mercado volunteer firemen to be given antiviral therapy and to stay within La Bendita for the next four days to be closely monitored for flu symptoms. Then she assigned six nurses, accompanied by the volunteer Mercado firemen, to go house to house to see whether any of the residents of La Bendita needed help. They reported in to her at six-thirty a.m.

At seven, she was starting to relax when one of her clerks told her to call the Deputy Secretary of the U.S. Department of Health and Human Services ASAP.

She told the clerk to organize a meeting of key staff at nine in the clubhouse, and made the call.

-/-/-

At nine a smiling Martin Bloom sauntered into the clubhouse. "Sylvia may be a little late for our meeting."

"Where's Gaspar?"

Chuy, who had darted in the front door, replied, "He and the Chief are on the phone with the Mayor of Mercado."

Sylvia scurried in through the back door. Ellen noted Sylvia's hair looked clean and her blouse and skirt were unwrinkled. "You've had time to shower and change clothes, unlike several of us."

Sylvia ignored Ellen's comment and pulled out a list from her folder. She didn't wait for Ellen to officially start the session. "Ten homemade bombs, I think you would call them Molotov cocktails, were hurled at the center's loading dock. It appears most landed in our open garbage dumpsters."

Ellen interrupted, "Why weren't the dumpsters closed per public health standards?"

Sylvia straightened in her chair and raised her eyebrows. "None of our garbage has left for seven days because we're quarantined. The lids on our dumpsters couldn't be closed because the dumpsters were full." She smiled, challenging Ellen to say more. "The fire trucks prevented the spread of the fire. The net result is we have less garbage and we'll have to replace the garbage dumpsters and perhaps repaint the back wall of the center. Oh, the refrigerated truck will need a new paint job on its cab, too.”

Gaspar had entered the clubhouse while Sylvia was speaking. “About the same at the clinic. We were hit with seven Molotov cocktails. The ambulance crew backed the ambulance away from the dock before it caught fire. Most of the garbage in our dumpsters was incinerated. The flames and smoke singed the back wall of the clinic pretty badly in places. The back door is warped. And there’s a third-floor window broken by the FBI. I already had the janitors board up the window.”

Sylvia wrote a note to herself. “I’ll have a building inspector look at both buildings after the quarantine is lifted, but that’s not our main problem. It’s food. We’re almost out of food.”

Ellen had been sorting through files and half-heartedly listening to Sylvia’s and Gaspar’s reports. With Sylvia’s last comment, Ellen jerked to attention. “How could that be?”

“You didn’t see those firemen eat.” Martin patted his abdomen.

“But most of the firemen were in the bosque, not inside La Bendita.”

“Yes,” Sylvia interrupted. “But their chiefs insisted we provide them with sandwiches and beverages.” She did not wait for Ellen to reprimand her. “I spoke to USDA and FEMA officials.”

Ellen sat silently and shook for a moment. “We gave food prepared in our quarantined area to those outside the quarantine. Ten of those men weren’t immunized against the flu.”

“Yes.” The determined look on Sylvia’s face challenged Ellen to say more.

“I guess I won’t mention this point to anyone,” Ellen muttered. “I hope no one thinks to ask.”

Gaspar decided it was his turn now. “It was rough on my patients last night being out in the cold because of the fire alarm. Even though they were out less than an hour and it really wasn’t cold, just cool.”

“We didn’t even try to take patients out of the center,” said Martin. “I decided to trust the fire crews. I figured a number of the patients in the center wouldn’t have survived the stress. They were too weak.”

“I didn’t lose any who vacated the building, although several relapsed a bit. But I kept four in critical condition inside. Two, a clerk’s husband and child, died anyway. Even antivirals didn't save them." Gaspar hung his head. "That's the first I've lost."

Martin glanced over at Sylvia. "Wish we had as good a batting average with those not receiving antivirals. Sylvia, what did we lose in the center?"

"As of an hour ago, one hundred and fifty-eight patients in the center — about one-half." She looked as if she would cry.

Martin didn't raise his head. "Now that's bad stats."

Sylvia continued, "We also lost forty-eight residents from the La Bendita community and fourteen others," said Sylvia. "That includes the two Gaspar lost last night."

"So, about sixteen percent of the residents in homes died," said Ellen. "That's about what they're seeing in El Paso."

Martin arched his back and almost looked triumphant. "But we shouldn't lose many more."

"So, our biggest concern now is new flu cases," said Ellen. "The residents mingled last night."

"Won't be a problem." Martin assumed his professorial voice. "Gaspar and Sara appear to have tracked down all the residents who were exposed to the flu. The mingling among non-exposed residents last night shouldn't matter.

"What about the volunteer firemen who weren't vaccinated?" Sylvia asked.

"They weren't in direct contact with anyone who had the flu. I countermanded your orders." Martin smirked at Ellen. "We vaccinated them and directed them to not enter homes where someone developed the flu in the last four days. That way they'll be ready for the next wave of the flu and weren't exposed to the flu virus." He paused and thought. "The one at the greatest risk is Sara."

Gaspar stood and began to pace. "She certainly was exposed to patients with the flu during the last twenty-four hours, but she was vaccinated and had some natural immunity."

"But her antibody levels were not optimal. However, if she gets the flu, she should survive."

Gaspar winced. "How about Cesar and Lalo? They had intensive exposure to Maria and Julia, but we couldn't control them. Remember, I lost two who had been on antivirals last night."

"If they get the flu, their symptoms should be fairly mild because they've taken antivirals for several days." Martin shook his head. "Of course, anything short of death or needing a respirator seems like mild symptoms to me now."

"Oh my." Gaspar wiped sweat from his brow. "The losses here have made you insensitive to the needs of patients."

"Just messing with you." Martin smiled. "They should at most get sniffles, headaches, and a low-grade fevers."

"Enough trivia." Ellen shook her head. "How did the residents react to the fire? Are they more restless than usual?"

Gaspar looked up to the beamed ceiling. "It's strange." He lowered his head and eyed Ellen and then each member of the group. "Ironically, the fires were good for this community. The residents worked together, maybe for the first time, last night to protect their homes. They generally seemed happier and more hopeful about the future this morning than yesterday when they picked up their orders of food. They certainly complained less about the food."

"Good." Ellen didn't feel like listening to Gaspar philosophize about the residents of La Bendita. "Chuy, how much property damage occurred last night?"

"The Petersons' and the Benders' houses were totally destroyed. Jane Lane's house and one on Aster lane were damaged severely. The insurance companies may declare them total losses. The Steeles' house, mainly the garage, suffered damage when a car parked in front of it blew up."

"Enough of the dry statistics." Martin gave an impish grin and rubbed his hands. "Chuy, buddy, can you tell me what really happened last night? How did the Petersons get the jump on the two FBI agents?"

"Not sure."

"How'd they get Jane Lane's car?" asked Gaspar.

Chuy shook his head. "Don't know. There was no evidence of a forced entry into her house or car. The Petersons must have gotten the keys. Of course, it was hard to tell with all the fire damage."

Ellen glowered. "There's a lot you don't know."

Chuy scowled.

"Tell me more about the blue car the kid saw," said Martin. "Was it blown up?"

"No, it was Jane Lane's car. We found it parked in the driveway of a resident who died of the flu. However, the Benders' car parked in the Steeles' driveway exploded about the time Lalo spotted someone at the wall. We think Peterson really doused the seats with gasoline or some other highly flammable substance and used some sort of remote control to set it off. There isn't enough left of the car to be sure without fancy chemical analyses."

"How many helped Peterson?" asked Martin.

"At least two — a shooter in the channel on the north and an arsonist in the bosque along the south wall."

"Did you at least catch these men?" Ellen asked.

"Not exactly. Asti, probably the best police tracker in the state, with the help of dogs and sheriff's deputies followed Peterson's trail after he shot his wife." Chuy noticed Gaspar, Sylvia, and Martin were staring at him in rapt attention but Ellen had returned to shuffling papers. "Anyway, they managed to track Peterson for three miles through the bosque. Peterson must have known the bosque well. He skirted all the firemen and ended up on a side road leading to Corrales. They found a charred body nearby. The Chief figures it was the arsonist."

Martin looked puzzled. "How did he know the body wasn't an innocent victim who stopped to pick up a hitchhiker? Or even Peterson?"

"Asti said it was obvious someone who was limping and bleeding was in the bosque last night. A sheriff's deputy at Post One was sure he hit the arsonist. The limper left clear tracks up to the area of the car tracks. We'll know for sure later today. The body was charred but bullets will still show up in the autopsy. The Chief's betting Peterson killed the arsonist to keep him from talking. It fits his pattern of leaving no witnesses."

"So, it's a hunch. You don't know." Ellen shook her head in disgust.

"Right, but the Chief's usually guesses right."

"That leaves you with nothing but a burned body in a morgue," said Ellen.

"Not quite. Albuquerque Police roused gang members from their homes and haunts in south Albuquerque around two this morning. They still hope to find the guy who escaped from the channel. He should be able to provide info on Peterson."

"So, you're nowhere in finding Peterson." Ellen smirked. Chuy's face flushed. Ellen guessed she'd put him in his place.

"Whatever happened to Howie Steele?" asked Gaspar.

"After all the shooting was over, the sheriff's deputies, who were stationed at the engineering shack, arrested him for breaking quarantine."

"Good. I'm glad someone took the quarantine seriously." Ellen smiled sincerely for the first time in the discussion.

"Actually, they used that minor charge to scare him into cooperating."

Ellen sniffed. "I assume they returned him to quarantine in his home."

"No, FBI put him in isolation at their headquarters after doctors at University Hospital set his broken arm. He fell trying to dodge bullets in the channel."

Ellen studied the animated faces of her crew as they continued to banter about the events of the previous evening. She feared they might ask about her awful conversation with the Deputy Secretary of the U.S. Department of Health and Human Services next. "Meeting's adjourned."

CHAPTER 41: Day Eight Continued — Sara

Light was filtering through the blinds in her bedroom. It was eight in the morning. Her head still ached and her nose still dripped. Now her throat was scratchy and her eyes burned. She took her allergy medicine and called her sister at work.

"Sara, sure glad you called me last night. I would have freaked out when I saw the headline story in the *Albuquerque Journal* this morning." Linda proceeded to read the story.

Sara interrupted occasionally to supply Linda with details.

Finally Linda asked, "Are you and Lalo in danger?"

"I doubt it. Peterson has no reason to come back here. The police appear to have enough evidence to arrest him for the murder of two FBI agents and his wife without testimony from any of us."

"Hmmf. Don't bet on it."

"Well, maybe they'll charge him with attempted homicide of Jane Lane. She'd make a pretty effective witness with one arm blown off, when she gets out of the hospital."

"Oh, you don't know. Today's *Albuquerque Journal* said she died of injuries."

"Strange. I talked to her by phone yesterday. She seemed upbeat and on the mend."

"Maybe emboli from her wounds hit a vital organ."

"Or maybe the newspaper was fed incorrect information as a way to protect her from Peterson."

"Aha. You do think Peterson is a threat."

Sara didn't answer quickly. "I'm more worried Lalo or I will develop flu symptoms."

"Were you careful?"

"I washed my hands a lot and wore gloves, masks, and paper outerwear in Julia's room. So did Lalo."

Linda's tone changed. "Try to avoid the clinic and center."

"Fat chance. I'm babysitting Lalo."

"Try…"

Lalo bounced through the doorway holding high a muddy pair of jeans.

"Got to go. Give Bug a kiss for me."

While Lalo surfed stations on her TV, Sara washed Lalo's clothes and called Aletha. At ten, she and Lalo finally set off to scrounge for food because the items in Sara's refrigerator were spoiled or unappealing to Lalo.

Lalo spotted Chuy as they moved toward the front gate and darted toward him. Sara was wheezing when she caught up with Lalo. "Excuse me, Sergeant. I don't know how to ask this. Lalo saw a lot yesterday."

"He was a real hero."

Lalo stood up straight and saluted.

"Lalo, why don't you stand in that line for food and see whether they have any for us even though we didn't order food yesterday?"

Lalo skipped over to the end of the line. He did jumping jacks as he waited.

Sara waited until Lalo was out of hearing range. "Did Lalo see too much? Will Peterson try to find him because he's a witness?" Sara did not wait for an answer. "I had two people read me the accounts of 'Leave-no-witnesses Jimmy' from the *Albuquerque Journal* this morning. I don't mean to be silly but…"

"Fair questions. Let's go talk to the Chief."

Gil climbed out of his car at the front entrance to La Bendita as Chuy and Sara approached the gate. "What's up?"

"Would Lalo be safer with Aletha?" When Gil didn't reply quickly, Sara added, "Remember I taught college classes for twenty-five years. I'm no good with eight-year-olds."

"How can I put this? Hmm." Gil looked over at Lalo. "He's a livewire. Aletha can't handle him. He got away from her once. You managed to find him and bring him here." He scratched his chin. "You're easier to talk to than Aletha." He adjusted his belt. "I don't want Aletha to call the governor again. Neither does he. We all think Lalo's better off here until the quarantine is lifted."

Chuy cleared his throat. "The other matter in the clubhouse."

Gil stared at Sara. "Do you like the boss lady? I mean Dr. Ellen Behren."

"Never actually met her."

"What?" Gil scratched the stubble on his chin.

"We communicated by email and occasionally by phone during the last week. I think I saw her last night."

"You seem to be able to get her to listen to you." Gil eyed Sara carefully as if he were trying to read her thoughts.

Sara kept her face motionless as she replied, "She's got big responsibilities here. It's a hard situation even without last night."

"Give me your gut feel."

Sara looked directly at Gil. "This assignment could be a career maker for her. She's young, smart, and ambitious. That adds to her stress."

Gil frowned.

Sara coughed violently. "Damn allergies. Okay, she's overly rigid about the rules and seems to lack empathy for staff and patients, but she took my advice on tracking leads. If I do say myself, we defined several important points for controlling the Philippine flu. And she did a good job of containing the flu within La Bendita."

"Hmm." Gil didn't look up from the ground.

"Okay, she's prickly." Sara emphasized the next words. "Especially if she's not treated with respect. She's not one of your minions who can't say no to you."

Chuy covered his smile with his hand.

"I hear you," Gil pulled at his belt again. "I know she knows a lot about quarantine rules and about preventing the spread of flu, but Doc and I have trouble getting her to pay attention to what Doc calls the big picture."

Chuy interrupted, "Like ragging Sylvia about open trash bins this morning."

Gil spit on the ground. "Exactly. Doc feels she listens to you better than to him. We hoped you might volunteer to help her. That way you could guide her a bit. You're here anyway."

"But Lalo."

"We thought of him, too." Gil guffawed. "We'll trade you. You handle the boss lady until the quarantine is lifted. Gaspar will find a nurse or aide to handle Lalo." Gil studied Sara's face. "She could even stay at your house and take care of him at night."

"I don't know."

"Doc's got several at the breaking point. A kid would lift their spirits."

"Aletha might..."

"We convinced her you needed a break."

J. L. Greger

Sara arched her eyebrows in annoyance. "In other words, I didn't need to come to you with questions. You would have come to me within an hour with orders."

Both Gil and Chuy smiled. Gil replied, "Not orders, just requests."

"Okay. But you didn't answer my original question about Jim."

Gil assumed a folksy tone with his voice. "You know those of us in public life learn to manage the press. We know one of Peterson's associates from last night, the sniper in the flood control channel, is still around. We want him and really all of Peterson's business associates to lose trust in him. Be scared he'll kill them too. That's why we called him 'Leave-no-witnesses Jimmy.' Sorta subtle propaganda." Gil noticed Sara's scowl. "Okay, not so subtle."

"What about those of us in La Bendita?"

"We're keeping guards on the gates and having the fire department volunteers patrol the perimeter."

Lalo ran to Sara. "They told me we could eat in the first-floor break room of the clinic. I'm hungry. Hurry."

Sara coughed again. "After we eat and Lalo sees his mom, I'll wander over to the clubhouse and introduce myself to Ellen." She added sarcastically, "Do I report in to you later?"

"No need. Gaspar will." Gil ambled back to his squad car.

As Sara and Lalo hurried to the clinic, the tickle in Sara's throat became stronger. She sneezed and then coughed violently.

Lalo studied her for a moment. "You, you sound like Mom did. Are you going to get the flu, too?"

CHAPTER 42: Chief Gil Andrews Reviews Day Eight and Nine

Gil climbed out of the old recliner in his office. Its brown leather had so many creases and scratches from wear that it looked like it was upholstered with a beige-and-brown houndstooth fabric. The recliner reminded him of himself — worn but still tough. Besides, it was a better place to think than the squad car. He'd spent too much time in the cramped vehicle during the last week. That reminded him. He left a note for his secretary to get his squad car detailed. It stunk of fast food, smoke, and sweat.

Now it was Wednesday evening. After working all night on both Monday and Tuesday, he'd announced to his staff he would go home early today. Instead he was waiting for a bigwig from the CDC to arrive. She'd insisted on talking to him privately before she toured La Bendita. Ellen couldn't lift the quarantine until this woman gave the okay. Gil waited.

-/-/-

Tuesday had been a roller coaster ride of high hopes and great disappointments.

The state pathologist had called around ten. The partially charred body in the bosque was tentatively identified on the basis of dental records as a known drug runner in the Zuni neighborhood of south Albuquerque. The pathologist found bullets in the man's right leg and head. Everyone assumed the charred body was the arsonist who limped after he was shot in the leg by the sheriff's deputy in the bosque. They also guessed Jim Peterson, aka Mazzone, shot the arsonist in the head to eliminate witnesses.

The police had swarmed the arsonist's trailer home in south Albuquerque. They scared his sister but had found no incriminating evidence except a couple ounces of cocaine.

Gil's old buddies in the Gang Unit of the Albuquerque Police had brought the drug runner's sister in for questioning. Gil convinced them to allow him to watch her interrogation. George Soto, the bureau chief of the FBI in Albuquerque, insisted one of his agents be present also.

The Albuquerque Police had shown her pictures of her brother's burned body and of Jean Peterson's head wound. They repeatedly called Jim Peterson, "Leave-no-witnesses Jimmy." They promised they wouldn't charge her for possession if she helped them locate the other shooter.

After an hour, the FBI agent had called his boss George Soto and talked for several minutes. Then he announced to the Albuquerque Police, "Soto figured you couldn't protect her and talked to the U.S. Marshals Service. They're sending someone over. They'll relocate her if her info is good."

The state police had found Tony Abolas, the shooter in the flood control channel, at his aunt's house in Belen about thirty miles south of Albuquerque three hours later. Abolas had been a drug runner for Mazzone for three years. He knew Jim Peterson as Jimmy Blanco or Mr. B.

"Hey man," Abolas had said, "Mr. B always says you make your own luck." Abolas explained Mr. B's escape plans. Both the shooter and the arsonist were ordered to create diversions on opposite sides of La Bendita. Both were instructed to park get-away cars at designated spots with keys in magnetic boxes under the right rear tire surrounds. Both were reminded to place gloves for Mr. B on the front seat of their cars and to wait outside the car until Mr. B arrived.

"Mr. B must have been real mad at him," Abolas said when shown a photo of his friend's charred body. "Mr. B don't like to waste time when he leaves a scene. Takes time to burn a body."

Abolas explained that he'd followed Mr. B's rules exactly. He waited near the SUV that he parked in the Wal-Mart parking lot for four hours before leaving around five on Tuesday morning to drive to the Rail Runner train station at Route 550. He knew Mr. B was angry when he spotted the SUV driven by his friend, the arsonist.

Upon further questioning, Abolas explained. Mr. B planned to drive one of the SUVs to Albuquerque unless both SUVs were compromised. If that occurred, he would ride the Rail Runner and pick up a third vehicle parked by the station in downtown Mercado.

As soon as Abolas mentioned the Rail Runner stations, Gil dispatched two of his officers to check out the described SUVs in the Rail Runner parking lots at Route 550 and in downtown Mercado.

The SUV in the lot at Route 550 was rigged. It exploded when the Mercado Police officers opened the door. The male officer was now in the hospital in critical condition and the female officer was in fair condition. Gil, Chuy and three other officers were now the total active police force for Mercado.

Despite threats from the agents and police, Abolas insisted he had no knowledge of Peterson's plan to rig the SUV at the Rail Runner station. However, he finally admitted, "Mr. B always kept certain supplies in our cars for emergencies."

The agents questioned Abolas for hours but got only vague answers even when they offered incentives. He had no idea that Peterson lived in La Bendita and didn't know his wife's name but admitted, "Mr. B always bragged about his whore at home." Eventually, Abolas named eight drug runners in return for the chance of being jailed "anywhere but New Mexico, Colorado, or Nevada" because he believed Mazzone had strong connections in those states.

In despair, Gil and those questioning Abolas debated whether to go home or continue their discussion over drinks at Kelly's or the Corrales Bistro Brewery. Chuy called before they reached a decision.

"Chief, Doc's been driving Rachel and me crazy."

"What's he's ragging on this time?"

"He keeps saying we haven't 'picked the brains' of the residents of La Bendita about Jim and Jean Peterson."

"Get to the point."

"Rachel and I met with the Crocketts, the Kents, and Susan Steele."

"I said, get to the point. I'm ready for a Corona."

"Hank said the only thing Jim could talk about was hunting. Marian thought Jim once mentioned a hunting cabin in Chama."

"Did you contact the Chama Police?"

"Yes. No one named Peterson or Mazzone owns property in Chama."

"Try Blanco. Hell, look for any Italian names."

"Okay."

"That's it?"

"No, the Santa Fe Police called. A car was stolen from a lot at the Santa Fe Rail Runner downtown station. The driver left it last night and couldn't find it when he returned around seven this morning. The state police found the car at a shopping mall lot in Espanola around noon. They checked it out."

"Won't be any fingerprints from Peterson. He has gloves."

"But they found smudges of blood on the side of the seat."

"How? He didn't get shot."

"Must have taken off his glove to pick his nose. There were several bits of blood in dried snot at the side of the seat. The state lab called. It's the same AB positive blood type as Peterson's. They'll do DNA tests but it'll take days."

"One for the records. Good old high desert air dries out the sinuses. You figure he headed from Espanola to Chama. Any cars missing in Espanola?"

"Of course, it's Espanola. The state police and Chama Police are looking for two in particular. Both were parked in the mall where Peterson left the first car."

-/-/-

Gil snapped back to the present. He tapped his fingers on the arm of the chair. Where was the damn official? He wanted to go home.

-/-/-

A real break in the case came around suppertime on Tuesday. Chama Police had found a cabin owned by an Angela Jean Ciccone in the town's records. George Soto had them secure the cabin and rounded up three of his agents. Within minutes, Soto and his agents jumped into a car and rushed with sirens shrieking to Chama.

As Gil raced behind the FBI, he made arrangements with an old friend, the Chief of the Chama Police Department, for someone to meet the two cars where US-64 N became NM-17 because it was easy to get lost in the backwoods around Chama, especially at night. The two cars roared up to the appointed spot about three hours later. A Chama police officer sat in a cruiser waiting to guide them to the Ciccone cabin.

The three cars had swerved and bumped along narrow, rutted gravel roads that wound through a dark pine forest. After twenty minutes of dust swirling around them, they'd skidded to a stop before a dirt path branched off from the gravel road.

A state officer emerged from an unmarked SUV parked by the side of the road. He led them down a dirt path through the pines. As they slipped and slid along the steep path, he said to Soto, "The Chama police department and the state police set up guards at the front of the cabin two hours ago after we got your orders."

Gil was surprised when he saw the cabin in the moonlight. It didn't look like the usual hunting shack. Dark green shutters with matching window boxes flanked the dark green front door of the log cabin. Rose bushes were planted around the front door. Tall, aromatic pine trees surrounded the sides and back of the cabin. Someone, probably Jean Peterson, had loved this cabin. The cabin looked much homier than the Petersons' house in La Bendita, at least as Chuy had described it. Gil also noticed the shutters on the lower windows were closed, but the shutters for the second-floor window over the front door were partially open. One of the cars missing from the Espanola parking lot was parked in front of the log cabin.

The Chief of the Chama Police approached Soto and Gil. He nodded at the cabin. "It's been like this for the last hour."

"Like what?" Soto growled.

"Smoke belching out of the chimney. Sinatra's voice blaring from the audio system. No lights."

"Was it like this when you first got here?' Gil asked.

"No. Then lights were on."

"Whoever is inside knows we're here," said Gil.

"Expect so."

Soto asked, "Did you try to get him out?"

"Not worth the effort. I read the sheet you sent me. He's down for what, four murders in the last day? Two were FBI. Looks like his options are a shoot-out, lethal injection, or life without parole. I don't want to waste my men or state police officers in a shoot-out." He turned to Gil. "Sorry to hear about your losses."

Gil had gulped. "Experience tells me Peterson, I guess I'd better call him Mazzone, has booby trapped this cabin, too."

The Chama Police Chief sighed. "I guess we'll have to starve him out."

Soto expanded his chest. "No, we'll act before morning."

Gil had sniffed the air. "Hate to mention this. Notice the smoke?" He waited a moment for everyone to smell the air. "That's not pinion, more like paper. Bet Mazzone's burning evidence."

"That seals it." Soto stalked away with his agents trailing.

The two small town police chiefs conferred quietly, but mainly watched Soto with both amusement and alarm as he had frantically used his cell phone.

After a few minutes Soto announced, "Washington wants us to get evidence to take down Mazzone's associates, particularly drug bosses in Nevada, Colorado, and Mexico. They want us to stop him from burning evidence. I've called for reinforcements."

Gil and the Chief of the Chama Police Department watched the FBI agents form a huddle like a football team around Soto. Gil broke off a small branch from a nearby pinion. The needles were dry. "Better get your fire crews out. Bet the bastard takes the cabin and a lot of forest up in flames."

"Crazy." The Chama Police Chief lifted his hat and scratched his head. "But sounds right. Still think starving him out is the best way." He spat at the ground. "I'll get my men ready. Gil, you'd better stick with us. It'll be safer than with those FBI jockeys, especially when they get reinforcements."

-/-/-

Gil's phone rang. The bigwig's plane was delayed. It had left Atlanta on time, but had stopped in Washington before starting toward Albuquerque. Gil returned to thinking about the highs and lows of Tuesday.

-/-/-

At ten Tuesday night, Soto had used a bullhorn to get a response from the occupant of the cabin. He failed. Sinatra continued to sing. The smoke continued to rise from the chimney.

Around eleven, the FBI agents began to doubt there was anyone in the cabin. One of them covered in Kevlar stepped from the trees onto the path to the house. He'd taken three steps when a rifle shot ricocheted off a tree behind him. Everyone assumed the shot came from the cabin's open upper window. Gil whispered to the Chama Police Chief. "Surprised he's such a bad shot with a rifle. Or he was just buying time. Wonder why."

Around midnight, two more carloads of FBI agents arrived at the site in Chama. While they conferred with the FBI agents on site already, two carloads of state police and four Chama fire trucks appeared. The Chama Police Chief turned to Gil. "Guess it's high noon now."

Gil shook his head. "Not sure I feel like Gary Cooper."

"Oh, I feel like him with an upset stomach. But I'm not sure I'll be as lucky."

They paced to where the FBI agents and state police were conferencing. Soto greeted them as they had approached the group. "Chiefs, I'm going to have sharpshooters shoot in between the open shutters into the loft window of the cabin. At the same time, we'll blast out windows and the door in the front of the cabin."

Gil remained silent for thirty seconds. "Don't like the plan. What if the cabin is booby trapped? You'll end up with nothing but burnt pieces and a forest fire. Why not use the fire trucks to blast the cabin with water before you let your sharpshooters work?"

A Chama fireman had been listening to the conversation. "It'll take a while to get the trucks in position. There are trees on both sides of the cabin. We'll only be able to blast the front and part of the sides with water."

Uncharacteristically, Soto had agreed.

Both of the small police chiefs sighed in relief.

"But we're going in no matter what in an hour," said Soto.

Gil spat on the ground.

-/-/-

Gil sat up straight in his chair and looked at his watch. He hated to even remember what had happened at two in the morning. Technically, it wasn't the low point of Tuesday; it was the low point of today.

-/-/-

The lawmen had focused spotlights on the front of the cabin. The fire trucks had shot streams of water at the front and part of the sides of the cabin. Then the gunfire assault on the front of the cabin began.

After ten minutes, the ground around the cabin sparkled under the searchlights with shattered glass and water. A couple of shutters hung limply at the windows. The rest lay in pieces on the ground. The stolen car looked a bit like Swiss cheese.

Soto signaled the fire trucks to stop dousing the cabin. He ordered his men to move toward the cabin. There were no gunshots. One agent kicked away debris from the opening that had once been the front door to the cabin and stepped into the cabin. Two other agents followed through the door.

They reported by walkie-talkies not seeing any evidence of anyone on the first floor even with their infrared search equipment. Then they reported the aroma of alcohol and gasoline everywhere.

Gil yelled, "Turn on those hoses now!"

The lead state police officer yelled to his men who were approaching the cabin, "Get the hell out of there!"

Soto hesitated before he yelled. "Run. It's booby trapped."

It was too late. The ground shook as flames exploded from the cabin, especially the back of the cabin. In less than two minutes the cabin was engulfed in flames even though the firemen continued to blast the front half of the cabin and its surrounds with water.

The Chama Police Chief commanded his men to work with the firemen. The state police retrieved their injured from near the house. Gil called the medical examiner's office and told them to come and claim the burnt bodies of the three FBI agents.

-/-/-

Gil got himself more coffee and studied three new faxes. Angela Jean Ciccone had a record. She'd been arrested for prostitution in New Jersey. No record she ever married Jim Peterson, James Mazzone, Jimmy Blanco, or for that matter anyone else. He wasn't surprised.

The second fax was from his friends in the Albuquerque Police Department. They'd found Peterson's computer at the repair desk of Best Buy at Cottonwood. His computer records suggested he had a big business operation, but the police hadn't decoded the names of contacts in the records yet.

The third fax was from the FBI. The fourth body in the cabin, presumably Peterson, had been so charred it could take weeks to identify. This troubled Gil. Usually the teeth, at least a few of them, were enough intact in the victims of house fires to help the police identify the victims, unless the body was doused with gasoline. Peterson didn't seem like the type to have doused himself with gasoline like a martyr. There was one more fact that troubled him. Firemen had found evidence of a sunken back door in the smoldering ruins of the cabin.

The phone rang. It was the woman who'd gone to the airport to pick up the bigwig from the CDC. "Chief, you'd better go to the Range Restaurant and get decent coffee. The Deputy Director of the CDC brought along the Deputy Director of the FBI and a few others."

"Are you stopping by the FBI office on I-25 before you come here?"

"No, they want to talk to you first. They also asked Doctor Gonzales to join you."

CHAPTER 43: Friday, Day Ten of the Crisis — Lalo Chavez, Sara, Lalo Again

Lalo dressed quickly, opened the door of the guest bedroom, and listened. Snores came from the living room. He thought the nurse assigned to help Sara until the quarantine was lifted, must be asleep on the couch. He tiptoed past her, sneaked into the kitchen, opened the utility drawer, and pulled out a hammer. He slid open the nearby patio door and ran.

-/-/-

Sara awakened to a noise. Someone had left the house through the sliding door in the kitchen. She wondered what Lalo was up to now and rushed to follow him. However, she teetered on her feet when she stood and quickly sank to the edge of the bed. She called for help.

The nurse rushed into Sara's room.

"I tried to get up but I was dizzy and nauseous." Sara shook her head. "You'd better look for Lalo."

"Lalo can wait. First, we take care of you." The nurse took Sara's temperature. "Oh dear."

"What is it?" asked Sara.

"One hundred and one. And it's only seven in the morning," The nurse called the clinic. "Get the ambulance to Sara Almquist's house now. We may have a new flu patient."

-/-/-

Lalo hurried along Willow Drive from Sara's house. He hadn't told Sara the whole truth about his fall in the bosque Monday when she found him. He hadn't tripped on the roots of the old cottonwood tree. He'd tripped on the corner of a rusty, padlocked metal box buried at the foot of the tree. He hadn't replied when Sara had called his name because he was busy covering the box up with leaves so she wouldn't notice it.

He'd heard Doctor Gonzales tell Sara his mom couldn't leave the clinic until Saturday or later. That meant when the quarantine was lifted, he'd have to go back home to Granny. He had work to do today.

He ran down Willow Drive, past the clubhouse, then down Marigold Lane to the low point in the wall. He climbed over the wall and peeked back over the wall. No one was in sight. He raced down the sandy path until he could see the gravel road leading into the back-emergency gate at La Bendita. A police car was parked by the gate.

He didn't want the police to stop him and he squatted and walked like a crab on the gravel behind the car. He continued until he got to the concrete abutment for the flood channel. He stood for a second and then slid down the side of the abutment.

He heard a siren becoming louder and louder. He flattened himself against the side of the abutment and heard the gravel rebounding from the road as one then another police car rushed past him.

He ran to the savanna. He looked toward the bosque and scanned for the old cottonwood where he tripped. He studied the distant trees and didn't see anyone. Finally, he spotted a gnarled cottonwood tree with rabbitbrush at its base at the edge of the bosque.

He sped toward it but slowed as he neared it because he didn't want to fall this time. He knelt at the roots of the tree, laid the hammer down, and pushed back the leaves. He dug into the dirt until he felt something solid.

Suddenly, he felt two big, gloved hands around his waist. In seconds, he was lifted entirely off the ground. He tried to kick backwards but to no avail. The man dangled him a foot above the ground.

"Kid, what are you doing?" The voice was rough and low.

Lalo gasped for breath.

"How did you know this was here?"

The man dropped Lalo to the ground and put his foot on Lalo's back. The weight on Lalo's back increased as the man pulled twine from a dirty white pillowcase and twisted the twine around Lalo's left wrist. The twine dug into Lalo's skin. Blood trickled onto his hand.

Lalo realized this wasn't a game anymore. He remembered a lesson at Cub Scouts and tensed the muscles in his arms and breathed deeply, as least as deeply as he could. The man pulled Lalo's right wrist behind his back too. Now the twine cut into both of Lalo's wrists.

"Been poking your nose where it doesn't belong." The man hobbled Lalo by tying twine around his ankles.

As the man finished digging up the rusty metal box, Lalo snuck a peek at him. Lalo turned his face back to the ground. The man kicked the box to lay about two feet from Lalo's head. He knelt, picked up the hammer, and raised it high. Lalo flinched.

The man laughed as he brought the hammer down. Lalo thought of his mom. The hammer crushed one of the rusty hinges on the box.

"Scared you, didn't I?" The man hammered more on the box. Lalo kept his face against the ground but squinted toward the box.

The lid twisted open. Stacks of what looked like money, real money not Monopoly money, poured out of the box onto the ground. Lalo noticed the bills weren't ones, fives, or tens. These bills had the face of a bald man on them. Lalo thought it was Benjamin Franklin, but he wasn't sure.

The man grabbed the bills from the ground and stuffed them into the pillowcase. He dumped the rest of the cash in the metal box into pillowcase too. He dropped the box on the ground.

Lalo heard a siren in the distance and then another.

"Bet they're looking for you. Would anyone look for you here?"

"Hope so."

The man laughed. "Do you know who I am?"

"Don't know. Didn't see you."

"Good answer. Let's keep it that way." The man tore off parts of the pillowcase and tied rags over Lalo's eyes and mouth. "If you're lucky, they'll find you before the coyotes do."

The gag stunk. Lalo felt like vomiting. His eyes stung under the mask.

Lalo listened to the man's steps as he departed. He was walking in the dry leaves not on gravel or sand. The man was going into the bosque not back to La Bendita. He was moving quickly but not running.

When he heard no more sounds, Lalo tried to scream. He couldn't make much noise with the gag.

He thought about the knot-tying and -untying lesson at Cub Scouts. A couple of the guys were really good at escaping after they were tied up. He tried to imitate what they did. He brought his knees up to his chest and tried to bring his wrists under his seat. He couldn't. He arched his back and tried again. Still couldn't. He tried again. His hands slipped under his seat. His shoulders and his wrists hurt. He rolled into a ball and slipped his wrists under his legs and feet.

He caught his fingers in the rag tied over his mouth and untied that knot. The fresh air felt great. He screamed, "Help! Help!"

No one came.

He pulled off the mask. His eyes stung. He bent forward and used his teeth to untie the knots around his wrists. The twine tasted like the rags smelled — smoky, bitter, burnt. He made progress on the knots but it was slow going. Finally, his hands were free and he untied his feet.

Lalo looked around. No one was in sight. He sighed, picked up the lid of the metal box and the rags, and trudged toward La Bendita. There was no need to be secretive now. He marched past the police car and to the back-emergency gate.

A startled state policeman grabbed his arm. "This community is quarantined. You can't enter."

"I just came from here a few hours ago."

"Don't smart off to me." The officer looked more closely at Lalo. "You're the kid who disappeared. We thought you were kidnapped."

"I was sorta." Lalo told his story to the officer and then to Chuy who'd been called to the gate to collect him.

"Do you think you could ID the man if you saw him again?" said Chuy.

"Sure."

Chuy called Gil. Soon the state police officers at the gate were tramping toward the bosque. Lalo assured them they could identify the spot where he found the box because twine, the bottom of the box, and a hammer were there.

Two FBI agents arrived and showed Lalo photos of men on a laptop computer. They watched Lalo as he looked at more than twenty pictures.

Lalo selected one of them. "That's him. See the big nose but his hair isn't gray and he has a beard now. He's a little skinnier than in the photo."

The agents called their boss.

Chuy called Gil. "Looks like charred body in the cabin wasn't Mazzone after all. Lalo's sure it was him." Chuy tousled Lalo's hair as he listened to Gil. "The kid's fine. Seems he learned a couple useful tricks as a Cub Scout."

After Chuy had said "right" a dozen times to Gil, he turned to Lalo. "You sure riled up the Chief and all the bigwigs."

Lalo shrugged his shoulders. "Why?"

"The local TV stations and papers were alerted that the quarantine was being lifted at ten. The bigwigs planned to make a statement and then fly back home. They had to cancel the announcement and stay here because of you."

Lalo cocked his head. "Really?"

"Well, then there was scare over Sara."

"What's happened to Sara?"

"They thought she had the flu. But now Doc Gonzales doesn't think so. Her fever's down already."

"Sara's tough." Lalo sat quietly for at least thirty seconds with a frown on his face. "So, why's everyone mad at me?"

"The bigwigs planned to go ahead with their announcement. Then a TV crew learned you were missing. Suddenly the only story anyone wanted was about you. The Chief had to advise the bigwigs the best way to control the swarms of reporters was to continue the quarantine."

Lalo gulped. "Now what?"

"We go to the front gate. There will be lots of people screaming at you. You smile and don't talk unless the Chief tells you okay."

Lalo nodded.

"If someone asks you who tied you up, say you don't know."

"That's not true. I heard you tell the Chief it was Mazzone."

"But we don't want the press to know. If Mazzone was sure you could ID him, he might come back for you."

Lalo puffed his chest. "I'd be okay."

"Yeah, but he might come back for your mom and brother, too."

For the second time today, Lalo felt scared. "How long before I see Mom and Sara?"

"You do as the Chief tells you at the gate. Then I'll take you to the clinic to see your mom and Sara while the bigwigs announce the quarantine is being lifted."

Chuy whisked Lalo from the back gate to the clubhouse in a police cruiser with the sirens blaring and then escorted him to the front gate. As soon as the reporters who'd been milling around the front gate caught sight of Lalo, they stampeded toward the closed gate yelling questions. One shouted above the rest," Do you know who kidnapped you?"

Lalo stiffened as he looked up to see Gil shake his head slightly. "No."

-/-/-

No one noticed a man in the baseball cap and dark glasses who smiled when Lalo answered the question. The man hoisted a torn, white pillowcase over his shoulder and ambled away.

CHAPTER 44: Seventeen Months Later — Sara

"Did you read the article in the *Albuquerque Journal* this morning?" asked Sara as she and Bug entered Linda's house on Saturday morning. Ever since Sara had arrived in the Albuquerque area, Sara and Linda had eaten dinner together on Saturday. Usually they ate out, but since the flu epidemic began at La Bendita seventeen months earlier, they'd taken turns making dinner. This week it was Linda's turn to cook.

"How could I miss it." Linda rummaged through a pile of newspapers and held up the front page. The banner read: *FLU OVER*. "The CDC estimated over a million people died of the Philippine flu in the U.S. during the last seventeen months. They noted the previous high had been eighty thousand deaths due to flu in the 2017-18 season."

"Might be a good time to celebrate. We could eat out today. A lot of restaurants have closed during the last year as people avoided public spaces. The Range in Mercado has barely held on and only because it started offering take-out services."

"Too late. The pot roast is done in the slow cooker and the table is set. I just need to slice the meat." She handed Sara the paper. "I know you only scan the headlines and the first paragraphs of newspaper articles, but you should read the whole cover story and the one in the science section. You're mentioned in both."

"The article I wrote with the scientist from Ames, Ellen Behren, and Martin Bloom got a lot of attention."

"No kidding. The cover article of *Science*. Got Martin promoted to full professor." When Sara picked a bit of beef that had crumbled as Linda sliced the roast, Linda growled, "Stop it." However, when Sara gave the bits to Bug. Linda said, "Why don't you sit down and read the paper."

Sara sat on the stool in Linda's kitchen with Bug at her feet. "Oh, this is nice. The CDC credits our discovery of a swine flu virus similar to the Philippine flu virus as the breakthrough that allowed the successful development of an effective and safe vaccine against the Philippine flu."

"Thought you'd be pleased. By the way, whatever happened to Ellen Behren. As I remember, she left La Bendita under a cloud."

"Yeah, so many public safety officers around New Mexico complained about her uncooperative behavior that the CDC demoted her. She sent me an email last month when she got a position as an assistant professor at Tufts University."

"Doubt she'll be a good teacher."

"Oh, I think she learned a lot from her experiences at La Bendita and ultimately saved lives, unlike George Soto, the director of the FBI office in Albuquerque. Gil was pleased when the FBI forced Soto retire."

Sara studied the second article in the newspaper. "The reporter really worked on this article. Talks a lot about La Bendita. Says, 'No other community suffered such a high death rate from the Philippine flu or contributed more to the eventual end of the epidemic.'" Sara studied the article. "I didn't know this. The reporter claims when drug companies ramped up their production of the experimental antivirals tested at La Bendita, they referred to these tests as the 'deadly experiments with the blessed' because La Bendita means the blessed in Spanish."

"Maybe the reporter of the article could give a talk at La Bendita. Your social director is always trying to arrange programs."

"Don't know if that's a good idea. At the HOA Board meeting this week, we debated a potential name change for La Bendita. Gaspar Gonzales and Sylvia Otega thought our name now had a negative connotation and hurt recruitment of residents to their health care facilities. I suspect the name also deters homebuyers, but Jane Lane, waving the stump of her right arm, made it clear that she didn't want the name changed."

"Bet Jane won."

"Yes, the motion was defeated." Sara picked up Bug and petted him. "Maybe, my neighbors would attend a program on the flu. Although they continue to worry about crime and gossip about 'outsiders,' most have come to realize a perimeter wall and gates won't protect them from all threats."

Linda placed the beef and vegetables on the dining room table and announced, "Dinner is served."

After all three had gobbled the beef, potatoes, and carrots with gravy, Sara said, "Oh, I forgot the real news. Aletha Bradley sold one of my large wall hangings for four thousand dollars this week."

"Okay your art work is becoming more popular that I expected."

"No, the point is the man who purchased it looked a bit like Jim Peterson — big nose, right height and age. He paid in cash and disappeared before the Santa Fe police officers Aletha called could arrive at her gallery to question him."

THE END

THE SCIENCE BEHIND THE STORY

The Philippine strain of the flu virus is fictional, but the biological and social responses to a potent new flu virus as described in the novel are realistic. The problems encountered in developing and testing new vaccines and antivirals in *The Flu Is Coming* may help readers understand why drug development is often slow and expensive.

There's a lot we don't know about viruses.

● Are viruses alive? It depends on how you define life. They're genetic material encased in protein but are incapable of reproducing unless they take control of a host cell.

● How common are viruses? They infect all cellular organisms — animals, plants, and bacteria. They occupy more of the earth's biomass than do cellular organisms.

● Are viruses always bad? Most viruses exist in their hosts without causing disease. Scientists use certain viruses as vectors to introduce genetic material into cells during gene therapy.

● When will the next deadly flu virus strike? All viruses are continually changing or mutating. In another hundred years, or maybe only one year, a strain of avian or swine flu virus may experience a sudden antigenic shift that makes it infectious in humans. Perhaps the next time, scientists will be better prepared and develop effective vaccines and antivirals quickly. Or perhaps next time, they'll be less lucky and the infection won't be controlled as well.

● If you doubt the horror of a flu epidemic, read *The Great Influenza* by John Barry. It's a factual account of the 1917-18 flu epidemic.

ABOUT THE AUTHOR

J.L. Greger is a biology professor and research administrator from the University of Wisconsin-Madison turned novelist. She likes to include tidbits of science in her thriller/mystery novels: ***Murder: A Way to Lose*** (1st prize in 2016 Public Safety Writers' [PSWA] book contest), ***Malignancy*** (1st prize in 2015 PSWA book contest), ***Riddled with Clues*** (finalist for a 2017 NM/Arizona book award), ***She Didn't Know Her Place,*** and others.

Her short story collections: ***Other People's Mothers*** (finalist for a 2017 NM/Arizona book award) and ***The Good Old Days*** focus on families.

Her website is **http://www.jlgreger.com**